HIS RISK

Center Point
Large Print

Also by Shelley Shepard Gray and available from Center Point Large Print:

The Loyal Heart
A Sister's Wish
Her Secret
His Guilt
Love Held Captive
The Gift

HIS RISK

THE AMISH OF HART COUNTY

Shelley Shepard Gray

CENTER POINT LARGE PRINT
THORNDIKE, MAINE

The text of this Large Print edition is unabridged.
In other aspects, this book may vary
from the original edition.
Printed in the United States of America
on permanent paper.
Set in 16-point Times New Roman type.

ISBN: 978-1-68324-746-3

Library of Congress Cataloging-in-Publication Data

Names: Gray, Shelley Shepard, author.
Title: His risk : the Amish of Hart County / Shelley Shepard Gray.
Description: Center Point Large Print edition. | Thorndike, Maine :
    Center Point Large Print, 2018.
Identifiers: LCCN 2018000809 | ISBN 9781683247463
    (hardcover : alk. paper)
Subjects: LCSH: Amish—Fiction. | Large type books. |
    GSAFD: Christian fiction. | Suspense fiction.
Classification: LCC PS3607.R3966 H58 2018 | DDC 813/.6—dc23
LC record available at https://lccn.loc.gov/2018000809

To my friend Kim Frazier,
who knows a thing or two
about taking risks

You are my hiding place; you protect me from trouble. You surround me with songs of victory.

PSALM 32:7

You can't change what is going on around you until you change what is going on within you.

AMISH PROVERB

CHAPTER 1

Saturday, January 27

Sometimes, the sound of a phone ringing still caught Calvin Fisher off guard. When his cell buzzed for the second time, he pulled it out of his back pocket. Thumb hovering over the screen, he intended to press Ignore, but then he noticed the area code.

Eight months ago, he promised he'd never ignore a call from Hart County again. As the phone buzzed a third time, the sound echoing through the alleyway, Calvin pressed the button to answer.

"Mark, is that you?" he asked.

"*Ack! Nee*, Calvin. It's Waneta," his sister-in-law said in a rush. "Oh, Calvin. I'm so glad you answered."

"Neeta, hold on one sec, 'kay?" With the phone still held to his ear, Calvin motioned to the men nearby that he'd be right back and started walking. "You okay?" he asked, already feeling awkward. *Of course* Waneta wasn't okay if she was calling him. She was Amish and didn't get on the phone unless she had a good reason.

9

"I'm not all right at all. Oh, Calvin, Mark and me just got back from the *doktah*."

He gripped the cell phone tighter. "What's wrong? Are you sick?"

"*Nee*, it's Mark, Calvin." She paused. When she continued, her voice sounded strained. "He's been feeling poorly for a while, you see, but he didn't want to let you know. Finally, he went to the *doktah* two days ago."

Waneta continued talking, hardly taking a breath as each word bled into the next so fast that he had to stop walking in order to understand her better.

"Dr. Hanna sent him to the hospital for tests, then he called us into his office this morning."

"What did the doctor say?" he asked as he resumed walking. Then, unlocking the front door of the apartment complex where he lived, Calvin trotted up three flights of stairs.

"Th-that Mark has cancer."

A wave of dizziness hit him hard. He stopped, gripping the worn metal banister so tightly that the edge of it cut into his palm.

"Calvin?" she asked hesitantly. "Calvin, are you still there?"

He closed his eyes. Waneta needed him. "I'm sorry, sis," he said, intentionally using his pet name for her in an effort to ease her worries. "I'm here. Um, what kind of cancer is it? Do you know?"

"It's *renal cell*–something."

"Say again?"

"Oh, I can hardly pronounce it. I'm sorry. Calvin, it's something to do with his kidneys." Sounding more perturbed, she continued. "Dr. Hanna gave us some literature and a phone number of a nurse who can explain things *gut*, too. But I don't know. All I remember him saying is that Mark has cancer and is going to need to have one of his kidneys removed."

He'd finally made it to his apartment. Unlocking the deadbolt, he strode inside and closed the door firmly behind. Then, as Waneta continued to talk about how worried she was, he did a quick walk-through just to make sure no one had been in his place since he'd left six hours ago.

When he was assured that everything was undisturbed, he sat down on the chair in the corner of his bedroom. Forced himself to remain calm and keep his voice steady. "Sis, where's Mark? Can I talk to him?"

"*Nee*. He's sleeping. Plus, I didn't tell him I was going to call you. This is Lora's phone."

"Okay. Is Lora there?" Lora was an old friend; they'd all grown up together. She, like him, had left the Amish faith, eventually marrying a deputy in the local sheriff's department. But also like him, she hadn't wanted to remove her Amish ties and live completely among the English.

Lora was a close friend to all of them.

"Um, *jah*."

"Put her on the phone, Neeta," he said gently. As he heard the phone switch hands, he attempted to pull himself together. But really, all he felt was numb.

"Calvin?" Lora said at last. "Hey."

"Hey. Waneta told me about Mark's diagnosis. Have you seen the paperwork? Did you talk to this Dr. Hanna?" he bit out in a rush, hardly able to think clearly. Taking another deep breath, he continued. "Have you talked to Mark?"

"I talked to both the doctor and Mark. The doctor is very sure, Calvin. Mark has renal cell carcinoma in his right kidney," she said slowly, the strain in her voice coming across like a taut wire. "They want to schedule an operation as soon as possible. Like next week. Can you be there?"

"Of course." Making the decision, he got to his feet. "I'll leave tomorrow morning."

"Thanks." Lowering her voice, she said, "Mark and Neeta are going to need your help."

"That's good because I want to help. Tell Waneta that I'll see her in the early afternoon."

"I'll do that." He heard Lora murmur something to Waneta and seem to move into another room. "Calvin, I need to ask . . . are you going to bring trouble here?"

He knew what she was asking. As far as she,

Mark, Waneta, and the rest of the world knew, he was still involved in a gang, and still did a lot of things that were illegal or brought on trouble of one kind or another.

"Hope not," he said, purposely keeping his tone light as he strode into the kitchen to get a glass of water.

"You hope not?" Her voice rose. "Calvin, if your being here is going to bring your gun-toting, drug-running friends, too, then you need to stay away," she hissed. "Actually, you should tell—"

He cut her off. "Gun-toting, drug-running friends?" he said with a forced laugh. "You make me sound like some kind of old-time gangster. Have you been watching black-and-white movies on TV again?"

"Don't joke about this," she replied in a steely voice. "You might be pretending that I'm as naïve as half the population of Horse Cave, Kentucky, but we both know that ain't me. I'm serious. You can't bring your problems and bad habits to your brother's doorstep."

As he filled his glass with water from the tap, he found himself wishing again that he could tell someone, anyone, what he was really up to. But because that wasn't possible, he kept his reply light. "Nothing's going to happen. Settle down before you get Waneta wound up. Everything's going to be fine." Before she could go off on him again, he decided it was time to end the call.

"Don't forget to remind Neeta that I'll be there tomorrow. Bye."

Calvin hung up before Lora could reply or give him another warning. After tossing his phone on the counter, he drained his glass, then filled it up again.

As he slowly set the glass on the counter, he was smiling to himself. Yeah, that's what he was drinking now when he got stressed out. Tap water. He wasn't sure if Lora would have been more shocked than relieved to see that he was no longer enjoying shots of tequila or a six-pack of beer when things got stressful. It hadn't been easy, but he had cleaned himself up.

Well, at least in private.

Out in public, though? That was a different story. His reputation depended on him being filled with vices and excuses.

"Cal?" a voice called from the outside hallway, followed by two heavy raps on his door.

Calvin grabbed his phone and crossed the room, taking his time to get his head back where it needed to be. He couldn't show weakness; he couldn't allow anyone to see an inkling of fear or worry, *any* strain in his eyes. He stopped, stood up straighter, exhaled, then pulled open the door. *"What?"*

"Boss wants you, Cal." Jenk, one of the men he'd been standing in the alley with, said. Stepping closer, he peered into his apartment.

"What's going on? You sure took off quick when you got that phone call." Grinning, he said, "You got someone in here or something? One of your old Amish buddies?"

"If I did, it ain't none of your business, right?" The gang knew he'd been born Amish but believed he'd been shunned by his family and had cut all ties with everyone else in the community. Still, more than one member of the Kings enjoyed jabbing him with his unusual past.

Jenk shrank back, stung. "No. 'Course not." Now looking at Cal warily, he shifted his feet. "So, you coming or what?"

By way of answering, Calvin pulled out his keys and locked his door. He kept his chin up and his expression blank as he walked with Jenk down the hallway. By the time he headed down the stairs, he was no longer thinking about his brother or Hart County or cancer. Instead, all he cared about was the reassuring weight of the pistol nestled against the small of his back, and the fact that no one else was loitering in the area wanting to talk to him.

When they finally stepped outside, his transformation was complete. To everyone in the back streets of downtown Louisville, he wasn't Calvin, the former Amish younger brother of Mark Fisher. Instead, he was Cal, the former homeless loser who had found a place inside one of the strongest gun-running gangs in the state of Kentucky.

He also was an undercover informant for the DEA.

And he now had less than twenty-four hours to make up a reason to leave that was believable enough to keep everything he did in this place, and far away from Horse Cave.

Otherwise, he wouldn't only be bringing his problems to his brother's house. He'd be bringing danger to everyone there, too.

CHAPTER 2

Thursday, February 1

Alice Yoder lived for little Jimmy Borntrager's hugs. At the end of each day of preschool, he would scamper to the door with his friends, abruptly stop, turn around, and then practically fling himself at her knees. Finally, after yelling "*Ich leevi dich*, Teacher!" in his husky, deep little voice, he would run outside to where his mother was patiently waiting.

Today was no exception.

Walking to the door, she smiled and waved good-bye to all her tiny scholars standing next to their mothers and grandmothers. Only when they departed in their buggies or on foot would she reply, "I love you, too, Jimmy."

Now, as she leaned against the doorframe and watched the last of her ten preschoolers disappear, she whispered it again. "I love each one of you *kinner*."

However, for the first time, instead of her heart feeling near bursting with love and gratitude, she felt a little melancholy. It was all well and good to love a classroom of four-year-olds. But one day soon, she would sure like to be uttering such a phrase to her own little boy or girl.

If she was honest, she was actually wishing to be saying those words to her own sweetheart, too. Walking back into her classroom, Alice wondered if that would ever happen. Here she was, twenty-two years old and had never had a sweetheart of her own. Not even anything close.

As she picked up stray picture books, crayons, sheets of paper, and plastic letters from the floor and atop various counters, Alice knew she was being ridiculous. She was only letting her looming birthday and a longtime friend's recent engagement get the best of her. The Lord would provide in His own time. And she was young, too. There was nothing wrong with being twenty-two and having never been kissed.

It only just felt that way. And, in her darkest moments, she would find herself doubting everything about herself—her looks, her personality, her past choices. Was the Lord angry at her because she'd done so many stupid things when she was a teenager, especially during her seventeenth year? She and her best friend, Irene, had been determined to stretch every boundary of their lives. They'd worn scandalous clothes. Flirted with Englishers. Made rash decisions. Caused a car crash.

Oh, that car crash.

Cold air, shattered glass, Irene's terrified expression. All that blood. The memories flashed back like an unwelcome guest depositing itself in her brain. Bringing with it so much guilt and pain.

It was nothing less than she deserved, of course. But since then, she'd worked hard to make up for all those mistakes.

But maybe the Lord had other ideas? Maybe He was attempting to remind her that she was never going to be able to make up for the things she'd done.

The possibility of that made her shiver. Not because she didn't doubt that she should be punished, but because there wasn't anything she could do about her past. There were many things one could do with one's life. However, erasing the past wasn't an option.

Shaking off the sudden case of doldrums, Alice finished cleaning up around the room, swept the floor, and took out the trash. Then, after getting a little snack, she sat down at her desk and prepared everything she would need for tomorrow's class.

It was one of her favorite days to celebrate, for it was Groundhog Day. Pulling out the little groundhog puppet she'd made last year, she gave in to whimsy and slipped it over her hand, then moved her knuckles so its little ears twitched. She couldn't help but smile at the sight. It really was a cute little thing.

"Playing with puppets again, Alice?" Ed called out from the doorway.

Embarrassed, she pulled the toy off her hand. "*Nee*. Just preparing for Friday's lessons."

Her eldest brother sauntered in, all confident and good humor. "Is Groundhog Day here already?"

After getting to her feet, she looked him in the eye and tried to appear scholarly. "Of course it is. Tomorrow is February second."

"Huh. I could have sworn we just celebrated it." He rubbed his faint beard like he was confused. But his eyes were twinkling.

"You're just jealous that you've got to work at the blacksmith's store all day instead of talking about the letter *g*, spring, and groundhogs," she said as she walked to the closet in the back of the room to retrieve her bonnet, cloak, mittens, and purse.

"That's true. I would be jealous, but Bethy and I are going to be in Pinecraft enjoying the Florida sunshine."

Well, she could tease him right back. "You're going to Florida? Goodness! I almost forgot." They both knew she couldn't have forgotten his trip even if she had tried. It was all he and Bethy had talked about for the last four months.

"I'm going to pretend I find that funny. Listen, I stopped by to let you know that John and Rachel offered to house-sit for the second half of our trip *if* you decide that you don't want to stay for a whole month."

He looked so earnest, Alice did her best to match his expression. "*Danke*, but I don't mind watching Valentine for the entire time. I've been looking forward to it . . ."

Feeling relieved, he pulled out an envelope. "Sorry. I don't know why I even asked. You always do what you say you're going to, so . . ." He smiled, though his expression faltered.

Obviously, he was remembering that wasn't quite the truth.

And Alice was as well. Remembering all too clearly the way she'd acted five years ago. She cleared her throat. "Don't worry, *bruder*. Everything is going to be just fine when you're gone. Why, I'll spoil Valentine so much, I bet she'll hardly realize you are gone."

"Don't tell that to Bethy. You know how she dotes on that cat." Pressing the envelope into her hand, he said, "Now, before you go refusing this, inside is the key *and* some money for food and things."

"Ed—"

"*Nee*. Don't argue. Take it. It ain't that much to compensate you for living in our *haus* for a whole month."

"I don't need to be paid to help you."

"Come on, little sister. You and I both know what will happen if you refuse."

"Mamm will try to get me to eat at home every night for supper," she said with a small grimace. Though her life might not be everything she dreamed it would be, she did love her parents. But their efforts to shield her from further pain created a new pain in and of itself. Alice yearned for some independence. It was a difficult thing to achieve, however, without hurting her parents. Because of that, she balanced precariously on the edge of keeping them happy and keeping herself happy.

Both of her brothers knew this and often had her stay at their houses when they weren't around.

After gazing at her for a long moment, as if he was mentally making sure his little sister was happy and healthy, he slapped his palm lightly on the corner of her school desk. "All right, Alice, I hate to say it, but I canna walk you home today. I promised my Bethy that I'd run to the post office for her, then we have a driver coming to pick us up. We have to take the bus from Louisville tomorrow morning, so we're going to spend the night in an inn over there."

Looking more than a little gleeful, he added, "I think the bathing suit she ordered arrived."

"She's going to wear a bathing suit at Siesta Key?" Bethy was everything proper. Never would Alice have imagined that Ed's wife would do something like that.

Her brother's eyes lit up. "Maybe. But don't tell Mamm. If she finds out, she's going to have plenty to say, even if it ain't her business."

Making a little locking motion over her lips, she giggled. "My lips are sealed." Walking around her desk, she hugged him tight. "Good-bye, Edward. Have a nice vacation. Don't worry about your *haus* or your cat. I'll take good care of both."

"*Danke.* Bye, now," he said as he turned and walked quickly out the door.

After spending another few minutes making sure everything was ready for the next day, Alice strode out the door. She needed to walk home, finish packing her bags, and head over to Edward and Beth's pretty two-story bungalow.

She might not have a vacation or even an exciting evening with a beau, but she did have a month of independence to look forward to. She needed to remember to count her blessings.

As she knew, things could be much worse.

THREE HOURS LATER, Alice was sitting on the front porch of her brother's home. As she'd expected, her parents had fretted and worried about her being on her own, but at last had hitched up the buggy and helped her move over to Edward's house. After numerous rounds of hugs, they left—but only after leaving a giant bag of food and paper products on the kitchen table.

Alice couldn't wait to tell her brothers about her care package. Their mother had an inordinate fondness for paper towels, tissues, and toilet paper. She stockpiled it like a tragedy was going to happen if someone sneezed and there wasn't a box of Kleenex nearby. Obviously, Mamm had been worried that Bethy and Edward didn't keep their cupboards as well stocked.

After her parents were gone, Alice made herself a mug of hot tea and came out to the porch with a new book. One of Edward's neighbors across the street had had a new baby. Sometimes they would take her out for a walk. Alice was hoping for a peek.

But it was the loud snap of a truck's door across the way that caught her attention. It was an old truck, light brown in color with a dented bumper. It was also parked right in front of Mark Fisher's house. He'd recently married Waneta Cain, and they were well known throughout the area.

Of course, everyone in the county had heard about what had happened to Waneta several months ago. She'd been attacked by an awful man. Mark Fisher and his brother had saved her. That in itself had been noteworthy. But because rumors abounded about Mark being suspected of hurting women years before, his heroism had caused even more talk.

Waneta's attack was all in the past now, thank the Lord. Since then, she and Mark had married and they were living a quiet life, just like the rest of the Amish in the area. Edward said that Mark and Neeta, as everyone called her, were friendly and kept to themselves. *Gut* neighbors.

She was about to open her book when she got a better look at the man who'd exited the vehicle. He was now standing almost directly across from her. Clad in jeans, boots, and a snug-fitting black T-shirt, he looked out of place. And . . . was he smoking?

She couldn't help but gape. He was striking. He was tall and looked muscular, had dark hair and a brooding expression. As if he sensed her staring at him, he turned and met her gaze.

She caught the color of his eyes. They were blue. So very blue.

Realizing she'd been staring, she resolutely opened her book. Pretended to read. But no words on the page registered. Instead, she seemed to be under his sway—the way he turned his head to watch a car drive by; the way he tapped his ashes into the top of a Coke can.

The way he glanced at Alice again.

For a moment, she was tempted to run inside and lock the front door. But that would be silly. Neither of them was doing anything wrong.

And, for Pete's sake, she was a schoolteacher now! She had nothing to hide. And was used to talking to all kinds of people.

With that in mind, she set her book down and

picked up her mug of tea. After taking a deep breath, she leaned back against the chair and sipped her tea. She felt pretty good about her actions, too.

Right until he put the last of his cigarette into the can and started walking over.

CHAPTER 3

Thursday, February 1

Calvin could tell himself that he wanted to talk to the woman because he was concerned about his family's safety. No one should be at the house. Mark and Waneta had just told him that Edward and his wife were leaving that afternoon for a month-long vacation in Pinecraft.

He walked across the street to get a better look at the person, a pretty Amish woman wearing a pale-gray dress with a pink wool cardigan. And as he approached, he knew there was only one reason he did so.

There was something about her that seemed different. Maybe even special.

Okay, that was stupid. Presumptuous, too. He didn't know a single thing about her.

All he did know, he realized, was that he wanted to meet her. She had lifted her chin when she caught him staring, right before she stared right back. He was so used to women shying away from him, her boldness caught him off guard. And, if he was honest, it amused him, too.

When he reached her front yard, he raised a hand, attempting to look friendly and nonthreatening. That was probably a hopeless endeavor. He wasn't a small man. He stood right at six foot two, just as Mark did.

He was also a strange Englisher. Most Amish women had a natural reticence around unfamiliar men.

"Hey," he said.

She got to her feet. "Hello. May I help you?"

She had caramel-colored hair and blue eyes. She also had just about the best voice he'd ever heard. Crystal clear, softly melodic and sweet. Until that moment, he hadn't realized that it was possible for a woman to have such a distinctly perfect voice.

Now he was even more intrigued by her. He also didn't want to scare her away by coming off too harsh or too forward. He needed to remember that he was back in Horse Cave, not in the back streets of Louisville or Cincinnati. She wasn't one of the women hanging around the Kings, hoping for a little fun for a couple of hours.

No. She was respectable. Not wanting to crowd her, he stopped at the foot of the stairs leading up to the porch. "My name is Calvin Fisher," he said. "I'm staying across the way with my brother and his wife. I was given to believe that this house was going to be empty for a while."

But instead of shirking back or being bashful,

she looked at him with interest. "You're kin to Mark?"

"I am. His younger brother. Now, who are you?"

"I'm Alice." Her blue eyes shone as she looked at him directly. "And this is my brother's house."

"You come over when he ain't home?"

"*Nee*. I come over when he asks me to house-sit."

"Ah. How long are you going to be here?"

Wariness snuck back into her gaze. "I'm curious as to why you are so curious about me. Why does what I do matter?"

It took every bit of self-control he possessed not to grin. This little gal was a firecracker. It had been a long time since he'd been around anyone who challenged him right to his face.

Especially not a young woman.

"No reason in particular. I guess I don't recall seeing you before."

"That makes two of us," replied Alice. "I have been here a number of times, but I can't say that I've seen you before, either."

He motioned to the wicker chair next to where she had been sitting. "Can I join you?" When she hesitated, he said, "If not, that's okay. I just think we could probably talk easier if I wasn't standing so far away."

She looked at him up and down again, almost as if she would discover all his faults. It made him feel strangely vulnerable.

"I suppose so," she said at last.

"Thanks."

She stayed on her feet as he climbed the steps. Then held her ground as she boldly lifted her chin to meet his gaze. "You sure are very, *very* tall."

He laughed. "I've been called a lot of things, but that's a first." Gesturing to the chair that was closest to where she'd been sitting, he said, "Okay if I sit in this chair?"

"It's fine."

After she sat down, she studied him again. "I'm going to be here for a month. Are you visiting your brother long?"

And just like that, all of his amusement fled. It was replaced by grief and worry and a complete sense of helplessness that rivaled all the feelings he used to have back when he was a child and at the mercy of his father's abuse and his mother's neglect. Briefly, he entertained the idea of either ignoring the question or giving Alice a vague answer.

But something told him that evading the truth now would give him consequences in the future. He needed to get used to saying what was wrong. To realize what was happening, and that there wasn't anything he could do about it, either.

"My brother was recently diagnosed with cancer. I'm not sure how long I'll be here."

Pure compassion lit her eyes. "I am sorry to hear that."

He ran a hand through his hair, ruffling up the ends. "Yeah. I . . . well, I was sorry to hear about the diagnosis, too."

She tilted her head to one side. "Where do you live when you ain't here?"

"Louisville. For the most part."

"For the most part?" she repeated. "Do you not live there all the time?"

"*Nee.*" There was no way he was going to start telling her all about his life with the Kings. She might be pretty, but he wasn't a fool.

"Ah. So you left the Amish and became English and moved to the big city."

"Pretty much."

Still studying him like he was fascinating, she tilted her head. "Do you like it?"

"Louisville?" he asked, answering his own question. "It's all right." Actually, the city was fine, as far as big cities went. But he wasn't living anywhere fine. He was in a run-down apartment a couple of blocks from the river.

She gave him a puzzled expression. "*Nee.* I mean being English. Do you like being an Englisher now?"

He was so used to people around here asking *why* he left the faith. They'd ask nosy questions, seemingly trying to understand what he wanted to have that he hadn't. Personal questions, about his feelings—did he feel it was so hard to be Amish?

31

They didn't want real answers. They didn't want to hear about living in the shadows of generations of tradition, faith, and rules. They'd wanted information, the sort that had been popular on so-called reality television shows.

He'd learned to give pat, meaningless answers. He'd been good with it, because he'd soon realized that no one had actually wanted to hear about how difficult his home life had been, or how much he'd needed to find a place for himself that felt safe.

All that was why he was caught off guard by Alice's question. She wasn't asking why he'd left. No, she was asking if he liked the change. It was a subtle difference.

"Yeah, I do. I do like being English," he replied after some thought. "I love my brother and respect his decision to remain Amish, but I think that being English is the right choice for me." He eyed her warily, half waiting for her to find fault with that.

Instead, Alice nodded her head, like he had made all the sense in the world. "That's *gut*."

That was her answer. No invasive questions. No sly recriminations. No guilt. Just acceptance.

Once again, a strange sense of peace drifted over him. He'd thought it was her pretty voice that had affected him, but maybe it was something more than that.

Maybe it was the easy way Alice accepted

him. It was refreshing and soothing, too. It also felt dangerous. Because he was fairly sure that if Alice really knew him, she would change her tune. Maybe she would be scared of him. Maybe simply be judgmental. She would have every right to be that way, too. She was a good woman. A lovely woman who no doubt had lots of admirers. And though he knew he could never pursue her in a romantic way, he also realized he was in no hurry to step away from her.

Which was one of the reasons, of course, that he needed to keep his distance. He was tainted by life and his hands were dirty from the things he'd done. They were never going to be clean enough to touch her.

Yet he was feeling a pull toward her. Like, if he was in her presence long enough, he would feel validated and renewed. It scared him. What would he do if he started wanting something more from her than he might ever receive?

Getting to his feet, he said, "I better go. Like I said, I just wanted to see who you were and introduce myself."

Her smile was almost angelic. Almost. "And that you did."

"I guess I'll be seeing you around."

"You will, though I won't be here all that often." She raised her chin a bit. "I have a job, you see."

"Oh? What do you do?"

"I'm a preschool teacher."

Of course she was. Could anything be better suited for a girl with such a sweet voice? "I bet those kids love you."

She laughed. "Some do, that is true. *Gut naught*, Calvin Fisher."

"Yeah. Good night." Just as he started walking across the street, his cell phone rang. After glancing back at Alice again, he clicked it on and brought it to his ear. "Yeah?"

"Calvin?" Andrew Mason, his DEA liaison asked, "is that you?"

Worry filled him as he wondered why he was being contacted. "Who else would it be?"

"Settle down. It didn't sound like you, that's all."

"How did I sound?"

"Like a nicer version of yourself."

He walked down the street, taking care to pass his brother's house and keep walking. "I must have had something in my throat. Why are you calling?"

After a pause, Andrew replied, sounding almost apologetic. "Look, I know you're seeing family on some kind of urgent matter."

"I told you. My brother has cancer."

"Of course you know we feel for you . . ."

"But?"

Andrew sighed. "How much do you need to be there?"

How much did he need to be with his brother while he underwent surgery to have an organ removed because it was cancerous? If he wasn't so indebted to the man, he would have hung up. "Why are you asking?"

"There's been some action with the organization. We've heard that two or three guys are vying for power and are interested in taking down everyone who gets in their way."

"Even if that was true, there isn't anything I could do, even if I was there."

"I think there might be. Our surveillance has heard your name come up more than once."

"I'm embedded, Andrew. Of course I'm gonna be mentioned."

"It's not in passing. We're hearing your name being spoken quite a bit."

There was a new underlying tension in his voice. "What's going on? Am I in danger?" More importantly, was his family in danger?

"Not at all. Actually, you should be real pleased with yourself. We heard West say he's thinking about making you a lieutenant sometime over the next couple of weeks."

"Really?" Though it was all an undercover mission for him, Calvin couldn't help but feel a little pleased. This was a big deal in the Kings. West Powers, the president of the organization, didn't promote members into his circle lightly. That meant that he trusted Calvin and was pleased with the work he'd been doing. It meant a lot of things. Respect. Security. And, yeah, even some freedom. As a lieutenant, he could do almost anything he wanted without anyone but West questioning him.

Of course, it also meant that it was going to be even harder to extricate himself from the gang when the time came. If it could ever actually happen.

"We need you back there. If they intend to promote you, we need that to happen. You can't do anything to mess that up."

When he'd agreed to the deal, when he'd agreed to become an informant in exchange for the DEA paying off his debts, Calvin knew it all would come at a steep price. He didn't care, though. If he hadn't agreed to be an informant, the Kings would have beaten him bloody before shooting him in the head. He'd owed them that much money.

In his darkest moments, he knew that being an informant was just a temporary bandage on his wreck of a life. No one could keep up a web of lies and secrets for an indeterminate amount of time. One day, he'd have to pay the price.

Of course, all this time, he'd imagined that the price would come in the form of him getting shot or killed.

But this? He didn't want to fail Mark again. He wanted, no, *needed* to be able to support Mark and Waneta right now. God had given him this opportunity and he wasn't going to mess it up. "Mark is going to have surgery on Monday to have a kidney removed."

"So when could you go to Louisville?" Andrew shot back.

Calvin swallowed, thinking he deserved every bit of Andrew's disinterest in his pain and worries. After all, he'd been a plenty disinterested person himself. Toward Mark—during the times he had to deal with their wreck of a father, and, on top of that, his reaction when Mark was accused of attacking an Amish girl. "I don't know."

A second passed. In the background, Calvin could hear Andrew speak to someone. Papers shuffled. "Okay, how about this?" Andrew said at last. "How about we sweeten the deal by giving you a new truck?"

A truck wasn't going to ease his conscience. But since those newfound principles hadn't saved his life, he tried to sound at least a little interested. "You don't think anyone in the Kings is going to notice me suddenly driving around in new wheels?"

"We've already thought about that. You can say that you got some of the money from the sale of the family house."

"But Mark didn't sell it."

"They won't know that. Or, if you'd rather,

37

just say that you went out and bought it. They're paying you enough to go buy whatever you want." Before Calvin could point out that no one in the gang was an idiot, Andrew continued. "If you had a decent truck, you could drive back and forth more easily while you're there—divide your time between your family and Louisville. Could you make that work?"

Everything inside of him wanted to tell Andrew no. His brother was what was important. Being the man he wanted to be was important.

But, as he thought about Alice and how he'd felt around her, he started thinking that it would maybe be for the best. Keeping some distance from the temptations here would be a good thing.

Then there was Mark and Waneta. He needed to keep them off the gang's radar. If West thought that Calvin's loyalty was in question, he could send someone to Horse Cave to check on him. Calvin knew that could happen because he'd spied on other members for West before.

And if a member of the Kings came to Horse Cave and started asking questions, it could inadvertently hurt Mark or Waneta. Maybe even Alice.

Coming back regularly could keep his head on straight.

It was also his job. Andrew had stuck his neck out when they'd hired him. It was also because of the DEA that Calvin was alive. He'd owed way too much money to the Kings before Andrew had helped him pay them off—and helped to cement his reputation as a ruthless man.

Then there were the Kings. They trusted him now, and that didn't come easy. There was even a part of him that felt good about it. Earning respect from that quadrant made him feel more worthy than he had during most of his life.

"Thanks, Andrew. Yeah, I'll take the truck. And I'll go back to Louisville tomorrow morning, but I'm coming back on Sunday. I need to be here for the surgery."

"And then?" he pressed.

"And then I'll go back and forth as much as I can."

"Thank you, Calvin. We'll have your new vehicle in the parking lot of the Hart Motel by six tomorrow morning. The key will be taped under the fender of the back right tire. A new phone will be in the glove box. When you receive it, destroy this one."

"Yes, sir."

"We're glad you made the right decision. Oh. And best wishes for your brother's recovery."

Before Calvin could reply to that, there was dead silence.

For some reason, it felt fitting.

CHAPTER 4

Thursday, February 1

I t took a minute, but by the time Calvin went back into the house, he had his emotions firmly locked back down.

"Sorry," he said to Waneta and Mark after petting Brandi, their shepherd mix, which they'd gotten from the shelter soon after they married. "I had a phone call I couldn't put off."

"No apologies needed," his brother said, but sounded surprised. "I know you left work to come see me, though it wasn't really needed. I'll be fine. There was no reason for you to disrupt your whole life just to sit around here and worry about me."

"Mark, don't say things like that," Waneta chided.

While Mark leaned closer to his wife and whispered to her, Calvin used the time to gather his thoughts.

His brother's unreserved belief in him was both humbling and unwarranted. Calvin couldn't think of anything that he'd ever done that would deserve his brother championing him.

Or, maybe it wasn't that Mark was championing him. Maybe it was more to the fact that his older brother didn't expect anything from him. That was more likely. Calvin made another promise to himself that he would one day raise Mark's expectations.

For the moment, he kept his silence, preferring to concentrate on his brother. He eyed him carefully, hoping to determine how he was feeling without being too obvious. Mark was sitting in the overstuffed easy chair in the corner of the room. Maybe he was pale? Maybe his eyes seemed to be a little duller than usual? In the dim room, lit only by natural sunlight from the windows, it was hard to tell.

Waneta had brought over a small table and put a plate with a sandwich and soup on it. It looked delicious. Now would be the perfect time to tell Mark how worried he was about him. How he wanted to be there for him no matter what. But though the words were in his head, they felt jumbled. Everything felt stuck on his tongue.

"I think my being here was needed," he said at last. "I'm glad Waneta gave me a call."

But instead of looking reassured, Mark looked irritated. "Calvin, I told ya. I ain't—"

"How about this, then?" he asked, cutting him off. "Maybe it wasn't needed for you, but it was for me." There. It wasn't what he wanted to say but was pretty close.

"Are you hungry, Calvin?" Waneta interrupted. "I made you a sandwich, too. It's in the kitchen."

"Thanks. That would be great." Turning toward the kitchen, he said, "I'll go get it."

"No need to do that. Sit down."

"I don't want you to wait on me."

"Now is a *gut* time to sit with your *bruder, jah*?"

There was iron in her tone. With her, at least, he knew it was the time to listen.

When she hurried back to the kitchen, Brandi on her heels, he sat down.

Mark chuckled. "*Mei* Waneta is a force of nature. Ain't so?"

Calvin smiled. "Absolutely."

After Waneta brought him his sandwich, along with a dish of sliced pickles that she'd obviously canned, he dug in.

The sandwich was roast beef and white cheddar on thick homemade bread. She'd added tomatoes, pickled onions and lettuce, and finally a generous swipe of horseradish sauce. It was so much better than anything he ever had in Louisville, and such a symbol of the love and care she had for his brother that he closed his eyes and gave a prayer of thanks to the Lord for the first time in ages. Even if nothing ever changed in his life, he was thankful that his brother was now the recipient of such love and care.

After he took his first bite, savoring the flavors, Waneta spoke again.

"You know, Calvin, when I heard you park your truck out front, I got everything all ready for you. But then I had to put it all back on the counter when you didn't come inside right away."

"Sorry. I, ah, had to take a phone call."

"*Nee.* I saw you were speaking with the woman sitting on the Yoders' front porch."

Mark shook his head at his wife, who was now sitting by his side. "Waneta, there's no need to bring this up."

"I don't care," Calvin said after he swallowed his second bite. "So you saw that, did you?" he teased.

"I couldn't help myself, what with you sitting up on the porch with her."

"At least you are being honest about your interest," Mark murmured.

Waneta ignored him. "Calvin, do you care to share with me who that was?"

He was tempted to tell her that he actually did not care to share that, just to tease her. But he was quickly discovering that, like his brother, he was helpless around Waneta's charms. "The woman is Alice Yoder, and I'm beginning to see that there aren't going to be a lot of secrets while I'm here."

Mark laughed. "You can keep all the secrets you want. But be warned, she's going to wheedle them out of you. Slowly but surely, I think my Waneta's turning into her mother."

"Mark, that ain't true!" Waneta exclaimed.

"It ain't a lie, neither," he retorted with a smile. While Waneta obviously attempted, and failed, to come up with a fitting remark, Mark continued. "Calvin, what I'm trying to tell ya is that just because she or I ask you questions, it don't mean you have to answer them. You don't owe us anything."

Even from across the room, Calvin could see that his sister-in-law was blushing. "If you've started peeking out your windows, I don't think I'm going to stand a chance to keep my secrets intact."

"I'm not that bad!" she protested. "Am I?"

"Not yet, Neeta," Mark replied.

Now that his plate was empty, Calvin stood up. He felt restless and edgy. He couldn't help grinning when he walked over to join them. "Alice is Edward Yoder's sister. She's house- and pet-sitting while they're on vacation. She's a nursery school teacher."

"Ah, yes. I had forgotten she was going to be there. She's a nice woman, Calvin," Waneta said. "Her parents are a bit of worrywarts and watch her like a hawk."

Mark nodded. "Edward told me once that he and his brother felt a little sorry for her, so they try to give her breaks every couple of weeks."

"Wow. If they're that protective, I'm surprised they let her work at the preschool," Calvin commented.

"I think she did it without asking them," Mark said. "You probably didn't get to talk to her long enough to discover this, but Alice ain't a pushover. She might look like a sweet young girl, but she's got a bit of a backbone."

Calvin chuckled. "I think I figured that out within the first two minutes of meeting her."

"Do you like her?" Waneta asked. Her expression brightened. "Maybe you two could get to know each other while you are here."

"I don't think that's going to happen." Even though he certainly had just been thinking that same thing.

Waneta raised her eyebrows. "But—"

"I went over there to see who she was. That's all."

"Our street is real quiet now, Cal," Mark said. "I can't think of anyone you should be concerned about."

There it was, spoken bold and almost as plain as day. Mark knew that Cal was not just a manager of an apartment building. Mark knew he watched everything with a wary expression.

"I'm not expecting any. It's just habit, I suppose."

"Like I said earlier, you don't need to explain yourself to us."

Realizing that he needed to tell them about his upcoming trip, Calvin said, "My boss called me when I was outside. I need to go to Louisville for some meetings. I'll be back on Sunday, though. I'm going to be here for the surgery, I promise."

Mark shrugged. "Don't worry on my account. We're fine here. All we're gonna be doing is getting ready to go to the hospital."

Mark's resigned tone of voice gave Calvin pause. "Are you worried about the surgery?"

Mark nodded. "*Jah.* Even though the doctors said it's the best way to get rid of the cancer for good, I don't like the idea of them taking out an organ. I can't help but think our good Lord intended for me to have two kidneys."

"He gave you doctors, too, Mark," Waneta chided. "And those doctors said that one of those kidneys is hurting you instead of helping."

Gazing at her, his voice softened. "I hear you, Waneta."

Calvin knew there were other worries, too. Such as Mark waking up after the operation to discover that the cancer had spread. Or that there would be complications during the surgery. Or even that Mark wouldn't survive it.

A lump formed in his throat, threatening to choke him. It simply wouldn't be fair for the Lord to take his brother when he'd done everything right all his life. But they'd learned at a young age that life isn't fair.

"I'm glad you will be at the hospital with Waneta," Mark said, looking at Calvin intently. "She's going to need someone to lean on and look after her."

"There's no need for Calvin to babysit me. I'll be fine," she said. "Then, of course, I know my parents will be there if I need anything." Looking down at the dog, who had just curled in a ball by her feet, she said, "Brandi will be here with me, too."

Ignoring her protests—and the idea of that shepherd helping much—Calvin stared right back at his brother. "I won't let you down."

Mark released a deep breath. "I know you won't."

Forcing a smile, he turned to his sister-in-law. "Get ready! You're going to have to put up with me for days."

"You really are planning to stay with us for the whole time?"

"I won't leave your side until you ask me to leave," Calvin promised.

Waneta opened her mouth, but closed it. "*Danke.*"

"Don't thank me for being a part of the family, Neeta. I'm glad Mark and I are better."

"Me, too." Reaching out, she clasped Mark's hand. "We are simply going to have to put our burdens in the Lord's hands and pray."

"That's right. That's all you can do. We don't

have to understand why I got kidney cancer; and we don't have to understand how or when the Lord will heal me. We just have to believe that He knows best."

Hesitantly, Waneta nodded. But as she met Calvin's gaze, he knew they were of the same mind. Even having such a strong and steady faith didn't guarantee that things would be easier.

The fear of the unknown was too great.

LATER THAT NIGHT, the old ghosts that used to haunt him returned. Again and again, long-forgotten moments of being hungry, dodging their father, and clinging to his brother flashed in his mind, making him feel just as dirty and unwanted as he'd felt back when he was five.

After drawing himself out of the nightmare, Calvin pulled off his sweaty T-shirt and got out of bed. Wished he could sleep somewhere else. Being back in this house, in his old room, dredged up too many feelings that he'd carefully hidden away during the last ten years or so.

He'd gotten real good at glossing over his childhood in his mind. Their mother had left because she'd been depressed, not because she had an alcohol problem and didn't actually like being a mother, as their father had told them repeatedly.

Their father had been discouraged because he'd never been able to hold down a decent job. Actually, he'd been violent and angry. He'd

49

belittled all of them and had taken comfort in drugs. Mark had done his best to shield Calvin from the worst of it.

And his brother? Mark had given up most of his childhood in order to protect him. Even getting hit so he would be safe. Calvin left because of the guilt.

But since that was far too painful on many levels, he had gotten good at simply saying that they'd drifted apart.

Calvin walked across the room, took a fresh T-shirt and put it on. Yeah, he had gotten real good at lying about his family, his roots, and himself. It had enabled him to survive on the streets. It had helped him find a place in the Kings, too.

And now? Well, it was no wonder he'd been able to become an informant for the DEA. He could lie so well he was able to almost make himself believe the lies.

But none of his acquired skills helped him when it came to being back in the room where he used to live. Even though Mark and Neeta had painted the room and bought a fresh mattress and dresser, Calvin felt as if he was being plagued by all the truths. They were playing games with his mind, venturing in at night when his defenses were at their lowest point.

Now he felt bare and vulnerable.

Doubts set in. What if he really had brought

danger to Mark? Or what if he hadn't been as careful as he should with his phone calls to Andrew? What if one of West's men was watching him even more closely? What would West do if he found out he'd been snitching on their business and plans?

Almost worse were his fears concerning his job. If he couldn't do everything Andrew and the DEA asked him to do, Calvin knew they'd demand he pay back the money they gave him. Sometimes he thought they'd even "accidentally" blow his cover. If that happened, Calvin knew he'd die a very quick—and very painful—death.

And just like that, sweat started pouring off his body again.

He walked over to his window and pulled it open. Closed his eyes as the bitter cold breeze hit his skin.

He knew he wasn't going to be able to go back to sleep anytime soon.

If he was alone in the house, he would have slept in a different room. Maybe on the couch in the living room. Maybe he would have even gone into Mark's room. He'd spent plenty of nights in there when he was small, needing his older brother's reassurance that everything was going to be better in the morning.

But it never was.

Feeling like he was being suffocated, he padded through the dark, quiet house and grabbed his coat. When he got to the front door, he let himself out. Ignoring the pair of chairs on the porch, he sat down on the steps and was able to exhale at last.

He was okay. He wasn't trapped in the house, waiting with dread for whatever came next. Instead, his bare feet were on the cool wood slightly damp from the night's mist.

He tried to clear his mind.

And found the perfect thing to keep his thoughts off his problems—the house across the street.

Where Alice was.

Staring at it, he was relieved to see that all the windows were dark. She was asleep. She probably slept through the night every night. Enjoying cheerful dreams about puppies or her preschoolers, or whatever women like her dreamed about.

At last he relaxed.

Leaning his head against the stair railing, he allowed himself to sit and think about Alice's dreams and how safe and secure she was in her bed.

Free from gangs and guns and drugs and fear.

Free from men like him.

CHAPTER 5

Saturday, February 3

"T hanks for meeting me here tonight," Alice's best friend, Irene Keim, said as she placed a garden salad and bowl of potato chowder in front of her. "I know it wasn't what we hoped to do, but I couldn't get off schedule."

Alice looked around the busy diner, then noticed that Irene's pale skin was flushed and her pale-blue eyes looked wary. With some dismay, she realized that her friend was upset. "Don't be silly," she replied in a rush. "I needed to eat and you need to work. Coming to Bill's works out perfectly. I can eat while you finish your shift, then we can walk home together."

Looking relieved, Irene smiled her thanks before going to help the customers at her other tables.

After praying briefly over her food, Alice placed her napkin in her lap. Then, just as she lifted her spoon, she noticed who was at the table next to her. Calvin Fisher! There in the flesh, looking completely at ease in a light-blue T-shirt and jeans, even though it was close to thirty degrees outside.

Once again, she was struck by his beautiful eyes. They were an unusual shade, lingering somewhere between blue and green. His dark hair seemed a little shorter, and he was freshly shaved. She wondered if all that was his attempt at dressing up. If it was, he'd done a real good job. The new haircut emphasized his cheeks and jaw. She didn't know if she'd ever met a man with such striking features before.

Just as quickly, she felt her cheeks flush with embarrassment. Why was she even thinking such things? His grooming habits were of no concern to her!

Then she realized that he saw her and was eyeing her warily. Well, of course he was. She'd been gaping at him like he was a new animal at the zoo. Hesitantly, she smiled.

Calvin looked startled for an instant before smiling back.

And just like that, all thoughts of chowder and salad fled her mind.

She tried not to watch him while he finished his meal, pulled out a worn wallet, tossed several bills on the table. Tried to tamp down the joy that threatened to engulf her when he walked to her table.

"Hey, Alice. This is a good surprise."

What could she say but the truth? "I think so,

too. I haven't seen your truck lately. I thought maybe you weren't spending much time around here . . ."

"I am. But, as I told my brother and Neeta, I needed to leave to take care of some things. I finished my work early."

"Did you get back today?"

"Yep." He smiled. "I just pulled into town. Actually, I was so hungry, I decided to stop here before I went home."

Unable to help herself, she studied him more closely. His expression seemed clearer. Or maybe it was his body that was more at ease? "I hope you are well?"

"I am." He looked around. "Are you waiting for someone?"

"*Nee*. My friend Irene recently started working here. We always eat together on Saturday nights. Since she had to work, I told her I'd eat here until she got done. She felt kind of bad about it, but I don't mind watching her flit around the tables. Sometimes, I find it's nice to watch someone else run around for a change. I'm usually the one doing that in my job." The moment she finished, she felt silly. He'd asked her a simple question, not for her life story.

But Calvin didn't seem to mind her chattiness at all. Instead, he was looking around the diner. "Is Irene the blond Amish girl in the navy dress?"

"*Jah*."

"She waited on me, too."

"Did she do a *gut* job?" She smiled, letting him know she was only teasing. Definitely not checking up on her best friend.

He chuckled. "She did just fine. Good enough for me to give her a good tip."

In spite of her reason for asking, Alice was really happy about that. Irene had had kind of a tough life. Most folks wouldn't think waiting on tables in a diner was an accomplishment, but for Irene it really was. "That's *gut*. Now, sit down so I don't have to keep looking up at you."

He sat, but gestured toward her soup as he did. "Don't stop for me. It will get cold."

Obediently, she picked up her spoon. "How is your *bruder* doing?"

A shadow crossed his eyes. "Waneta called me yesterday and left a message. She said that Mark was fidgety but otherwise all right. They're going to go ahead and admit him into the hospital on Sunday afternoon. I guess they want to do some tests and monitor him closely before Monday's surgery."

"That all sounds hard. I'm real sorry, Calvin."

"Thanks. I keep trying to tell myself that it's out of my hands, you know? Waneta is worried, of course, but Mark seems to be at peace."

"And you?"

He blinked. "Me?"

"How are you? Are you at peace?"

He shrugged. "I don't think I remember how to be at peace . . . But I'm hopeful at least. I'm worried about him, but I have to have faith that everything is going to work out." He paused again, looking as if he was trying to search for the right words. "Right?"

She nodded. Took another sip of soup. "I'll pray for him tomorrow and Monday, too. I'll pray for all of you."

"Thank you. He's going to need all of our prayers." His gaze softened on her for a moment. Long enough for her to practically feel the heat of that visual caress. Then, seeming to need to gather himself together, he stood up. "I'll let you go. It was good seeing you."

He was acting so formal! "It was good to see you, too, but you might want to get used to it. I'll be living across the street from you for at least another three weeks."

"I haven't forgotten." Right as he was about to turn, he paused. "Hey, how are you getting home?"

"I'm walking home with Irene." She smiled.

But instead of smiling in return, his brow creased with concern. "Does she live on our street?"

"*Nee*, but close enough. I live only about ten minutes beyond her apartment.

"So who is going to walk you the rest of the way?" His gaze hardened. "You aren't walking by yourself, are you?"

"Of course I am." Maybe on another day she would have reminded him that she was neither his responsibility nor a child. But it was obvious that his concern came from a good place. "*Danke* for caring, Calvin. Don't worry about me. I'll be fine."

But instead of looking placated, he looked irritated. "Don't thank me for caring about you, Alice."

Not knowing what to say to that, she sipped her drink.

Calvin pressed his palm flat on the table. "I know it's not my place to say this, but you need to be careful."

"Because?" He really was being a bit ridiculous.

"Things can happen that you don't expect. Don't forget that."

A chill wrapped around her. She'd lived in Horse Cave all her life. Never once had she worried about walking around by herself. Until now.

She lifted her chin again. "I'll be thinking about you and your family, Calvin. Please let Waneta know that I'm more than happy to help her if she needs anything. I can bring you all a meal or even do some cleaning or laundry. Anything at all."

"I'll let her know, but you won't be needing to do any laundry, Alice," he said before he grabbed a black wool coat hanging on a nearby hook and walked away.

Unable to help herself, Alice turned her head to watch him disappear down the sidewalk. When he was out of sight, the entire room seemed a whole lot dimmer and far more noisy. To her surprise, she realized that she hadn't been aware of anything other than Calvin when he took the seat across from her.

If she closed her eyes, she knew she could describe in detail the way his T-shirt stretched across his shoulders. The way the sleeves hugged his biceps. The scar across his knuckles. The scar near his bottom lip. The way he smelled, a combination of peppermint, tobacco, and soap. Why, she could even recall each nuance in his expression. Never had she imagined that two eyes could convey so much.

She felt his loss like a tangible thing.

Not quite sure how she felt about that, Alice stabbed a piece of iceberg lettuce with her fork. She really needed to stop thinking about him so much. Really! Dwelling on a man like him could only lead to trouble.

Fifteen minutes later, Irene was at her side, ostensibly to bring her a fresh glass of iced tea. Alice was pretty sure that it had more to do with her curiosity than anything else.

"Who was that man? I've never seen him before," Irene stated the moment she set down the glass. "And how do you know him anyway?"

"He's Calvin Fisher. He's my brother Edward's neighbor. Kind of."

Her eyes widened as she slid into the booth, right where Calvin had been sitting. "Fisher? Wait, he's Mark Fisher's brother?"

"He is."

Irene cleared her throat. "Alice, surely you remember the rumors about Mark?"

"I would prefer to remember how all those rumors were false. Besides, Calvin is Mark's younger brother. There aren't any rumors about him."

"Oh, I'm sure there are, we just haven't heard them yet."

"If that is the case, I'm glad about that. I don't want to know. He's nice."

Irene leaned back in the booth and folded her arms across her chest. "Why was he sitting with you?"

"Because I asked him to." Alice knew her answers were abrupt and vague, but she was in no hurry to gossip about the man, especially since she didn't know him all that well. Then there was the fact that Calvin was worried about Mark. He needed a friend.

Staring at her intently, Irene raised her perfect blond eyebrows. "What did he have to say? Did he just want to tell you hello?"

"Not exactly. His *bruder* is having surgery on Monday morning. I was concerned about how

60

he was doing, which is the same way you would have been," Alice added before Irene could say otherwise.

"Oh."

"*Jah. Oh.* Now, may we please drop this subject?"

"I would drop it . . . except that I saw how you were looking at him."

"And how was that?" she asked before she realized that she didn't want to hear Irene's description.

Her palms started to sweat as she began imagining what the rest of the restaurant had observed her doing. Oh, no! Had she been showing on her face *every* emotion she'd been trying to curb? She really hoped not. The last thing she wanted was for people to be commenting that she'd made a fool of herself with Calvin—in front of a crowd at the diner.

"You were staring at him like you were smitten, Alice."

"I am not smitten. He is simply a nice man." Realizing she sounded rather defensive, Alice attempted to put a little bit more force behind her words. "He's going through a difficult time, too. He needs a friend."

Irene studied her. Finally, she said, "It doesn't matter if he used to be Amish. He's English now."

"I happened to notice that."

"No need to be sarcastic."

"There is also no need to point out the obvious," Alice explained. "I know who Calvin Fisher is, and I know he isn't Amish anymore." Before she inadvertently said anything else about him, she cleared her throat. "Now, I think we have talked about him enough. When can you get off?"

For the first time since Irene joined her, she looked unsure. "That's what I came over here to tell you. Alice, I'm really sorry, but May asked me to stay later. One of the other girls has a sick baby at home and they're shorthanded."

"How much longer, do you think?" A feeling of dread came over Alice as she heard the heaviness in her tone. But she was preparing herself for the worst. The restaurant had gotten really full since she'd sat down.

"Probably another two hours." Irene winced. "At least."

Two hours? "I don't think I want to wait that long," Alice said. "I'm sorry."

"I didn't expect you to," Irene replied. "Besides, the other customers are going to need your table, right?"

Alice tried to summon a grin. "Right."

Glad that things were smoothed over, Irene smiled. "At least we got to talk, though, right?"

"*Jah*. We did." Alice hoped she sounded more positive than she felt. Because she really didn't feel like they got to catch up. All they'd done was talk about Calvin Fisher—and that had gone nowhere fast.

Realizing that she was now going to be walking back to Edward's house by herself, she felt a flicker of unease. Calvin's warning felt fresh and ominous. She opened her wallet and pulled out a ten-dollar bill. "I better get on my way."

"Truly? I have five more minutes of my break."

Since the door to the restaurant had been opening and shutting quite regularly for the last fifteen minutes, Alice thought Irene cutting her break short might actually be something of a blessing. No doubt the other servers needed help and Irene was brand-new there. Surely, she would want to be busy and make a good impression on the owners. "I've got a long walk ahead of me. I should be going."

Irene stood up, fished in her pocket, then handed Alice her bill. "Here you go, then. See you tomorrow. My aunt Ruth is hosting church."

"*Jah*. I'll be seeing you then." She stood up and hugged Irene good-bye, but there was a new tension between the two of them. It was obvious that both of them were aware of the slight change. They'd come a long way from the girls they'd once been. Back during their *rumspringa*, both of them had been sure that no one understood how they felt.

63

Just as they had been *abundantly* sure that no other members of their families had ever experienced any of the same emotions that the two of them had.

Together, they'd pushed boundaries so much that Alice would feel her cheeks heat in embarrassment every time she recalled their escapades. Oh, they'd done so many things that brought her shame.

But their worst was when they'd gone off with an English girlfriend for the weekend to Nashville. They'd lied to their parents about where they were going, and to themselves about what experiences they were craving.

It had all come crashing down on them that weekend. Literally. Remembering the car accident, she winced.

By the time they'd come back to Horse Cave, Alice and Irene felt like they were different people. They'd vowed to be different, vowed to never again encourage the other to do something that would harm themselves or other people.

Alice had gotten in big trouble. She'd been grounded for over a month. And Irene? Irene had never talked about what happened to her. That had to be why Irene had made such a fuss about Calvin. She was worried Alice was being tempted again.

But that wasn't the case at all. It was because of her past that she knew the value of accepting others with an open mind. It was hurtful to be judgmental.

After gathering her purse and tote bag, she slipped on her pink sweater and black cloak and started walking to Edward's house.

When she'd been looking forward to walking with Irene, the long walk had sounded like a wonderful-*gut* way for them to catch up. Now it just felt long.

And since the sun was beginning to hang on the horizon, it also felt a bit dangerous. Especially when an unfamiliar fancy-looking SUV with tinted windows slowly drove past her.

Then drove by her again—this time in the other direction—and so slowly that it almost came to a stop on the side of the road before accelerating and zipping out of sight.

Though it was silly, she felt as if the people inside had been staring at her. And not just in passing, either.

Feeling more and more ill at ease with each step, she started looking around her. Fearing the shadows. Feeling like she was being watched.

She began looking down side streets, trying to remember if any of them had streetlights, trying to figure out which ones would get her back to Edward's house more quickly.

But her mind kept getting muddled.

Oh, but this was all Calvin's fault. He was the one who said it wasn't safe for her to walk alone. His warning had stuck in her head and was spinning around practically daring her to prove him wrong.

When another car passed, she looked at it nervously, her heart in her throat. It didn't even matter that it wasn't the black SUV, she still felt conspicuous and vulnerable. She bent her head and increased her pace.

Only another thirty minutes now. If she walked really fast, maybe only twenty-five.

When she heard another vehicle approach, then start to slow, tears pricked her eyes. She was almost running now. She was afraid to look to see who it was. Was it that black SUV again?

If it was, what was she going to do? She wasn't near anything. Only fields and a run-down lot that was filled with a bunch of old rubber tires and a mean-sounding barking dog.

Now her heart was beating so loudly, it was practically all she could hear. Until the hum of an electric window sliding down sounded next to her.

"What are you doing, walking on this street all by yourself?" a very familiar voice called out.

She whirled around. Calvin must have arrived just seconds before. Why was he there?

Opening his door, he got out and grabbed hold of her arm. His hold was firm but not painful. "Why did you lie to me earlier?"

"Calvin—"

Visibly attempting to calm himself, he exhaled. "You know, don't say another word. I can't even handle it right now."

"But—"

"Just get in," he said as he forcibly escorted her to the passenger side and opened the door. "You're coming with me."

A mixture of emotions filled her. Relief. Anticipation. Wariness. And, finally, confusion.

What was worse? Getting in Calvin's truck or walking by herself?

At the moment, neither seemed like a good option.

CHAPTER 6

Saturday, February 3

C alvin knew Alice Yoder was a gently bred, sheltered Amish girl. He also knew she wasn't stupid. But at the moment he couldn't decide whether to enfold her in his arms or shake some sense into her.

Since neither of those options were possible, he made do with yelling at her instead.

"Alice, you lied to me. You told me you weren't going to be walking home by yourself."

Right before his eyes, her shocked expression transformed into one of fierce irritation. She folded her arms over her chest and glared. "Well, *hello* again, Calvin. I'm so glad to see you again."

Had any woman ever been so exasperating? "You don't want to start playing games with me."

"Who said I was playing? It seems like you are the one playing games, acting like you did when you left the diner almost thirty minutes ago. What happened? Did you decide you had nothing better to do than stop and yell at me on the side of the road?"

Calvin loved Alice's gumption. Loved that she

didn't take any flack from him. But that didn't mean he was going to back off, not when her safety had been in jeopardy.

He didn't care that they were in the middle of Horse Cave, he still knew that women weren't safe walking alone. Especially not this close to nightfall. Thinking back when he'd first run away from home, his pulse started racing. He knew from firsthand experience that there were a lot of men who hoped and prayed for situations like this.

Then, too, was the added danger that was likely his fault. Alice probably hadn't even been aware of it, but he was sure he'd just seen a dark SUV driving down the street. That was what West drove. It was practically a calling card of the Kings' leadership.

Seeing one of those decked-out Suburbans in the middle of Kentucky cave country? Just when he happened to be there? It was too much of a coincidence for his comfort.

When he'd left the day before, he'd been sure that everything was all right. But maybe he'd been wrong. He needed to get on the phone and figure out what was going on. But first, he needed to get Alice home.

"Buckle up, Alice."

After hesitating a moment, she put on her safety belt. Once she was settled and safe, he pulled out onto the now empty stretch of highway and picked up speed. Already, he was feeling better. One glance at Alice told him that she wasn't feeling near as pleased. She was wearing a mutinous expression. Actually, it looked like she was trying real hard to not snipe at him.

Again, instead of feeling irritated by her show of spunk, he was impressed. This little thing, so pretty in her pink sweater, had more grit than most men he knew. Rarely did anyone talk back to him like she did.

Though it would probably be better to let her stew in silence, just like before, he couldn't resist riling her up a bit. "Care to tell me what you're thinking?"

She folded her arms across her chest again. "*Nee.*"

He tried hard not to smile. "You sure? I know you're irritated with me. You can yell at me if you want, you know. Don't hold back. I can take it."

"Calvin, there's no need for us to discuss anything."

Hearing something new in her voice, he caught sight of her folding her hands in her lap.

Noticed they were trembling.

All of his amusement and anger evaporated. She wasn't simply being spunky, she was upset. He was fairly sure that he heard a quiver in her voice. Had he been too harsh?

Thinking back to the way he'd chewed her out,

he knew the answer to that. Of course he'd been too harsh.

He should have remembered that she wasn't like any woman he'd had contact with in recent years. She'd been handled with care and looked after all of her life. She wasn't used to being treated callously or yelled at.

Embarrassment, mixed with tenderness, flowed through him. He might have enjoyed her strength, but he hadn't meant to hurt her feelings. He certainly didn't want her afraid to speak to him. He was tempted to reach out and curve his hand around hers. Comfort her. Say anything he could to make her feel better.

But that wouldn't do.

They were never going to have a future together. One day she was going to realize he didn't have a respectable job. No, it was far from that. He spent most of his days procuring illegal weapons.

Among other things.

He needed to apologize and then step away from her.

Keeping both of his hands on the wheel, he even made sure he stared straight ahead. "I'm sorry I yelled at you, Alice."

"You yelled and you acted like you were trying not to laugh at me."

"I know. I'm sorry. I don't know why I'm acting this way," he lied. "But seeing you out on the road alone scared me half to death. I can't take the thought of you being hurt."

"I was fine."

But he noticed that she didn't sound all that convincing. Darting a look her way, he realized that she wasn't just shaking. There were tears in her eyes.

She wasn't just upset that he had yelled at her. She really had been afraid. Knowing that erased the last of his efforts to keep his distance and his concerns to himself.

"What happened? What has you so spun up?"

"It was probably nothing," she said, right before she swiped a hand across her cheek.

Wiping away fresh tears.

The action broke his heart. "Alice, I'm not going to drop this. Actually, I'm about to pull over to the side of the road and wait until I find out what did happen. I'll wait all night."

She turned her head, examined him closely. "You truly mean that, don't you?"

Not trusting his voice, he nodded. It was taking all his willpower not to pull her into his arms and wipe away her tears himself.

"I . . . well, I guess I started thinking about how you were worried about me. It made every car and truck that passed by seem suspicious. I started feeling scared."

He didn't doubt her words, but he knew that wasn't the whole story. "And then?"

She took a deep breath. "A little while before you showed up in your truck, a black vehicle drove by. Twice."

"What did it look like? Was it a truck? A car?"

"*Nee*, it was one of those SUVs. It had dark windows, too. When it drove by the second time, it slowed down. I thought it was going to stop."

Unable to help himself, he released the death grip he had on the steering wheel and reached for her hand. When she didn't fight his touch, he carefully curved his fingers around her own. "You okay now?"

"I think so." Her hand tightened under his, then relaxed. Then it flipped. He felt her soft palm curve around his hand. It felt so small against his own.

That movement, along with her answer, eased the tension in his body. She was beginning to trust him. And that? Well, that made Calvin feel almost whole.

Even though the situation was his fault. If he hadn't been there, the Kings wouldn't have come to Hart County.

"I'm sorry this happened, Alice."

"What are you sorry about? It's not like you had anything to do with that SUV driving around."

"I know, but I'm sorry it happened."

"Me, too." Taking a breath, she smiled slightly. "But it's over now, right? That SUV is long gone? . . ."

"Right." After pulling to a stop in front of her house, he placed his other hand over hers. "You may not completely trust me yet, but I want you to know that you can depend on me. If you ever need something, all you have to do is ask."

Looking down at their hands intertwined together, she pursed her lips again. Then nodded. "All right."

"All right? You're going to give in that easily?" He hoped his words would make her smile.

And she did. Pulling her hands away from his, she said, "You remind me a little bit of how things are at school."

"In your preschool?"

"*Jah*. Especially little William."

Part of him felt offended. Here, he'd just vowed to be her protector and she was comparing him to a four-year-old. "And I remind you of him because? . . ."

"William is always so scrappy. He never wants my help right away. I have to coax him to listen to me. I have to sometimes even remind him that I know best."

"Wait a minute. You're saying that I am acting like you do with William?"

"*Jah*." Her eyes sparkled. "That ain't a bad thing, though."

"Don't worry about me being offended, Alice. I actually think that you just gave me one of the best compliments I've ever received in my life."

He unbuckled. "Now, stay there and let me get the door for you. And then I'm going to check the inside of your brother's *haus*."

"Just to be sure everything is all right?"

"*Jah*," he said softly. "Just to be sure."

When she gazed at him with trust in her eyes again, he felt like he was everything. Everything that he'd ever wanted to be.

CHAPTER 7

Tuesday, February 6

The unfamiliar squawk of sirens woke her up. Lying on the hard mattress in the middle of Edward's and Bethy's guest bedroom, Alice tried to get her bearings, then flinched as she heard another set of sirens ring out.

After making sure that Valentine wasn't scared—and the white-and-gray cat wasn't, he was sound asleep on the end of the bed—Alice threw on her cozy flannel robe and got out of bed.

While the sirens continued in the distance, she peeked out the window. But of course there was nothing there. Even in her dazed state, she had known that no emergency was taking place on the street.

Stifling a yawn, she looked at the bedside table, where Bethy had thoughtfully left a digital clock, flashlight, and book of devotions. It was only five in the morning.

Glancing out the window again, she peered into the darkness. The sun was still asleep and the dark winter morning held only shadows. All she could surmise was that a bit of snow had fallen overnight. It made the neighbors' lawns glisten and the streets turn powdery white.

It was a perfect morning to sleep in, especially since her preschoolers didn't come to school until noon on Tuesdays.

Well, she was awake now. Disappointing— she'd intended to sleep until at least eight. But now that she was up, Alice wandered downstairs, walked into Bethy's beautiful kitchen, and put the percolator on the stove for coffee. Ten minutes later, still feeling like something was amiss in the world, she threw on her sheepskin slippers, one of Edward's thick coats over her robe, and walked out the front door.

The acrid scent of smoke was in the air.

A house must have caught fire. She scanned the area, looking for wisps of smoke, but saw nothing. Only that thick blanket of darkness that the middle of winter brought.

Then she heard a muffled click and spied a faint orange glow. It brought her attention back to the house across the street. And with some surprise, she realized she was watching Calvin Fisher stepping out of a shiny truck.

It might have been dark, but the faint glow from his cigarette and the distant streetlights brought out the fact that he looked different. He had a dark knit cap on his head and what looked like an old army-green jacket over his shirt. Jeans.

Boots. When he brought the cigarette to his lips again, she could have sworn that he looked tired.

Unable to help herself, she watched him hold the cigarette between his thumb and index finger, exhale, then bring it to his lips again.

For some reason, she couldn't stop watching him. Oh, not because she was shocked that he was standing outside smoking so early in the morning. After all, he'd been smoking the first time she saw him. Then, the last time they talked, there had been that faint scent of cigarettes on his skin and clothes.

Or maybe it was that she and Irene had had their fair share of cigarettes. She almost smiled at the memory. When she'd first inhaled, she thought she was never going to be able to take a full breath again. She'd coughed like the naïve girl she was.

Though it was rude, she continued to study him. When she saw him carefully extinguish his cigarette and toss it in a can, then grab a backpack, she couldn't help but stare at him in wonder.

Why, it looked like he'd been gone all night.

After clicking his key fob, he looked in her direction. Met her gaze. Froze for a second.

Then, to her dismay, he started walking over.

Alice wasn't sure if she was more embarrassed about how she looked or the fact that he caught her watching him like she had every right to do so.

By the expression on his face, she was pretty sure she'd just made a bad mistake.

"What are you doing?" he asked as he strode up the steps. "It's kind of early to be standing outside in the cold, don't you think?"

Alice knew that she should say that she was sipping coffee and enjoying the morning. Except it was about twenty degrees out, there was smoke in the air, and only the streetlights prevented them from being completely in the dark. She resigned herself to tell him the truth.

Surely, that was better anyway. She'd learned a long time ago that practicing deceit only created more pain and embarrassment.

Holding her cup with both hands, partly to keep them warm, partly to have something to do, she shrugged. "I heard the sirens. They woke me up."

His hand tightened on the soda can he still held. "They were that loud?"

"There were a lot of them. What happened? Do you know?"

"Yeah. A car caught on fire right outside of town."

"Really? I thought it was a house. I didn't realize cars could catch fire, too."

"Of course you wouldn't have. You hang around horses and buggies." His smile showed that he was teasing.

Usually, she would have laughed that comment

off. Coming from a man like him, who was raised Amish, they both knew that most Amish weren't deaf and blind, too. But his voice held a new edge to it, and she wasn't in the mood for jokes. "You tell me, then. Why did it burn up?"

"Why are you asking me like I was there? I only drove by and saw the commotion."

"Why do some cars burn up?"

"I don't know. Engines get overheated. Wires get torn. People do things they shouldn't."

"Was anyone hurt?"

He shrugged. "Probably. An ambulance was there."

"I hope that whoever was inside will be okay."

He tilted his head, looking at her closely. "Why do you care?"

His question caught her off guard. "It's human nature to be concerned, Calvin. Don't you feel the same way?"

"Not really. If it ain't my problem, I try not to worry."

"I'm pretty surprised to hear you say that. What, with your *bruder* so sick and all."

Some of the ease in his expression vanished. "That ain't the same and we both know it."

She felt her cheeks heat. He was right. Suddenly, she was aware that she'd been jabbing at him. "I'm sorry."

He shrugged again. "Don't worry about it. I'm a little keyed up. I guess you noticed."

She lifted her coffee cup. "I need more *kaffi*. Would you like some? I made plenty."

"No. Coffee's the last thing I need." His voice drifted off. "You care if I smoke out here?"

She should. This wasn't her house. "You going to put those ashes in that can?"

"I will if it will make you happy."

"Then I guess it's okay with me."

"*Danke*," he muttered as he set down the backpack, pulled out a red package of cigarettes, a lighter from a pocket, and lit one quickly.

She watched his eyes close as he inhaled, and it told her everything she needed to know. He was stressed out. "What have you been doing? Why are you up and dressed so early?"

He raised his eyebrows. "Why are you asking?"

That was probably a good question. "No reason."

After he took another fortifying puff, he sat down on her stoop, just like he intended to stay there awhile. "Go get your coffee, Alice."

She turned and hustled back inside. Valentine was now sprawled across the kitchen counter. She meowed when she saw Alice.

Alice knew the cat well enough to know that she wasn't greeting her. The cat was annoyed that she hadn't been fed yet. Walking to the cabinet, she pulled out the box of Meow Bites and poured a generous amount in the cat's bowl.

Then, before she convinced herself that nothing

about sitting on the front porch in her robe and Edward's coat—with a smoking Calvin Fisher—was good, she poured herself another full cup and walked back out.

He was lighting another cigarette.

"You are sure smoking a lot. Do you smoke this much every morning?" The moment she said the words, she wished she could take them back. What was wrong with her? Though she often spoke her mind, even she wasn't usually so brash.

"*Nee*. Only when my *bruder* is in the hospital."

So that was where he'd been. "I'm sorry. I should have asked about Mark first thing. How is he?"

"Don't worry about it, you had other things on your mind." He shrugged. "When I called to check, the nurse on duty said he was still asleep, and that the next twenty-four hours would tell a lot."

"So you are waiting."

"*Jah*. Neeta is there with her parents. After I shower, I'll head up and join them." He smiled then. It was unexpected. "You sure ask a lot of questions."

"I'm sorry. I do, but I sound rude even to my ears."

"It doesn't bother me."

"Sometimes I can't help myself. It's a product of being around four-year-olds all day, I'm afraid. They ask a lot of questions of me."

83

"That's a good reason, but something tells me that you ask so much because that's how you are. You're a curious girl."

"Maybe so." She frowned, considering it. "I need to learn to curb my tongue, though."

"Why?"

"Because it hasn't done me a lot of favors."

"I'm sure your tiny scholars don't mind," he said with a smile.

"You're right. They don't. But no man wants a wife who asks a lot of questions of him."

With a frown, he tossed the last of his cigarette in the can. "Who said that?"

"No one in particular. It's just a given."

"Maybe. Or maybe you've been hanging out with the wrong men."

That startled a laugh out of her. "What are you saying? That you would want a girlfriend who asks a lot of questions?"

He shrugged. "I wouldn't care if she did. It's not like you have to answer everything."

She realized then that he hadn't been answering everything she asked. Actually, he was real good at evading and redirecting. "I'll keep that in mind for future reference."

He smiled then. "Alice Yoder, you are a piece of work." As he stood up, he leaned toward her, bringing with him the scent of tobacco and a faint aroma of cologne. "I'm real glad you were out here this morning."

"Why is that?" she asked before she could stop herself.

"You made everything seem better." He flashed a smile again. "Kind of like this morning's sunrise."

She turned to the east, only saw the faintest hint of a glow. "Calvin, the sun hasn't risen yet."

"I know. But the hint of it is there. Some mornings that's enough, ain't so?"

She was still puzzling over that when he picked up his backpack and strode across the street. She watched him walk toward the back entrance and toss that can of cigarette butts in the trash, then unlock the door and walk inside.

After he was gone, she looked at the approaching sunrise again. The band of light was wider.

As she sipped her coffee, Alice decided to watch it grow. And while it did, she gave thanks for another day and tried to concentrate on the lingering scent of Calvin's cigarettes instead of the smoke from the car fire in the distance.

CHAPTER 8

Thursday, February 8

Another two days passed before Alice saw any sign of life over at the Fishers' house. She'd certainly been looking, too.

This wasn't something she was proud of. She knew better than to think too long about a man that was so unsuitable—knew better than to not only be attracted to him but to even have a friendship with him.

Yet having this knowledge didn't change her behavior. Actually, it seemed that it was out of her hands.

She found herself looking for Calvin's truck every time she ventured outside. She'd also found herself gazing out her windows late at night, hoping to see lights shining in the house. But so far, she hadn't seen anything at all.

Alice figured everyone was at the hospital. She had no idea how long one stayed at the hospital after having a kidney removed. She wished she would have thought to ask Calvin that. But because she hadn't, she was forced to simply hope and pray that the surgery had gone all right and that Mark Fisher was simply recovering.

When she wasn't thinking about the Fishers or taking care of Valentine, Alice was as busy as ever with school. This week her tiny scholars were learning about George Washington and Abraham Lincoln. She'd even checked out a book from the library about President Washington extolling the dangers of lying.

She'd been pretty proud of that lesson. She'd read the book out loud and led a discussion about lying, the children sitting on the ground around her in a semicircle. Their eyes had been wide with the idea of such a great man telling tales.

Since then, her little scholars had taken the lesson to heart, too. Now they couldn't seem to stop telling her the truth about everything—from what they thought about each other, to unusual things their parents liked to say and do, to their many likes and dislikes. More than once Alice had had to pinch herself so she wouldn't burst into laughter . . . or wince, after learning something that obviously wasn't meant to be shared.

Yes, she had indeed ended up finding out a bit too much information about her students' families. However, all that sharing did have a silver lining.

It kept her mind off of all the other things that were happening around Horse Cave.

The first incident had been the mysterious car fire that she'd smelled on Tuesday morning.

She'd gotten chills when one of her students' parents relayed that it had been a black SUV. The picture in the newspaper showed only a burnt shell, but the journalist also had provided a photo of what the car usually looked like.

It looked just like the one that had passed her before Calvin picked her up. She couldn't help but wonder if it was the same one.

But even the awful car fire didn't worry her as much as Mark Fisher's recovery did. Maybe it was because she stared at his house every morning . . . or maybe it was because Calvin was his brother—still, every couple of hours, Alice would find herself thinking about him. She hated being so close to his situation but not close enough to actually help him or his family in some meaningful way.

All she could do was wait and worry. Was his condition worse? She hoped and prayed that wasn't the case. Should she consider walking down to the phone shanty and giving the hospital a call?

Now, here it was Thursday evening. Though she had a book open in her lap, she couldn't help but spend more time gazing out the windows instead of at what was written on each page.

Finally, giving up all pretense of reading, Alice stood at the window and peered across the street.

She knew she shouldn't be concerned, but she was. All sorts of terrible things kept running through her head. Maybe Mark's surgery went badly. Or there were complications afterward.

Or they found even more cancer. Then, too, she couldn't understand where all of their family was. Though the Fisher boys didn't have any more relatives, she knew that Waneta did. Why was no one stopping by?

Why, her own brothers, their wives, *and* her parents would have practically moved inside her house if her husband was having such a serious operation.

Now she was kicking herself for not getting any more details about Calvin's hospital visit. She could have tried to call to check on the Fishers or, at the very least, offered to cook them meals or clean their house. Anything to help out.

Just as she was about to turn away, Calvin's truck pulled into the driveway. And then, there was Calvin! At last!

Before taking the time to second-guess herself, Alice ran to the front door, threw it open, and hurried over to see him.

She reached his side just as Calvin was unlocking the front door.

He stiffened in surprise, then gradually, he relaxed. "Hiya, Alice. What's going on?"

"Oh, Calvin, what isn't?"

Immediately, his expression grew concerned. He reached out and clasped her arms. "What's wrong? Did something happen to you?"

"Not at all. I'm fine. I've been worried about your brother. Is Mark okay?"

He swiped a hand over his face. "He's as well as can be expected. At least, that's what everyone is saying." With a sigh, he rolled his shoulders, like he was trying to get the kinks out.

The gesture looked so weary, her heart went out to him. It must have been a terrible couple of days. "Did they get all the cancer?"

He shrugged. "The surgeons said they thought they got it all, but they took all kinds of samples of other tissues so we don't know for sure. I'm learning that even at the hospital, everything takes time."

"I'm really sorry."

Calvin blinked, looking surprised. "There's nothing for you to be sorry about. It's been difficult, but we have to just keep praying and hoping that what the doctors say is true. They say a lot of patients can recover just fine from this kind of cancer. And that they can live a long life on just one kidney, too."

His words might be sure, but she heard a hoarseness in his voice that told how he was really feeling.

"Is there anything I can do for you? What about Waneta? I had assumed she would be coming back here every night. Or her parents would."

"Neeta's been sleeping at her parents' *haus*. That's where she is now."

"Where have you been sleeping?"

Looking at her more intently, he murmured, "I've been at the hospital, Alice."

"I didn't think they had extra beds for visitors."

"They don't. I've been sleeping in the chair next to Mark's bed."

"You've been sleeping in a chair? That can't be comfortable." Remembering their early morning conversation and his chain-smoking, she said, "Have you been getting any sleep at all?"

He averted his eyes. "Not a lot. But some. Don't worry about me." A small smile lit his features. "I've slept in worse places, Alice. I'll be fine."

"Oh. Of course," she mumbled, suddenly embarrassed. Calvin Fisher was a grown man, a very capable man, and here she was, talking to him like he was one of her preschoolers. When was she ever going to learn to talk to men like they were men and not small boys under her care?

When he didn't say anything more, just looked at her in that almost-tender way of his, Alice backed up a step. She was such a foolish girl. "You know what?" she asked, far too brightly. "I bet you're tired. I'll let you go get to sleep."

He rubbed the back of his neck. "I am tired, but all I've been thinking about for the last couple of hours was taking a hot shower. I feel like my shoulders are full of knots."

He was about to shower. In spite of being a grown woman, she felt her face flush. "Well, good night, then," she said in a rush.

"Hold on. Let me walk you home."

Next thing she knew, he had her hand firmly clasped in his. As much as she liked holding his hand—and she really did—she felt foolish. "It's only across the street, Calvin. I think I'll be able to navigate my way just fine."

"Humor me. I like making sure you are safe," he said as they walked up the four steps to her front porch.

"Thank you for looking out for me," she said softly.

When they got to her door and she opened it, he leaned against the frame. "Listen, by tomorrow afternoon, we should get a better idea of how my brother is doing. What time do you head home from school?"

"Usually, around three or four."

"How about I meet you there and take you home?"

She almost protested, saying how there was no need for him to go to so much trouble. But then she saw something in his gaze. He needed to have this chore. "*Danke*, Calvin. I would like that. My school is right near Floyd's Pond. It's just at the top—"

"I know where your school is, Alice," he interrupted. "I'll be there at three thirty."

Her insides gave a little burst of happiness, even as she told herself that this was not a date. "*Danke.*"

For the first time since she'd greeted him, he grinned. "You're welcome. Good night."

"Night."

"Don't forget to lock this door. I'm going to stand here until I hear the bolt click."

"Calvin, there's no—" But before she could finish her thought, he jerked open the door from her grasp and rushed inside. Just as he slammed the door shut and bolted it, she spoke. "What is—"

"Quiet!" Looking around the neat but rather sparse living room, he pointed toward the couch. "Get behind the couch. And stay there. Whatever happens, don't come out until I tell you to."

"But—"

"For once, listen to me without arguing, Alice!" he said harshly as he walked back to the window.

Very afraid now, she practically crawled behind the couch—and couldn't help but peer at him.

He was crouched near the window, muttering to himself. When he contorted to pull his cell phone out from his back pocket, she noticed for the first time that he had something nestled in the small of his back.

She blinked, at first sure that her eyes had deceived her.

She might be naïve, but even she knew what that was.

Her lungs tightened as the reality of their situation set in. Calvin Fisher had brought a gun into her house, and she was fairly certain he intended to use it.

CHAPTER 9

Thursday evening, February 8

His heart was pounding so loud, Calvin swore he was about to have a heart attack.

Why had the head of the Kings just driven down the street? He knew he wasn't mistaken, either. It wasn't just any black SUV—plus, the sight of it would have taken anyone by surprise here in the middle of rural Kentucky. That sedan had a ton of polished chrome, and was tricked out with darkened windows and black rims. He'd never seen another car quite like it.

As Alice shifted restlessly behind him, Calvin forced himself to ignore her unease and concentrate on why West was there. No, he was forcing himself to come to terms with the only reason West would have come here himself. He was no doubt there to kill him.

Calvin's cover must have been blown—that was the only thing that made sense. It would explain why West, who usually stayed out of sight and only left his home heavily guarded, would come to Horse Cave in person. With only Smith by his side.

Smith was West's bodyguard, confidently the only person handing out West's directives. Smith wasn't the man's real name, of course. No one had ever told Calvin what it was. He had heard rumors that he'd gotten the name because he could blend into the background unnoticed. Others said it was because the guy was a good shot—so it was Smith, as in the gunmaker Smith & Wesson.

All Calvin knew or cared about was that the guy was smart and clinically cold. Nothing seemed to ever shake him up.

Which was the exact opposite of how Calvin felt at the moment. If Smith or West had come to kill him, then neither would have any problem shooting him in front of Alice.

Alice would see that, too. And because she was so obstinate and impulsive, just about anything could happen. Maybe she'd even rush out and get caught, get herself hurt, too.

Sweat broke out on his temple. Slid down his back. If Alice was harmed, it was on his shoulders.

When he was coming back to Horse Cave, he realized there was a strong possibility of bringing his garbage with him and tainting his brother's life. Now he had not only done that, but he could be hurting Alice, too.

When his hands started to shake, he inhaled deeply. He needed to get a grip on himself before he made things worse.

"Calvin, what are you doing with that gun tucked into your back? Is . . . Is someone outside on the porch?" Alice asked after several more minutes passed. "Should we go into another room and hide? Or—"

"Hush," he said. If they were in another situation, he would be grinning. There she was, hunkered in a ball behind the couch—and what was she doing? Offering helpful suggestions.

He would have been proud of her if he wasn't so afraid he was about to get her killed. His little preschool teacher was no shrinking violet. Instead, she had a bossy, take-charge streak that was a mile long. No one, not even gang members, it seemed, was safe from her efforts.

When he heard her sigh, his smile faded. He needed to tell her something, anything to help her settle. But though he knew that, Calvin couldn't bring himself to speak. After all, what could he say?

Then all thoughts left him when he saw the black Suburban pass again.

Knowing that West's slow drive-by was the only warning he was going to get, Calvin clenched his phone. He was going to need to call him. And then he was going to have to go outside and wait for him to return.

But first, he had to do something about Alice. Since there really was no story that he could fabricate that would shine any sort of positive light on this situation, he elected to give her the skeleton version of the truth.

Walking away from the window, he carefully knelt by her side.

She looked stressed out—and afraid of him. He hated that, and had no one to blame but himself. He should have never talked to her so much. He should have never made her think that he could ever be someone she could trust or befriend.

Taking care to keep his voice even, he spoke, knowing all the while that he was going to have to be quick. "Alice, a member of the, uh, organization that I'm in just drove by the house. I need to go out there to speak to him."

"Are you sure? Is it safe?"

There she went again, trying to manage him. Trying to protect him.

It was so humbling, it took everything he had to keep his voice even and easy. "I'll be fine. You stay put, though."

"I don't understand. If they are your friends, there's nothing to be afraid of, is there?"

"I don't want them to see you."

"Well, I don't like being down here."

He almost smiled. That was what he liked about her. This girl had gumption. In spades. "You know what? You should probably go to another room." Seeing a narrow staircase leading to the basement, he pointed to it. "I want you to go down to the basement and stay there until I come back for you."

Her eyes widened before she shook her head. "*Nee*. I don't want to go there. Ed never got it finished. There are tons of spiders."

"I want you to be safe." When she still looked like she was going to put up a fuss—honestly this girl could give a number of men he knew a run for their money—he hardened his voice. "Don't argue, okay? Just do it."

She bit her lip, looked ready to voice her displeasure yet again, then turned around and headed down the stairs.

Hoping that he had scared her enough that she was going to stay put, Calvin strode toward the door and walked to the front porch, jerking the door shut behind him. With one hand, he pulled out his pistol; with the other, he lifted his phone, about to dial.

But he paused for a moment, and tried to see himself as West and Smith might. He was wearing old leather Nikes on his feet, worn jeans on his legs, and a long-sleeved Henley on his body. A black ball cap was on his head, serving to shield his eyes and his expression.

Still one of the guys.

As the seconds passed, his pulse raced, and every doubt and worry that he'd ever entertained rose up and threatened to choke him. What had he done, coming back here? Putting his brother and Waneta in danger. And now putting this innocent woman in danger, too?

Hadn't he learned that he couldn't have everything? Especially not a future.

He scanned the road again. Listened for an approaching vehicle. Felt his heartbeat slow as he sorted through options—wondering if he left right now and didn't return, if that would be enough for his family and Alice to be safe.

Cal's keys were in his pocket. He could simply leave. After a while, Alice would creep upstairs, go back to her parents' house, and chalk up the experience as the reason she shouldn't trust a man like him.

Then the car returned. Driving just as slowly. Probably not a degree over the twenty-five-mile-an-hour speed limit carefully posted at every intersection.

Then it pulled to a stop in front of the house.

Pocketing his gun, he stepped down the front steps just as both the driver's and passenger's side doors opened. Calvin tensed, then forced himself to breathe slowly as he saw that it definitely was West who had arrived. And there, just as he'd suspected, was Smith standing by his side.

Both men were dressed much the same as he was. Jeans. Long-sleeved knit shirts. Black ball caps. But West had on expensive leather loafers and Smith had on thick-soled work boots. They looked as out of place on the street as Calvin felt half the time.

They were also staring at the closed door suspiciously.

"Never thought I'd see you greet two members of your family with a gun in your hand, Cal," West drawled as he took care to walk to the neatly lined walkway that led from the street to the steps where Calvin was standing.

"A man can't be too careful," Calvin replied. "Especially when the visit is unexpected."

West glanced at Smith. "Oh, yeah. I was gonna tell you to give Cal a call and let him know we were coming. Huh. I guess I forgot."

Smith said nothing, only stared at Calvin with that carefully blank expression that more than one man he knew had learned to dread.

"What can I do for you?" he asked when they stopped in front of him. "Why are you here?"

"What? You aren't going to ask us in?" West murmured.

"Maybe he doesn't want us around his girl," Smith supplied.

Calvin stayed silent, feeling slightly better about the situation. The men were prodding him on purpose, just to see what he was about. If they had wanted to hurt him or if they suspected him of snitching on them, he would already be in the car or bleeding on the sidewalk. Their boss liked them to be efficient in everything they did.

Slowly, West smiled as he took off his sunglasses. "Do you have a girl in there, Cal? You hiding her from our prying eyes?"

"Yes to both."

Smith looked amused. "Come on, now. You know that we wouldn't hurt her. We just want to see what she's like. Is she pretty? Don't you want to show her off?"

"She's not that kind of girl."

West slid his shades back on. "Oh, yeah? What kind of girl is she, then?"

"She's no one." He locked down his panic and eyed them both. "Why are you here?"

"Someone told Smith that maybe you weren't just taking care of your brother while you were here. He thought maybe you had other business." His voice got harder. "But now it's obvious that this business is personal. Looks like you got yourself a honey in the country." His voice hardened. "Or am I mistaken?"

Thinking quickly, Calvin realized that their suspicions about the girl actually were to his benefit. If they thought he was distracted by a woman, then they wouldn't think that he was doing anything for the DEA.

"Her name is Alice," he said slowly, taking care to keep as much to the truth as possible. "She's Amish and shy. We, ah, used to know each other before I left. I guess there's still something there."

Though Smith was staring at him in disbelief, West nodded like he understood. "Makes sense to me. I had a girl like that once. Girls like that, nice girls who don't want anything . . . well, they're real hard to resist."

"I'm not going to let her be a distraction."

"Can you trust her?" Smith asked.

"She's Amish," West said. "She isn't going to start texting her friends that Cal here is hiding out."

"You're right. She ain't going to do any of that. And now that my brother is out of danger, I'll come back for part of this week, too."

West stared hard at him. "You know what? I think it might be better for you to hang out here another week or so. We've got a deal going down on Friday and the police have been trailing us around like we're leaving them bread crumbs. If you show up to oversee the job, they're going to think something's up."

"I understand."

Some of the tension in West's body eased. "Glad to hear that." He pulled out an envelope. "Here's your take for the week. I figured you might need it, with your family being here and all."

"Thanks," Calvin said as he shoved it in a back pocket. "I won't let you down."

West shoved his hands in the back pockets of his jeans. "I know you won't. The Kings come first, right?"

"Always." Calvin smiled tightly, hoping he didn't look as sick as he suddenly felt inside.

Because there was no mistaking what West meant. Men who didn't always put the Kings first learned to regret that decision.

He'd seen that happen more than once.

CHAPTER 10

Thursday evening, February 8

I rene Keim was a great many things, but a fool wasn't one of them. At least, she hadn't thought so until today.

Lost in thought in the back of Bill's Diner, she kept replaying her recent conversation with Alice. Either she had completely misunderstood Alice's story . . . or she had completely been wrong about Calvin.

If that was the case, then she'd been wrong about just about everything else that she knew to be true.

Alice had steadfastly ignored all her warnings about Calvin Fisher. First off, he came from a bad family—even worse than hers, and that was saying a lot. While her parents had been mean and verbally abusive, his parents had been blights on the whole community. They'd constantly ignored their church community's rules while being first in line for handouts.

Then Calvin had taken off when he was fourteen and done who knew what. And though he was now helping his brother Mark, there were still lots of rumors around Hart County about him. They were disturbing rumors, too. Rumors that he not only had left the faith and considered himself English, but had taken up with dangerous people, too. Some whispered that they not only disobeyed the law, they carried weapons and dealt drugs. Why, any one of those things should have been reason enough for Alice to stay far away from Calvin.

Then there was his older brother Mark's past. Oh, sure. He'd only been suspected of hurting Bethany Williams years ago. Another man had later been charged for that.

But didn't it mean something that he'd even been suspected of such a thing? Irene felt pretty sure that a good man, a real man of honor, would never have garnered such a tarnished reputation.

All that was why Irene could hardly believe it when Alice told her yesterday that she had become friends with Calvin Fisher. Irene talked until she was blue in the face about the many reasons why she should keep her distance from the man. But instead of listening, Alice had only laughed off Irene's fears and told her that she shouldn't gossip so much.

"Irene, you going to gaze out the window all day or go wait on customers?" her boss, May, said.

Irene jerked to her feet. To her embarrassment, during the last lull in customers, she'd hopped onto one of the red padded stools at the bar near the kitchen and allowed her mind to drift off. "I'm sorry." Scanning the area, she noticed a pair of men sitting in the back booth. "I'll go right over."

May didn't say anything, but Irene could feel her irritation. And no wonder! Irene had only been working at the diner a couple of weeks. She wasn't going to be working here another two days if she didn't pay more attention to her job.

After double-checking for her pad and pencil, she hustled over to them. Her footsteps slowed when she realized that the two English men were boldly watching her approach. Sure she was about to hear a slew of complaints, she spoke quickly. "I'm so sorry you were kept waiting. I don't have any excuse, either," she admitted, remembering how her mother had once told her it was best to be honest. "My mind drifted off."

The skinnier, younger man snickered under his breath but said nothing.

Just as Irene felt her neck heat with embarrassment, the older man's eyes warmed. "It ain't a thing, sugar. We got time."

She blinked, realizing that he might have been older than the skinny man, but he wasn't *old*. Most likely he wasn't much past thirty. The moment that thought entered her mind, she realized why she'd been thinking such a thing at all. She found him attractive.

It had to be his voice. It was dark and thick. Not scary, though. No, it was more like he didn't talk a whole lot and his voice was out of use. Feeling relieved, she smiled at him, liking how his dark-brown eyes seemed to look at her like there was no one else worth paying attention to in the room.

"Are you ready to order? Oh! Would you like to hear about the special?" She couldn't help her own hesitant tone of voice. This particular special was not her favorite, but a great many people seemed to like it.

"What is it?"

"Liver-and-onions."

The younger, skinny man swore under his breath. But not low enough that she didn't hear him. And though she'd heard such cursing before, it did take her off guard to hear him saying such things in the middle of the diner.

His cursing, along with the appraising way he was looking at her, made her hand tremble a bit as she pulled out her little pad of paper. "Do you know what you would like to eat?" she asked, hoping to get out of his space.

"Yeah. Get me a burger and fries and sweet tea."

She wrote that down. "And you, sir?" she asked the older man.

He was glaring at the skinny man but darted a look her way. "I'll take the fried chicken with

110

the potatoes and green beans. Is it any good?"

"It's real good. Bill makes it fresh every morning." She smiled.

His eyes—lovely and deep—warmed back again. "Good to know. How about you get me a tea, too?"

"Sweet?"

"Unsweetened. You got that?"

She nodded as she went through the motions of writing it down, though she had a feeling she'd remember their orders for the rest of the day. "I'll be right back with your drinks."

"No need to rush. We're all right," he said slowly and quietly. Then his voice hardened. "But wait a sec, 'kay? Smith here has something to say to you."

Surprised, she looked at the other man. Gone was the smirk and the oily attitude. Instead, he looked, well, contrite. "I'm real sorry for offending you, miss." After a darting look at the man across from him, Smith swallowed. "I won't do it again."

Irene was so stunned, she only nodded before turning on her heel and rushing back to fix the drinks and put in their orders.

"Burger and fries plus the chicken with beans and mashed potatoes, Bill," she said as she handed him the ticket.

"Everything okay over there, Irene?" he asked as he slapped a beef patty on the grill.

"Yes." She smiled tightly. Then got the drinks together.

When she returned to the men, the older one was watching her again. The younger one was tapping on his phone. "Here you are," she said. "Unsweetened tea for you and sweetened tea for you. Oh! And straws!" She set them on the table with a little flourish.

Oh, brother, but she was acting the fool!

The brown-eyed man's lips twitched like she'd amused him. "Thanks."

For a second, she felt like he was waiting for her to start a conversation with him. But what was really strange was she actually was thinking about doing that.

Luckily, the door opened and two groups of customers entered. One was a family of six and the next was another pair of men. She pulled back a sigh as she watched May seat the family in Lora's section and give her the men—and as she watched, she felt a little ball of dread inside.

These men, she knew.

They were Foster and Tim. They were Amish and had grown up near her. The men were best of friends, just as she was with Alice. Their school hadn't been big, but the four of them had never been close.

Things took a turn for the worse when Tim tried to court her and she pushed him off, rather rudely. In front of other people, too. He hadn't taken kindly to it and never let her forget it, either. Even though all that had been years ago, Tim still acted as if she'd gone out of her way to embarrass him just last week.

Stifling a sigh, she walked over to take their order. As luck would have it, May had placed them in the booth right next to the two Englishers.

"Look who's here," Tim said to Foster snidely. "Irene Keim."

She schooled her expression and reminded herself that she only needed to serve the men, not have conversations with them.

"Hiya, Foster. Tim." She said this as pleasantly as she was able. "Can I get you a drink while you look at the menus?"

"Water," Foster said.

Tim didn't even look up from his menu. "I'll have a Coke."

"Bill's got liver-and-onions today, too."

Foster nodded. "We need some time."

The door opened again and still more people entered. May put the elderly couple in Lora's station and seated three women about her age in the booth next to Foster and Tim.

Irene rushed around as best she could. She got the two Amish men their drinks and delivered the Englishers their meals.

The women were easy, ordering soup and fresh rolls. It was obvious that they were using the time to catch up. To her surprise, the Englishers

113

ate slowly, too. Well, the older, kinder man did; the younger one ate, then returned to whatever he was doing on his phone.

But the problem came from Foster and Tim. They wanted more to drink. Then for her to take their orders. Then they changed their minds and ordered something else. Then, to her dismay, Tim said he didn't like his and changed his order again.

Bill took it in stride but did look irritated.

When she brought Foster a fresh glass of soda, he glared at her. "When did you start working here?"

"A couple of weeks ago."

"Do your parents know?"

He said it loudly enough for the Englishers to hear. What the Englishers didn't know, of course, was that it served as an insult to her. Her parents were dead, and even if they'd been alive they wouldn't have cared what she did.

They hadn't cared about much she did, as long as she stayed out of their way. Now she lived by herself in a basement apartment in the town's only apartment complex.

"You know the answer to that," she said tightly.

"You're still all alone."

"I'm fine."

"It didn't have to be like that, you know. At one time, you could have gotten a husband. Before you lost your way. Now it's likely that no one would have you if you begged. But we could give it a try. You feel like begging, Irene Keim?"

His voice drifted enough that one of the women gasped. Even the Englishers looked at the men in surprise.

Her embarrassment was complete. Keeping her head down, she forced herself to walk to the counter, grab the Englishers' and the women's checks, and Tim's second meal.

After she delivered it all, May touched her shoulder. "I'll finish up their bills, Irene. Why don't you go take a little walk? It's nice outside."

She needed this job. No way was she going to "take a walk" just because someone spoke harshly to her. "I'll be okay."

"You aren't in trouble. Go on now. I'll put your tips in a safe place."

Realizing that May wasn't exactly giving her a choice, Irene nodded, grabbed her sweater from the hook by the door, and walked outside. Usually, she would have put on a coat. It was February, after all. But the temperature was in the upper thirties and the sun was out.

Actually, the brisk air felt good against her skin. Needing some space to get her bearings, she turned right and kept walking to the corner of a building on the opposite side of the diner's main parking lot. Where hardly anyone ever parked their cars or buggies. It was her favorite place to take a break, though. It was so quiet and peaceful. Five or six pine trees dotted the corner.

Leaning against the building, she pressed her hands to her face and wondered if she was ever going to be able to outrun her past.

"You okay?"

She jerked her head up and saw that the older English man had caught up to her. His friend was nowhere to be seen.

Wariness filled her, especially now that she realized just how tall he was. Probably a couple of inches over six foot. And right on the heel of feeling wary, she thought of something else. He was standing only a few feet away from her. Slightly more than arm's distance. But his brown eyes were kind. Not harsh like they'd been with his friend nor unamused like they'd been when she was late taking their order.

Yes, kind. Like he cared about her.

"I'm fine, thank you," she said.

He didn't look like he believed her. But that was no surprise, because she didn't believe her words herself.

"Those men mean anything to you?" he asked.

She almost shook her head, but his grave concern felt so good, she told him the truth. "One of them wanted to date me a couple of years ago. I refused him. He took it hard."

"He is still holding a grudge, huh?"

"It's more than that. I . . . Well, for a time, I

made some mistakes. Everyone found out. Those men enjoy bringing it up."

"They sound like, ah . . . jerks."

She laughed as she realized that he purposely cleaned up his words for her. "They are. They've always been." When he smiled, she added, "Do you know anyone like that? Who always acts like a bully? Someone who never changes his spots, year after year?"

"Yeah. I do." He shoved his hands in his pockets. "Want me to beat them up for you?"

He almost sounded serious. Smiling, she shook her head. "No, thank you."

He stepped closer. Then, to her surprise, reached out and wiped off the tear that had escaped her eye. "You're a pretty thing. Sweet, too. Don't cry over men like that, 'kay? Trust me, they ain't worth it."

His touch had been gentle. The callous on his finger brushing against her skin felt soothing. "Thanks for coming over to check on me," she said quietly. "It was nice of you."

"You got someone who looks out for you now?"

Before she thought the better of it, she shook her head. When his eyes narrowed, she felt stupid. "I'll be fine."

"You won't be fine for long, if that's the kind of thing you're putting up with."

"Today was rough, but I'm usually a better

waitress." Remembering she wasn't supposed to call herself a waitress, she gulped. "I mean *server*."

"No offense, but I don't think working at this diner is the right job for you."

"I used to work in a warehouse for less money. So, this is a good job for me. I'll get better."

"Do you got a phone?"

She shook her head. "I'm Amish."

"But there's a phone here that you can use, right?"

She nodded.

"Okay, then." He fished in a couple of pockets and pulled out a card. "This has my number on it," he said, handing it to her. "If you ever need something and don't know who to ask, call me, Irene."

He was looking at her intently. While her insides were getting all mushy again, she knew she couldn't just take a strange man's card and follow his directions as if she did things like that. "Why?"

He paused, as though not expecting her to question him. "Because looking out for you would make me happy."

"But don't you live far away?"

"Only by two hours. That ain't anything, sugar. If you need me, I'll get here." While she gaped at him, he continued on. "Now, look. I'm gonna come back in a week or so. Sometime before that, you call and leave a message for me. Tell me how you're doing. Don't forget."

"I don't know how I feel about that."

He blinked, then folded his arms across his chest. "What do you want to know?"

What didn't she want to know? And more importantly, why was she even still talking to him? "Are you West? Is that your name?"

"It is."

She fingered the card. Noticed that it had a motorcycle emblem and a bunch of numbers, and one name. "Don't you have a last name? Or is that your last name?"

"It's neither, but it's what everyone calls me."

Well, that was as clear as a mud puddle. "I still don't understand why you came over here to find me. Or why you want me to call."

"All you need to know is that those men won't be bothering you again. Now I gotta go, but I'm expecting you to call. If you don't, we're going to have to have a talk about that when I come back here."

He was bossy! She should be offended. Maybe even worried about how presumptuous he was being. But instead of either of those things, she was merely curious. "If I don't call, what are you going to do?" she whispered.

"If you don't call, all we're going to do is this."

"This?" She waved a hand, feeling like she was treading water in a deep pool.

"This. Talk, sugar. That's it. Don't you worry. I'd never lay a hand on you. You understand? I don't hurt women."

"Okay."

That seemed to be important to him. "Do you believe me?" he pressed. "I don't want you scared."

"I'm not scared of you." And miraculously, she wasn't.

"Good. Now, chin up, sugar. Things are going to get better. You ain't alone anymore."

And before she could respond to that, he turned and walked over to a dark SUV that his friend had just driven up. While she looked on, West got in the passenger seat, closed the door, and Smith drove off.

She watched the small cloud of dust that the car's tires kicked up dissipate before making her way back to work. Just before she walked inside, she slipped the business card in the pocket of her dress.

And realized that she felt much better about everything.

Though she knew she should only feel scared that such a scary man had taken an interest in her, Irene decided to worry about that later.

For now, all she knew was that she wasn't alone. And for her, that was a very good feeling.

CHAPTER 11

Friday, February 9

C alvin had grown to love his sister-in-law. Waneta was easygoing, generally cheerful, and had given him another chance to prove himself with her and Mark.

He would always appreciate that.

And because of what he owed her, there was usually nothing she could do that he would ever find fault with. Until today.

She'd spent much of the day at the hospital pacing and fussing, questioning nurses, and generally making herself sick with worry. Privately, he couldn't fault her. There were so many things that could prevent Mark's recovery: One of the tests could show that the cancer had spread, or his other kidney could start failing, unable to handle the stress of losing its other half. Or Mark could get an infection—and with his weakened autoimmune system, a whole new set of dangers could set in.

Calvin was there not only for himself, though; he was there to give his sister-in-law support. That meant he needed to act as if everything with his brother was going to be fine.

In some ways, this subterfuge was even more challenging than his undercover job. But still, he persisted. He tried to reassure, distract her, and even pray with her. None of those things helped.

He felt so sorry for her.

But as the hours passed, he began to feel a little sorry for himself, too. It was a thankless job, attempting to calm someone who didn't care to be calmed down. Exhausting, too. If he didn't get a break from her restlessness, he was going to snap. "Waneta, how about you go home for a couple of hours?"

She turned on her heel, pausing in midstride. "Why on earth would I want to do that?" she asked after double-checking that her husband was still asleep.

"Because we both know if Mark saw you like this, he would be concerned. He would want you to rest."

She inhaled, obviously prepared to list the dozen reasons why she shouldn't leave the room. But Calvin had some ammunition that he'd been saving for this very moment. "Before Mark's surgery, I promised him that I'd try to look out for you."

"And that's what you're doing?"

"I am." He wasn't lying, either. Mark actually had gripped his hand hard and made Calvin promise that he would always look after Waneta if something happened to him. That was one of the easiest promises he could make, especially since he planned to do it anyway. He *wanted* to be there for his brother and sister-in-law. He wanted to help them, to do something of worth.

So that's what he was trying to do. But he was also looking after himself. He would be able to be the man he wanted to be . . . if his dear sister-in-law wasn't getting on his last nerve. "You need to leave for a while," he said as forcefully as he could while still keeping his voice low. "It's time."

Her blue eyes narrowed, refusal shining in their depths. "But you've been here much longer."

He also was much better at sitting and waiting. If there was anything his adult life had taught him, it was the value of patience. "I'm going to have to go back to Louisville for a couple of days. You'll be on your own then. Why don't you go see Lora or your parents for a couple of hours? I know they are all probably real worried about you."

Her expression brightened. "Lora did say she was working at Bill's Diner today. I bet my parents might want to go there with me. I heard the special is liver-and-onions again. My mother loves that."

Carefully schooling his features so he didn't grimace, he said, "See? There you go."

Neeta's expression brightened a bit more.

Feeling like he was making progress, Calvin pulled two twenties out of his wallet and handed them to her. "Why don't you go get some lunch or a shake and visit with all of them for a while? I'm sure they'd be glad to hear your updates. When you come back, Mark will be awake and you'll have something to talk to him about."

She nibbled her bottom lip. "I could do that. Mark does like hearing about my parents' latest projects. But you keep your money. I'll use my own."

"You need cash for a driver and food."

"But—"

"Let me keep my promise to Mark, Neeta." When she still hesitated, he said, "Mark gave me this money before he left for the hospital, so you would have some if you needed it."

Her brow wrinkled. "He didn't want to give it to me?"

"He was worried you'd be flustered or wouldn't want to use it on yourself."

She glanced at her husband. "Mark is so wonderful."

"*Jah*. He is. He's wonderful-*gut*," he said drily. "So take it, okay?"

After a lengthy hesitation, she took the money. Then, after gently brushing her hand along Mark's brow, she walked out. Calvin might have been mistaken, but he was pretty sure that her step was already a little lighter.

Feeling pleased with himself, he exhaled.

"I didn't know you could manage my wife so well," Mark said.

Calvin popped his head up. "How long have you been awake?"

"Long enough to hear you lie to her about that money," he said weakly.

"It wasn't anything. I didn't want her to worry about paying for a driver. That's all."

"*Danke.*" His eyes closed again.

Standing by the bed, Calvin asked, "How are you doing? Do you need anything?"

"Some water would be good."

Carefully Calvin poured some ice water into the plastic glass and positioned a straw in the middle of it. "Here you go," he said as he held the cup for him. "Sip carefully, okay?"

Mark did as he was told, then leaned back with a heavy sigh.

Calvin thought he looked pale. "Are you in pain? Do you want me to call for the nurse?"

"Not yet. Why don't you sit and talk to me instead?"

Calvin sat down. It was moments like this when he felt the chasm in their relationship most of all. He could work beside Mark easily. He'd had no trouble pitching in and helping Waneta prepare for Mark's hospital visit.

He was even good with doing what Mark asked him to do. But sitting by his side made him uncomfortable. They didn't have that ease of relationship anymore.

Or maybe they never did. He couldn't remember very many times during their childhood when they weren't in some kind of crisis mode. Either one of their parents would be acting strangely and Mark would be helping Calvin stay out of their way—or he and his brother were in need of clothes, school supplies, or food.

The older Calvin got, the more he came to appreciate all the sacrifices Mark had made for his good.

"Anything special on your mind?" he asked, half hoping that Mark would need him to go ask a question of one of the nurses.

"*Jah.*"

"Name it, then."

After an interminable moment, Mark murmured, "How 'bout you tell me who your friends are now."

A dozen lies entered his head, each one promptly cast aside. He didn't want to lie to Mark. But he didn't want to disappoint him right to his face, either. "Ah, what friends?"

"The ones in Louisville. The ones you are always texting or seeing."

"You know I'm part of the Kings. That's not a secret."

"*Nee*, but I thought you were going to get out of that gang."

126

"Getting out ain't all that easy." For most people, it meant death.

"How are you going to get out?" Mark's gaze turned direct. His eyes were clear and piercing, making Calvin shift uncomfortably, just like he used to when he was a young boy. "What will you have to do?"

"It doesn't matter, because I'm not going to get out anytime soon." He held up a hand. "I owe West. He took me in when I was in a pretty bad place. I make a good living working for him, too."

"But aren't you still doing illegal things?"

"Not so much," Calvin said lightly. "We should talk about something else. So, um, are you in much pain?"

Mark grunted. "I'd rather talk about you. If you don't want to leave, I get that. But you don't have to lie about it."

"I don't want to argue, brother. Years ago, we each made our choices. Mine happened to come with some consequences that I have to live with. But I'm making sure that they don't touch you or your wife."

"Drugs and guns . . ."

"Neither of those things are going to touch you."

"I heard you tell Waneta that you were going back soon."

"Yeah, I tried to get out of it, but I don't have much choice. I won't stay long, though."

"They won't mind if you come home again?"

"The Kings aren't a Boy Scout troop, but they aren't all bad, either. West values family as much as the next guy."

Mark pursed his lips together. "I don't understand it, but I am glad you've been here. I've been resting better knowing you are with Waneta."

"I'm glad I've been here, too," he said, relieved he could finally say something without lying. "I wouldn't have wanted to be anywhere else."

Before Mark could start another topic, Calvin pressed the call button.

"May I help you?" a tinny-sounding female voice asked.

"Yes, my brother is awake."

"That's great. Someone will be right in."

"I'm getting the feeling you did that on purpose," Mark said drily.

"Of course I did. Waneta would be mighty upset with me if I didn't try my best to take care of you."

"Huh."

Luckily, a nurse came in with a cart and prevented Mark from pressing him for more information.

"Hello, Mark," she said with a smile. "Let's see how your vitals are doing." She smiled brightly as she reached for his arm. "The doctor said if you continue to show improvement, you might be able to go home in a couple of days."

"Not tomorrow?"

She clucked as she pressed two fingers on his wrist. "That's up to the doctors, Mr. Fisher. But we wouldn't want you to leave before you are ready, right?"

"Right."

When Mark looked at him with raised eyebrows, Calvin winked. "I'll go stand outside."

Mark pulled his arm out of the nurse's grasp. "But we'll talk later?"

"Of course, *bruder*. I'm here all night. We'll talk all you want," he said before walking out into the hall.

Only then did he release the breath he'd hardly even been aware he was holding. His brother was going to be all right. He hadn't messed up anything with him and Waneta yet.

So, yeah, he would definitely talk with Mark. He'd talk with him all night long, if he wanted.

It just wasn't going to be about anything that could get either of them killed.

CHAPTER 12

Wednesday, February 14

The minute Alice walked onto the front porch, intending to walk to the street and retrieve Edward's mail, she realized that she should have looked out the window first.

Calvin Fisher was standing outside again. As if he'd heard the screen door creak, he looked directly at her but didn't speak.

That was a good thing, because she had no idea what she would say anyway. All she seemed to be able to do was stare back.

He wasn't smoking this time. Instead, he was just standing there, looking at her. Or maybe he was simply staring out at the world and she happened to be in his line of vision.

She stood stuck for a couple of seconds like a deer on the edge of a street. She wasn't ready to see him again. She'd seen a gun tucked into his clothes the last time they'd been together.

He was obviously dangerous. Dangerous to know and dangerous to be around.

But still, there she stood. Watching him in a bold way.

The sun was slowly setting on the horizon, seeming to cause shadows to play across Calvin's features. There was only one streetlight and it hadn't come on yet. She couldn't see him all that clearly. The longer she watched him, the more she started worrying about him.

She was almost disappointed that he wasn't smoking. She'd started to become used to the way he fussed with both his cigarettes and his lighter, and got the impression that the constant motion relaxed him as much as tobacco did. Now? He looked too still and silent. She wondered if he was worried about his brother or was bothered by something else.

Yet again, she might have just been imagining things. Maybe Calvin was perfectly fine and was simply enjoying the peace and quiet.

Determined to simply complete her errand and get back inside, she started walking. And, if he happened to say something to her, she would reply politely.

But that was it.

Chin up, she walked down the driveway to the mailbox. Opened it to see that her suspicions were correct. It was fair to bursting with mail and catalogs. Yes! She'd been absolutely right to get the mail for her brother and sister-in-law. It wasn't a made-up errand at all.

Knowing that gave her the fortitude to sneak another peek at him.

Unfortunately, she didn't end up being sneaky at all. Calvin was still staring right at her.

Which made her all the more flustered.

She waved, hoping to look pleasantly surprised to see him, but no doubt failing miserably. "Oh! Hiya, Calvin. I hope you are well?" Yes, she did indeed call out to him from across the street.

"I'm all right. What are you doing?"

"Nothing much. Getting my *bruder*'s mail." Standing beside the box, she smiled at him. Practically willing him to invite her over.

He didn't disappoint. "I just made a pot of decaf coffee. Would you like any?"

"Oh! *Jah*. Kaffi sounds wonderful-*gut*. I mean, I'll be right there," she called out before rushing inside to put the mail away. Valentine the cat looked at her like she'd lost her mind.

Alice felt herself blushing. "I know what you're thinking, cat, and you would be right, too. I'm being a little impulsive and very forward. Mamm would be displeased. But I'm only being neighborly."

Valentine eyed her silently, then held out a paw and licked it.

"I know. Words mean nothing compared to my pushy behavior. But it's not too awful. I mean, I hope not. There's no need to look so disapproving," she chided before rushing back outside.

By the time she got through his front door,

Calvin already had two cups on the coffee table. Beside them was a little plate with a sugar bowl, spoon, and a jelly glass full of milk. "You made me a coffee service?"

"Don't tell anyone. Every man I know would laugh at me. But I figured girls always like sugar and milk with their coffee."

Since she was known to take a generous helping of both, she had to smile. "I won't tell anyone. But I do appreciate it. *Danke*."

He shrugged. "Don't thank me for this. You coming over helped me out. I'm not used to sitting here all alone. I was standing out there, feeling like the evening was going to last for hours."

"How is your *bruder*?"

"He's going to be okay. The initial tests came back negative for traces of cancer in other parts of his body. It looks like they got it all when they took that kidney. But he's sore and having a difficult time bouncing back."

"He needs to be patient."

Calvin grinned as he waited until she fixed her cup of coffee, then poured his own cup. "That's going to be hard for him to do. He's used to doing things, not lying in bed all day."

"And your sister-in-law?"

He set his cup down. "She's a nervous wreck, Alice. I've tried to help her talk with the doctors, and even encouraged her to let me speak to them first so she doesn't have to, but that doesn't help.

134

She takes every warning that they give her and magnifies it in her mind."

"I bet a lot of people do such things."

"I'm sure they do. I find myself doing that, too. I don't blame her, of course, but it's hard to know what to do."

Struck by how worried and unsure he sounded, Alice's heart went out to him. "I'm sure that Mark and Waneta are thankful you are here. It is comforting to have family around in situations like this. I think you being with them now, might be enough."

"I don't know. I want to take on more of Waneta's burden or help pay for Mark's bills."

"Will they let you do that?"

"I think they will, but even that hasn't been easy." He stared down at his cup, which was almost empty. "I owe Mark a lot."

"Why?"

"He practically raised me." After a second, he shook his head. "No, that ain't right. He did raise me."

"Where were your parents? Oh! Did they pass away when you were young?"

"Oh, no. They were around, not that it mattered." After glancing at the front door of his house for a long minute, he spoke again. "Our parents weren't the best. Actually, they were pretty bad. Our mother wasn't happy and our father had a lot of issues."

135

"Issues?"

"He drank. He was bitter and lonely. He abandoned our faith. When my mother eventually left, Daed took all of his frustrations out on us."

"That sounds painful."

He blinked. Then he nodded. "It was."

He was being so honest—so brutally honest, it took her off guard. Both because of the fact that she didn't know anyone in their circle who'd been through so much at home; and also because, even if they had gone through as much, they didn't admit it.

"I guess I shocked you."

He'd been so frank, she didn't want to make light of that by toning down her response to it. "You did."

"Do you want to head back home? If you do, I won't blame you."

He wasn't lying. His expression was carefully shuttered. Almost like he had already prepared himself to accept her rejection. That, of course, was such a shame. What kind of life did a man have to have for him to always think the worst was about to happen? To expect to be rejected?

"Of course not, Calvin. I'm not going to walk away just because of something you said. Certainly not because of the way your childhood was. That ain't your fault."

"You mean that, don't you?" His voice was soft, almost hopeful sounding.

Hesitantly, she nodded. "You couldn't help what your parents were like." Instinctively, her voice came out soft, just like when she was with her tiny *kinner*. He needed a gentle tone *and* a good dose of reassurance. There was nothing wrong with that. Everyone needed to feel that way at one time or another.

Calvin picked up his cup and sipped slowly, looking like he was taking a moment to think about what she said. Alice used the time to sip her coffee, too. While she did, she couldn't help but reflect that he made excellent coffee. Better than hers, she thought. She also noticed that his feet were bare just below the frayed cuffs of his jeans; and that visible under his gray sweatshirt was the collar of a sparkling white undershirt.

He looked different, all covered up. More approachable, she assumed. Less scary.

"I've never met anyone like you, Alice."

His statement was sweet but a bit too pat. "I'm not the only Amish girl you know."

"This is true, but you are the only Amish girl I know who I've ever wanted to share so much with. *Danke*."

"You are welcome, Calvin."

"I'm glad you came over. If you hadn't, I would have gone over to knock on your door."

"Really? You would have done that?" she blurted, hating that her voice sounded both breathless and extremely hopeful.

Ack, but she was acting desperate.

"Yeah." When she smiled, he rushed on. "Not just to talk to you, either." He cleared his throat. "You see, I wanted to let you know that I was going to be gone for a few days again. I'd like to give you my cell phone number. You could call it if you notice anything strange over here."

"You're going to be gone yet again?" Ack! Could she sound like a more lovesick fool? Horrified with herself, Alice pressed a palm to her lips. "I mean, I'll be happy to give you a call if I notice anything out of the ordinary, not that I've had much of an opportunity to watch your *haus* or anything."

"I've got to head up to Cincinnati. Something is going on there that I can't ignore."

"Of course. But you are coming back?"

"Oh, yeah. Hopefully, I'll be back by the weekend. Maybe I'll see you then."

"Maybe." Hoping to not sound so desperate, she added, "I'm not sure what I'll be doing."

He stepped closer. "Well, if you are home and you happen to see me and you want to talk again, that would make me real happy."

"Why is that?"

"Because I've been watching your house, Alice," he said, his voice turning lower, and maybe a little bit warmer sounding, too. "I find myself glancing at your windows in the evening to see if you are still awake. I check in the morning to make sure you get out of the house in time for school."

She was so touched and so taken aback, she said the first thing she could think of to respond. "I'm never late for my job. I take my *kinner* and their education seriously."

He laughed, but not in a mean way. Instead, it sounded as if he was holding some secret close to his heart and laughing at his own private joke. "I know you would never be late for them. Just like I know they are blessed to have such a caring teacher."

His praise embarrassed her. "They are the blessings."

His gaze warmed. "Yes, they are." He took a breath, almost as if he was steeling himself to continue their conversation. "When I come back in two days, maybe we can talk again. I mean, if you would want to."

"I would."

"*Gut.* You can tell me more stories about how your little students have been doing."

Every bit of her body seemed to respond to his words just a little too intently. Because she was feeling more awkward about that by the minute, she attempted to regain some distance between them. Before she practically melted next to him. "Just as you'll share what you've been doing when you're gone?" she teased.

But her attempt at razzing him fell short.

Instead of joking right back, his expression turned carefully blank. "*Nee.* Not like that."

And just like that, this confusing conversation that was so filled with double meanings and hidden feelings veered into another direction again. Now—instead of simply wanting him to see her as a woman worthy of his time, instead of yearning for him to feel for her as she did for him—Alice realized she ached to be someone more.

Someone he could lean on. Whom he could be completely honest with. "I can take whatever you tell me, Calvin. As you know, I'm stronger than I look. I'm a preschool teacher, after all."

Those beautiful eyes of his, that combination of blue and green, so intense, warmed her.

She felt her lips part. Was . . . Was there something new in his expression now? Something more personal? Something deeper?

After their gaze held a moment longer, Cal said, "I know you are strong, Alice. You are strong and have a good heart."

"I only try."

"But that's the problem, you see. I ain't like you."

"How are you, then?"

"Weak." The word came out harsh and direct, sounding almost like a curse word. "Alice, where you are concerned, I'm not that strong at all."

He was tall and strong and had a capable, confident air about him. "You aren't weak, Calvin."

"That's because you don't really know me. If you did, you would know that I was right."

Slowly, she got to her feet. She felt bereft, even though she knew that he had every right to keep his secrets and shouldn't expect him to tell her things he wasn't comfortable sharing.

But it still felt like a rejection of sorts. Like she was never going to be the person he reached out to when he was in need.

After they said good-bye and she was walking back to her house, knowing that he was watching from his porch, likely just to make sure no mysterious mystery man swooped out from the shadows and grabbed her, Alice felt a little empty.

It was one thing to know that a man wasn't ready to be hers. It was a whole other thing to realize that it was never going to happen.

CHAPTER 13

Thursday, February 15

C alvin didn't have the time now to drive all the way to Cincinnati, but it couldn't be helped. West had recently formed an alliance with a gang there, and someone needed to make sure that everyone involved in loading the guns and ammunition onto the boats was doing what they said they were going to.

They certainly weren't the first group of men to utilize the Ohio River to transport guns. They were probably one of the most successful, however, and that success depended upon everyone working smart, keeping their mouths closed, and not taking any unnecessary chances.

Calvin's job during this trip was to check out the new warehouse the Kings had purchased, make sure the members running it weren't being stupid. He knew it would be his job to remind both their members and the men in the other gang that West wouldn't take failure lightly.

The upside was that when he got there, he was staying in his regular hotel, which meant he could speak to his contact at the DEA fairly easily. The

DEA had a decent-sized office in Cincinnati, thanks to both the fact that the city was within a two-hour driving distance to Columbus, Indianapolis, Louisville, and Charleston; and that a lot of guns and drugs could now be trafficked on the water. Security wasn't so tight in the small ports, and there were innumerable areas for a boat to pick up supplies and carry them down to Louisville without anyone being the wiser.

He stopped by his motel to tell the DEA he'd arrived. This was their code, which Calvin had at first thought was ridiculous, and more than a little over the top.

When he'd first gone undercover, he was tempted to point out that neither West nor any of the other members were going to be monitoring him so closely, but wisely kept his mouth shut. But after seeing what happened to a member who'd been viewed as disloyal, Calvin was glad for all the subterfuge. Being both alive and in command of all his limbs was a good thing. It must have worked, too—so far no one in the Kings had been the wiser.

After letting Andrew know that he would be staying at his regular motel, Calvin drove to the oldest section of the city, a previously German area called Over the Rhine. The narrow streets might have been charming once; now they only highlighted the fact that the area was in desperate straits, no matter how many people tried to say that it was in transition.

Though there were some refurbished lofts and restaurants, most of it was run-down, vacant, and filled with people willing to do almost anything to survive.

That was what the Kings were counting on.

He parked his truck in a secure lot, tipping the attendant well. Then he started walking, taking note of the area—and allowing anyone who was looking to see him. After going another block and scanning the area, the tension in his body eased. Everything looked the same. Surrounding him were the same crumbling red-brick buildings, graffiti-riddled fences, and cracked sidewalks littered with debris. On one of the stoops sat old Mrs. Johnson, who tried so hard to keep an eye on the kids in the neighborhood. Two doors down, a homeless man was sipping coffee, his alert expression at war with his ill-fitting clothes and air of despair.

And just beyond the chain-link fence was a group of five men, all of whom knew his name. He talked with them for a few minutes before moving on. The area smelled like smoky fireplaces and vending carts, all faintly tinged with the smell of yeast and hops from the brewery a few blocks over.

It was familiar and noisy. Ugly and a myriad of colors. It was like he'd never left.

Aware of the many eyes focused on him, Calvin kept his gait loose and his expression blank. His gun was secure in the small of his back and his cell phone in one of his front pockets. He was dressed like he always was now, no matter if he was in Horse Cave or in the city. Worn jeans, tight T-shirts, thick-soled boots.

The clothes didn't matter. Instead, what did was the attitude. His way of looking around with enough force and confidence so that no one would think twice about messing with him.

Once again, they didn't. Two men on the sidewalk, one of them Jenk, raised his chin when Cal approached. That surprised him. Usually, West traveled with Jenk or Smith. Trepidation filled him. Had he been found out?

"Fisher," Jenk said.

"Jenk. Hey," he replied.

Calvin made sure to keep his pace slow and look at the men directly in their eyes, all while keeping his own expression blank.

When he got to the entrance of the warehouse, the front door was being guarded by a teenager. He couldn't have been more than sixteen or seventeen. "Cal Fisher," he said.

Immediately, the kid opened the gate. His eyes stayed averted, almost as if he feared that Calvin was going to slug him if he didn't move fast enough.

Such a thing once took him off guard. At other

times, he was ashamed to admit he'd felt a certain amount of satisfaction.

Now? All he could think about was what Alice would say. He didn't have to wonder what she would think. He knew she'd be disappointed in him.

Now he was wondering how, when Mark was healthy again and he returned here to his old routines, he was ever going to forget about her responses or opinions. She seemed to have settled herself firmly into his life.

As he passed through the gate, Calvin forced himself to stop thinking about Alice. Doing so would only make him weak. If he was thinking about her, he could almost imagine his expression softening. And if that happened, then all of his hard work to change his life would be for nothing.

And then? Well, he'd be dead.

He buzzed the front door and waited for the intercom.

"Name."

Leaning into the speaker, he complied. "Cal Fisher."

There was another buzz followed by the door opening. One of the Kings' prospects was on door duty. One of his favorites, a kid by the name of Brandon, going by the name Bear.

"Hey, Cal," he said. "West said for you to go on up to three."

"West is here?"

Brandon said nothing, just turned away to keep watch on the street.

The third floor held three or four bedrooms, West's warehouse office, which Calvin had never seen him use, and the conference room.

As he walked, his footsteps echoing around him, his pulse raced. Every bit of what had happened so far had been unexpected. He'd been told to check on the men here, foster the alliance with the other gang, and make sure everyone knew that West took things seriously.

No one he knew was supposed to be here, certainly not West himself.

Each step toward his boss's office felt like a yard. By the time he got to the door, every beating that he'd seen or participated in raced through his head. When he'd first joined, Calvin had been sure many of the stories were simply talk. Stories to inspire fear in the ranks.

But he'd also seen enough evidence to know they were true.

He could be about to be reprimanded for being gone so long, told to visit some of the projects and other areas where they were selling drugs, or be shot for being an informant.

Then there was the rumor of him being promoted.

When he got to the third floor, he bypassed the four closed doors and stopped in front of the conference room. As expected, another member stood in front of this door, waiting for him. What was unexpected was that it was Smith, West's second in command.

"Hey, man," he said, passing on his signature half smile, the consequence of a knife fight he'd been in when he was ten or eleven. "Good to see you."

"Thanks."

"You carrying?"

"Yeah." He waited, knowing better than to reach for his weapon without an invitation.

"I'll take it, then."

After Calvin handed over the gun, Smith looked him over. "Got anything else?"

"Knife," he said as he leaned down and pulled it out from its sheath on the inside of his boot. He tossed it on the ground. "That's it."

"All right, then. Let's get this over with." As usual, Smith's expression was blank as he frisked him.

Arms outstretched, Calvin stayed motionless as Smith's hands moved over his torso. It was moments like this he was so glad that Andrew had his back about his refusal to wear a wire. Every once in a while, some new guy would bring it up, acting like it was a great idea. But Calvin, having been through this process so many times, argued that he could never let his guard down.

"All right. You're good," Smith said, almost sounding bored. "Go on in."

Calvin searched Smith's face for a hint of what was about to happen. He saw nothing but the same expression he always wore when he was around other gang members.

Then, because he knew there was nothing to gain by hesitating a second longer, he strode inside the vast room. To his surprise, West was sitting by himself in front of a conference table. The desk's top was conspicuously bare. All that lay on top was the boss's hands. They were folded together, looking almost relaxed.

When he heard the door click shut behind him, Calvin pretended that his pulse wasn't racing and that every nerve ending didn't feel frayed. Instead, he kept walking forward. Whatever was about to happen was going to happen whether he was ready or not.

All he could hope was that he'd have enough fortitude to not make a fool of himself.

"It's almost eleven," West said. "When did you arrive?"

"About fifteen minutes ago." He hoped no one knew that he'd first stopped at this motel room.

"Ah." After looking at him a minute longer, he said, "How's your brother?"

"He's all right. Recovering. Doctors say they can't find any more cancer."

"That's good. I'm real happy for you."

Calvin didn't know where the conversation was going, but he allowed himself to relax slightly. He was pretty sure if West had thought he was an informant, Smith would have already shot him. "Thank you, sir."

"Are you going back there soon?"

"I hope to."

West stood up and walked around the desk. He was dressed much the same as Calvin was, snug T-shirt, faded jeans, thick boots. But where Calvin's build was lanky, West was built like a linebacker. He was thick and tall and solid muscle. The man could pack a powerful punch, and Calvin had witnessed the damage he could do more than once. However, it wasn't the threat of violence that made most men wary around him. Instead, it was the intelligence that shone in his dark-brown eyes.

"Cal, you've been in the Kings for several years now. Several members are alive because you've had their backs. Business is good and I know that you've been treating each transaction like it matters. It hasn't gone unnoticed."

"Yes, sir."

Pulling out an envelope from his back pocket, he handed it to Calvin. "It's time to reward your loyalty." His lips curved. "We're making it official now. I want you as a lieutenant."

It had actually happened. He had reached the top of the organization. He would have even

151

greater access to West and the hidden business dealings that went on.

If he took the money, there was also no turning back. No man left the organization after this point. With some dismay, he realized that Andrew couldn't help him now if something went wrong.

He certainly wasn't going to be clean enough or good enough for Alice now. Not now. Not ever.

But he had known that. He might have pretended otherwise, but at the end of the day, he supposed, it didn't matter. Years ago he had made his choice. He'd decided to survive instead of wither away.

Now he could choose to make a difference— before he was killed—or to be killed now.

He might be wrong, but he didn't see a choice. As he folded his hand around the envelope, he smiled.

"Thank you, boss. I won't let you down."

West's brown eyes warmed, looking almost kind. "Don't worry, Cal. If I thought you would, you'd have never gotten this far."

Calvin laughed before they both sat down to get to business. The sooner he finished with West, the sooner he could report to the DEA.

And then he could head back to Horse Cave to watch over his brother and concentrate on staying away from Alice Yoder. Now that he was in the organization even deeper, everyone he was close to was at greater risk.

He knew that, too. He'd had girlfriends around in the early days with the Kings, when West was still checking him out and wasn't certain Cal could be trusted. No way would West shy away from coming after Alice if he thought Calvin needed additional coaxing.

CHAPTER 14

Monday, February 19

Alice was starting to think that she needed to get paid more—especially when a child's parent decided to take all his anger with the world out on her.

It all started when Mary Ruth's father arrived late again to pick up his daughter. Alice knew it was normal for a parent to run late every now and then. After all, everyone was busy and no one could be everywhere at one time. But John Yutzy was late a lot—always. Once a week, sometimes more than twice.

He had begun arriving later and later, too. Whereas he used to only arrive ten or fifteen minutes after all the other parents left, he now was showing up thirty minutes after the scheduled pickup time.

Today, when it was closer to forty minutes, Alice knew she had to say something.

"Mr. Yutzy, if you canna find a way to pick up Mary Ruth on time, I'm afraid I'm going to have to ask that she not attend preschool here anymore."

The look he sent her was filled with disdain.

"You'd really do that? Punish a child because I'm out making a living?"

Though she could practically feel Mary Ruth cringing behind her, Alice didn't back down. She'd already tried to speak to Mary Ruth's father more privately. He'd rebuffed her gentle reminders in such a way that she was now afraid to be alone with him.

"I enjoy Mary Ruth very much. I would hate it if she had to leave, too. But you are taking advantage of my time. It's unfair to your daughter, too. She worries when you aren't waiting for her with the other parents."

" 'With the other parents,' " he mimicked as he stepped closer with ire in his eyes. "Look at you, acting so full of yourself. Always actin' as if you are better than the rest of us."

His tone was so venomous, Alice yearned to shuttle Mary Ruth back into the schoolhouse and shut the door. But she didn't dare. Mary Ruth would be terrified, and such an action would only make her father angrier.

"We both know that isn't true," she said quietly. "Now, if you are ready to go, I'll help Mary Ruth get her lunch pail." Leaning down slightly, she curved an arm around the child's slim shoulders. "Mary Ruth, are you ready to get your pail and head on home?"

Mary Ruth was just nodding when her father yelled again.

"Don't you touch her!"

Immediately, Alice removed her hand. Keeping her voice gentle, she said, "Why don't you go in and get that pail, Mary Ruth? I'll be right here waiting."

Without looking at her father, the child hurried to the doorway. Just before stepping inside, she whispered, "Can I get my goat, too?"

"Of course, child. It's yours."

When Mary Ruth went inside, her father stepped even closer. "What is she talking about?"

"Oh. I gave all the *kinner* tiny plastic goats today," she said, trying to keep her voice easy and smooth. "We're working on the letter *g* this week."

When Mary Ruth came out, her pail in one hand and the white plastic toy in the other, her father shook his head. "You drop that now, Mary." Mary Ruth's hand opened instantly and the goat fell to the ground.

The quick compliance, combined with the heartbroken expression, fairly made Alice's heart break, too. "Mr. Yutzy, all the *kinner* got one—"

"We don't need no charity from the likes of you, Alice."

"It wasn't charity, Mr. Yutzy. All the *kinner* got the toy."

"You shouldn't be offering such evil items anyhow. You should be teaching them to grow up to be decent women, not be tainted by your worldly influences."

Just as Alice scanned the area, hoping for someone to help her, she heard Irene's voice. "If you don't stop yelling at Alice, I'm going to tell Sheriff Brewer," she called out.

With a jerk, the man turned on his heel to face her. "You should stay out of it."

"How can I?" Irene asked as she walked forward, her expression looking haughty. "I've been dealing with you all my life. You've never given me much choice."

"Stay away from me and my family," threatened Mr. Yutzy. "If you don't, I'll make sure you'll regret it."

Not liking the way Mr. Yutzy was acting toward her friend, Alice tried to calm everyone down. "Irene, everything is going to be all right. You don't need to get involved."

Irene curved a hand around her shoulder. "*Nee*, I'm not going to let him continue to berate you." Glaring at the man, she said with renewed force, "Alice, you've done nothing to deserve this treatment."

And just like that, his temper snapped. Grabbing Irene's arm, Mr. Yutzy started pulling at her, hard. "Don't tell me what I should and shouldn't do, girl."

As Irene cried out and attempted to pull her arm away, Mary Ruth started crying.

Everything was spiraling out of control.

Feeling like the pressure in her chest was making it difficult to breathe, Alice looked from Mary Ruth to Irene. "Please stop!" she cried. "We all need to calm down."

"*Nee,* what we need is to get on our way." Mr. Yutzy released Irene and then gripped his daughter's wrist, jerking her toward him. "Come on," he ordered.

Mary Ruth, with each foot practically tripping over the other, struggled to keep up with her father's long strides.

Alice clenched her hands as she watched the pair escape the schoolyard. As much as she wanted to run after them or yell, or even burst into tears, she made herself stand stoically. There was nothing more that she could do. She was only Mary Ruth's teacher. In their world, it was the parents' prerogative to discipline a child how they saw fit.

Even though she knew that if the other children's parents were there, they, too, would be shocked and saddened by Mr. Yutzy's actions.

Alice, still watching, felt thanks seeing in the distance that Mary Ruth's father eventually released his grip on the girl's wrist. But then she saw her little student shake her arm slightly before bending her head as she followed him down the road.

When they disappeared from sight, Alice bent

and picked up the abandoned goat. After absently wiping off the smudge of dirt on it, she placed it in her pocket.

"Alice, I canna even believe him! That poor child. What are you going to do?"

Feeling like she was about to burst into tears, she held up a hand. "Can I have a minute?"

Immediately, Irene backed down. "Of course. I'll go in and start cleaning up."

"There's no need for that."

"I don't mind, Alice. Take your time."

After Irene went inside, Alice walked to the side of the schoolhouse, pressed her hands to her face, and tried to stop shaking. For a moment there, she'd been so frightened, both for Mary Ruth and for herself. It made her think of Calvin and her reactions to him.

Yes, she and he were very different from each other. He was no doubt dangerous—but she'd *never* felt frightened of him. No, instead, she'd almost felt like he would be willing to take care of anything that bothered her, by any means necessary . . . all in an effort to protect her.

Just that quickly, she remembered exactly what he looked like bending at the window—with a gun tucked at his back.

How could that be all right?

Curving her arms around herself, Alice closed her eyes and prayed for Mary Ruth and for her father, too. Prayed that God would give him the sense of peace that he so desperately needed. Finally, she gave thanks for Irene being there.

After a couple more deep breaths, Alice felt like she finally had a grip on herself. She walked back to the schoolhouse.

Irene was sitting in a rocking chair when Alice joined her. Crossing the room toward her, Alice smiled. "I don't know why you were here, but I'm sure glad for it."

Irene's smile didn't quite meet her eyes. "Me, too."

Alice faltered. "What is wrong? Are you hurt?"

She experimentally moved her arm. "I'm fine. I'm more concerned about how you handled things."

"Me? What did I do?"

"Nothing." Glaring at her, Irene said, "You didn't do anything, Alice."

Stunned that Irene was acting as if she was to blame, Alice felt her temper rise. "I couldn't. John Yutzy is her father. I canna interfere."

"That's no excuse. It's obvious he has been abusing her. He's mean, Alice."

Alice couldn't disagree with anything Irene was saying. But what could she do? If she interfered with how parents treated their children, no one would want her to be their child's teacher. And the bishop could even get involved. "Her mother is at home. She'll look after her."

"Oh, yeah. I'm sure she'll do a real good job of

161

doing that. Her husband is probably mean to her, too."

Alice imagined Irene was right. But interfering wasn't going to change anything. And it wasn't like Mary Ruth came to school bruised and beaten every day. "I'm the children's teacher, Irene. It's my job to teach them things, not interfere with how they are being raised."

"That sounds like an easy excuse."

"I suppose I could go to the preacher and ask him to intervene," Alice said.

Irene nodded slowly. "If you want to do that, I'll go with you."

"All right." Feeling inadequate and helpless, and not a little bit defensive, Alice raised her eyebrows. "Is there a reason you came over here?"

"There *was*. I wanted to see if you'd come over for supper. I bought a roast at the market the other day and some things to make a chocolate cake."

In spite of their difficult conversation, Alice's mouth watered. Irene was a fine cook, much better than Alice. "Do you still want to do that?"

"Honestly, I think I'm too upset. I'm going to go on home."

Disappointment settled in. "Irene, what happened ain't my fault."

Irene's lips pursed together, then she shook her head. "You're right. It ain't your fault. But I can't help but think that you could have done something, Alice. That little girl is only four. By you doing nothing, you're subjecting her to years of situations like this. All you do is tell me how much you love teaching and love your students, too."

"I do. You know that."

She threw up her hands. "I guess I expected better from you. I thought you actually cared about being something more than just a sweet teacher who passed out toys."

"That's mighty unfair." Alice's eyes filled up with tears. All kinds of arguments churned inside her, but she was so upset, she was afraid that every word she said would come out wrong.

"I agree," Irene said, sounding exasperated. "It's *mighty* unfair. It really is."

When Irene walked away, Alice felt the tears slide down her cheeks. Never would she have imagined that such a wonderful day could have disintegrated into one of the worst moments of her life.

She'd been so afraid of Mr. Yutzy. And felt guilty about Mary Ruth, too.

But that didn't mean she shouldn't *sometimes* intervene in extreme situations.

Ashamed that she half agreed with Irene but had no one to explain herself to, she seemed to give up and sat down in the rocking chair. If she shared what had happened with her parents, they would encourage her to quit her job. That was

163

always their remedy whenever they were worried about her welfare.

Her brothers would be more understanding, but they'd probably want to go over to the Yutzys' house and try to fix things themselves.

Which would only make things worse.

Only then did she allow herself to think of the one person who she wished was nearby. Calvin Fisher.

She was certain that he would have listened to her side of the story. He wouldn't have gotten mad at her.

Maybe he would have even given her a hug and told her that he knew she had done the best that she could.

But since he was gone, she did the only thing she felt she could. Alice leaned against the back of the chair and cried.

CHAPTER 15

Tuesday, February 20

Thirty more minutes. Irene had just thirty more minutes before she finished her six-hour shift at the diner and could finally go home. She'd clocked in at six that morning. Soon, it would be noon. She'd have the rest of the day to do whatever she wished.

Waiting another half hour wasn't much time at all . . . which was why it was really too bad that it felt like an eternity.

As she carried a stack of dirty dishes back to the kitchen, her arms screamed in protest, right as her feet let her know that they were sore, too. Unable to help herself, she groaned.

Lora, who was wiping down one of the counters, paused. "You okay, Irene?"

"I'm fine," she replied, pasting a smile on her face.

Instead of looking reassured, Lora straightened. "Want some help with that?"

"*Danke*, but *nee*. I've got it."

Lora raised her eyebrows at the obvious lie but didn't say anything as she went back to her task.

Irene was grateful for that. She was too tired to concentrate on anything other than her job.

But Irene kind of doubted that thought, realizing that she was simply just too tired to concentrate generally.

Irene knew she couldn't blame her exhaustion and bad mood on the customers. Everyone had been rather kind and forgiving when she forgot to refresh their coffee or didn't stop to chat as usual.

Maybe they realized she was having a difficult day and gave her space and understanding, Irene mused as she put the dirty dishes in the bin by the sink and returned to her station. If that was the case, then they were being far more lenient than she'd been yesterday afternoon with Alice.

Remembering the judgmental way she'd acted, and the hateful things said, made Irene feel terrible. Alice was her best friend. She was doing her job, too—and knew a lot about working with preschoolers *and* their families.

Irene did not.

All she'd thought about in that moment was how difficult it was to watch both Alice and that sweet little girl get berated by John Yutzy. Before she'd given a second's thought to the consequences, she'd barged in like an avenging angel determined to protect Alice and the child with one fierce statement. Part of her was sure John Yutzy would back down when she confronted him.

Yet he did not.

So instead of helping, all she'd done was make things worse. Alice was hurt and frustrated, Mary Ruth lost her toy, and her father still got his way.

And she? Well, she now sported five dark fingerprints on her arm. Mr. Yutzy had grabbed her so hard, her arm was actually a little swollen. It was also throbbing from carrying heavy trays and coffeepots all morning. She knew better than to complain, though. Her injury was no one's fault but her own.

"Miss? More coffee, please?"

"What? Oh, sure." After hurrying to retrieve a coffeepot, she refilled a couple's cups. Just as she turned around, the door opened and her heart practically stopped.

Because there he was. That scary, quiet, intense, large Englisher who had given her his card the other day. The man who she'd spent too much time thinking about . . . when she wasn't staring at his card.

Unable to stop herself, she paused to gaze at him. He was wearing a stark white T-shirt and dark jeans. A black leather jacket hung on his shoulders. He looked like he was dressed for a fine spring day instead of the middle of winter.

He also appeared just as heart-stoppingly handsome as he had been the last time he'd come in.

No, that wasn't exactly right. He seemed more attractive than he had before—because now she wasn't afraid of him.

He had also come alone.

She swallowed, realizing that she most definitely wasn't looking at him in fear anymore. Instead, it was true anticipation. Had he come inside to see her?

As she refilled another table's coffee cups, she peeked at him again.

May was seating him in the back against the wall. It wasn't technically Irene's station, but there was no way she was going to pass up the opportunity to speak to him once more.

"I'll take that man who just sat down, May," she said as she returned the coffeepot to the counter.

May looked relieved. "Thanks, Irene."

Feeling excited, she picked up a pitcher of water and approached. Then realized that he was staring at her intently.

Before she could stop herself, she was smoothing back the hair from her brow.

The man gazed at her movements. Then, just as the smallest hint of a smile teased his lips, he stilled. A second later a new, thunderous expression appeared on his face.

Concerned, Irene rushed forward. "Are you all right?" After setting the pitcher down, she ran a hand along the Formica tabletop. "Is something wrong with the table?" she asked as she inspected it for crumbs or a spill.

Instead of answering, he pressed his palm over hers. Effectively stopping her swiping motion.

Actually, effectively stopping the rest of her words. And any future ones forming in her brain. His touch didn't hurt. Though his palm was warm and large and calloused, she knew he was taking care with her. As if she was fragile. Or as if he was worried that she would be afraid of his touch. It was all rather endearing and rather sweet. But it was confusing, too.

Feeling like every person in the restaurant was watching, she tried to tug her hand away.

He didn't allow that to happen. "What happened to you?" he asked, his voice even rougher-sounding than usual. "Who did this?"

With her hand still held captive by his own, she looked at her dark-green dress sleeve. It seemed clean enough. So did her apron.

Try as she might, she couldn't see anything wrong. "Who did what?"

Still holding her hand in place, West used his other hand to slide her sleeve up. *"This,"* he bit out.

Though she now knew what he was referring to, she followed his gaze like she, too, was making a new discovery. Under the florescent lights, her bruises shined brightly. If anything, they looked even darker than they had that morning. The skin around the marks was discolored and swollen.

Embarrassment heated her cheeks. Had all of her customers noticed the marks, too? Was that why they'd been so patient with her?

"Irene, answer me."

But how could she? This was none of his business. She didn't even know him. And even if she did, what could he do? No doubt he would probably tell her that she shouldn't have stuck her head, or her arm, out where it didn't belong.

She shook her head. When surprise flared in his expression, followed immediately by a narrowing of his eyes, she pasted a smile on her face. "Would you like some water? Or, perhaps, coffee? It's freshly made."

"It's West."

"Pardon?"

"My name's West. I told you last time I was here. Don't you remember?"

"I do." Of course she did. But that didn't mean she was going to start speaking to him so familiarly. "Would you care for water or coffee?"

His lips pursed. "All right, then." Exhaling, he scooted out of the booth. "I guess I need to be more clear."

"*West?*"

"This is what is going to happen. You and me are going to go have a talk."

"No, I'm working."

"That's not an option," he said as he removed

170

the pitcher from her hand and set it on the table. "I'm offering to give you some privacy. Do you want to go tell your boss that you're going to step outside, or should I tell her?"

"You can't come in here and start ordering me around."

"All right, then, I'll tell her."

And just like that, he started walking over to May.

Ack! He was going to get her fired. Feeling like everyone's attention was on them, she scurried to his side. "West, you must stop."

He did. Kind of. "Glad we're making progress. Now that you're saying my name, you can go tell your boss that you and I need to have a conversation. That it's real important and can't wait."

"But—"

"Go tell your boss, Irene. I mean it."

But, like a cantankerous child, she only glared at him.

After waiting for another couple of seconds, he nodded. Then, to her dismay, he walked toward May. Irene rushed to follow, a dozen apologies running through her head. "May, I'm sorry—"

He cut her off. "Excuse me, ma'am."

May immediately turned to him. "Yes?"

And then, to Irene's amazement, he spoke quietly. "I know Irene is working, but I need to speak to her outside for a few minutes. It's important."

May looked at her in concern. "Is everything okay, Irene?"

She knew why May asked the question. West did look pretty scary. And the impatient way he was standing next to her conveyed a lot of tension. Her boss was simply trying to figure out where that tension was coming from.

But she realized then that she wasn't afraid of him. Instead, she just didn't know how to handle his heavy-handed ways. "*Jah*. I promise that everything is fine. West is just, ah, concerned about something."

May visibly relaxed. "If that's the case, why don't you clock out? You only have ten minutes left and you never took a break. You can leave for the day."

What could she say to that? "Well, um . . ."

"That's a great idea, isn't it?" West interjected. He even smiled at May. "Thank you for letting me take her early."

"Irene works so hard, it makes me happy to see that she has a good friend in you," May replied.

They both looked at her then.

Irene looked back at them both, feeling frustrated and confused. But, goodness! Was May actually blushing? "See you soon, Irene."

May's smile grew wider. "Enjoy the rest of the day, dear."

Irene stared at West again. His arms were folded across his chest. He looked immovable.

Like a mini mountain right there in the middle of Bill's Diner.

He was unexpected and harsh. She was also beginning to get the feeling that he didn't easily take no for an answer. He could change like a chameleon and quickly gain the regard of other people.

Her mother would have called a man like him slick. Someone who was untrustworthy.

But she also had noticed something else about him, too, and that was that he didn't seem mean. Not to her, anyway. With some surprise, Alice realized that she wasn't worried about being alone with him again.

It was because of that that she finally looked up at him with a sheepish smile. "Let me get my things and I'll meet you outside."

"I'll wait for you by the door."

Honestly, did he have to correct everything she said? "There's no need—"

"Take your time, Irene. I got nowhere else to be."

Irene felt her pulse race, just from the way he was saying her name. It felt personal and tender . . . and, maybe, also intertwined with a hint of aggravation.

It should have been awkward, but all it really did was make a lump form in her throat. Maybe it was because everyone always assumed she was fine. No one expected much from her. Not anymore.

Looking down at her feet, she forced herself to come to terms with that.

And the knowledge that she'd begun to think she didn't deserve anything more, either. That was why she was having such a hard time accepting his concern or allowing herself to become emotional about the bruises. She'd learned that expressing her anger or fear or pain didn't change the fact that she was a lot of people's afterthought.

May chuckled, bringing her back to the present. "He's a fine-looking man, ain't he?"

Embarrassed, especially since she couldn't disagree, Irene hurried to the back area where her personal items were neatly kept in a wooden cubby.

West Powers might not mind waiting to talk to her again, but she didn't want to wait another minute.

CHAPTER 16

Tuesday, February 20

Standing just outside the diner's entrance, West was struggling. Not wanting to frighten Irene's boss, he'd made sure to keep his expression easy. But now that he was away from the crowd, he was fuming. There was no doubt in his mind that he looked like it, too.

He had to get himself under control before Irene came outside to meet him. The last thing he wanted to do was frighten her. He would never harm her. Of course he wouldn't. But she didn't know him well enough to realize that his anger was directed at someone else.

Counting to thirty, he clenched and relaxed his hands several times in an effort to remove some of the tension that had taken over his muscles when he'd first seen Irene's bruises. His reaction—and the way he was choosing to deal with it—was unusual.

Okay, it was more than that. It was completely out of character.

West was thirty-three years old, the Kings' leader, running a number of profitable businesses.

Some were legal but most were not. He was hard. He'd learned from an early age that being soft and showing weakness only brought pain. His mother had made sure to teach him that lesson over and over again.

He was also smart. West could read people and was able to look beyond someone's appearance to ascertain what their motivation was. That God-given trait was what had led him to come out to see Cal in Horse Cave in the first place. There was something about Cal that didn't ring true, and he'd wanted to know what it was.

When West first saw him on the porch, the puzzle about him made more sense. Cal might have said he had cut ties with his family and community, but it was obvious that he hadn't done that entirely. Smith was amused, too, seeing Cal standing so properly on the front porch of a girl's home. Likely, an Amish girl.

West had felt nothing but relief. He already knew he could trust Cal, that he wasn't hiding secrets or being deceitful to the Kings. Instead, Cal was attempting to come to terms with his past . . . and, perhaps, figure out how a girl fit into his present life.

That was something that West could understand and relate to.

That relief had been all he'd been thinking about when he and Smith had stopped at Bill's Diner about two weeks before.

And then he'd met Irene.

He'd been instantly attracted to her. Attraction to a pretty girl wasn't anything new. But the feelings and thoughts he'd been having about her were unlike anything he'd experienced before. It was like he was seeing a woman in a whole new way for the very first time. He wasn't looking at her in terms of her assets. Actually, he wasn't even giving much attention to her figure or her features, other than having a general impression that she was well put together.

No, it was something else. A quietness about her that filled some of the gaps in his soul. And the fact that she was struggling to do a good job. Her little waitressing job meant something to her.

He'd spent the weeks doing his best to forget her. He was glad that he'd given her his card with his phone number on it. If she needed him, he would be there. But other than that? Well, he didn't need a soul to tell him that the two of them needed to stay far apart from each other.

But he hadn't been able to do that. Last night, when one of the girls in the clubhouse just about offered herself to him, he found himself comparing her to Irene. It wasn't fair to either of the women, and he ended up leaving the clubhouse early, seeking the solace of his empty house. He was hoping being alone would give him some insight as to why he was so infatuated with an Amish server in a Kentucky diner. But no answers came. Instead, he tossed and turned all night.

All that was why he decided to come back. By morning, he thought he had turned in his effort to remove her from his head, and wanted to prove to himself that this was so.

But now, instead of that, here he was trying to convince himself not to beat up the man that had hurt her.

"I'm so sorry you had to wait," she said as she rushed through the door. "I . . . well, I decided to get cleaned up."

Irene's face was still damp. No makeup, nothing artificial on her pretty face. Only bright eyes and perfect skin looking soft to the touch. He knew he shouldn't notice either.

He pushed off from the side of the building that he'd been leaning up against. "I told you that I didn't mind waiting. I meant it."

Relief settled in her gaze before tension flared there again. "I don't understand why you wanted to see me in the first place."

Oh, Irene knew exactly why he did. But if she wanted to play it that way, he could do that, too. "I only wanted to talk to you. That's all." West searched her expression and was relieved to see that she still didn't seem apprehensive around him. "Where can we go to talk privately?"

"I don't know where you would like to go."

Unable to help himself, he rubbed her upper

arm. "It's sunny out, but not right here in the shade. We should go someplace else. Will you get in my truck? Would you trust me enough to do that?" A mini war waged inside of him. He wanted her to trust him enough to get in his truck, but the other part of him was wanting to call out warnings to her. She should know better than to get in a truck with a man like him.

"I don't know . . ." she said hesitantly.

"I'm real proud of you, Irene. You're right not to accept right away. But think about it, I came here to where you work. Your boss knows you're with me. I'm not sneaking around."

Some of the wariness in her gaze disappeared. "You're right."

"I passed a hiking trail about two miles back. Do you know of it? Maybe we could go for a walk?" He was so glad that he had come by himself. There wasn't a soul in the Kings who would have recognized him making an offer like that.

He wouldn't blame them, either. He had never asked a woman to go for a walk with him in his life.

"Oh! That's Widow's Trail. It's a pretty place. Real peaceful, too. There's a pond there that we used to skate on."

He couldn't resist smiling at that. She went walking on trails and hung out around ponds when she was feeling stressed. It was so clean. So opposite of how every other man or woman he knew handled things. "So, are we good? Will you come with me? I know it's cold, but the sun is out."

"I won't be too cold."

Since she still didn't move, he kept talking. "I won't keep you long. Then, after, I'll drive you home."

After a few seconds—which felt like an eternity—she replied. "*Jah*, West. I'll come with you."

"*Jah*?"

"That means yes. In Pennsylvania Dutch."

"You know two languages? When did you learn that? In high school?"

"No, I learned that first." Smiling softly, she added, "All of us Amish learn to speak Deutsch before English. We start learning English when we go to school."

"Looks like I've got a lot to learn about you. Come on, then. Let's get going."

After taking care to stay by her side but not touch her, he opened the door to his truck and helped her inside. Then he got in his own side and drove to the trail he'd mentioned. It had a blue Kentucky sign next to it, signifying that it was a scenic viewpoint. A historical marker, too, which probably had something to do with its name. A lot of people would probably take the time to read about it.

He couldn't care less, he just wanted to be someplace where she wouldn't be afraid to walk with him and they could have the privacy he wanted.

After they got out of his truck, he stuffed his keys in his front pocket, ignored his ringing cell phone, and let her lead the way down a grassy field toward the trailhead.

The ground was neatly raked and taken care of. Though he saw two other vehicles in the paved lot, there was no sign of any people. They were far enough from the road that even the noise from passing cars was muted. He couldn't remember ever feeling so apart from the rest of the world. His gun was in his truck's glove box. He felt vulnerable without it, but he hadn't wanted to scare her by pulling it out.

"I haven't been here in months," she said as they started down the trail.

"Because it's been too cold?"

"Yes, but for other reasons, too." After peeking up at him, she continued. "Once, when I was very young, my mother would take me on a picnic here." Looking sheepish, she added, "Later on I came out here with my friends when we were teenagers."

The right thing to do would be to let her ramble on about the trail and her family. He was even interested in her stories. He wanted to know more about her. About who she'd hung out with. Shoot, he even cared if she'd come here with some Amish boy. He had a feeling he was going to be interested in pretty much anything she wanted to tell him.

But he wasn't that kind of man. After another minute or so, he stopped in a sunny patch and reached for her hand. "Let me see your arm."

"You aren't going to let it go, are you?"

He shook his head, deciding that it was safer than telling her that they hadn't even *begun* to talk about it.

After a moment, she presented it to him. "Here it is, West," she murmured. Like she was giving him a special gift. It was kind of cute.

However, he didn't smile. Instead, he kept his gaze on her arm while he carefully pushed up her sleeve. She could practically feel the tension emanating from him.

There, in the bright sun, the marks looked even darker. Examining it with him, Irene frowned. "I think it looks worse out here in the bright sunlight."

"Who did this?"

"It wasn't anything important. We should just forget it."

"You've got a series of fingerprints on your arm, Irene. It's swollen. Whoever did this could have really hurt you. I'm not going to forget about it."

"It's not that bad."

West was torn between yelling at her, holding her close, and laughing. She was exasperating. It

182

brought on a wave of tenderness that he hadn't known he was capable of.

He settled for sliding one finger under her chin and forcing it up. "Irene, I'm not going to let this go. Someone grabbed you hard enough to hurt you and leave marks. Who did it?"

"It wasn't anyone you would know."

"Didn't think it was. But you haven't answered my question."

She pulled from his grasp and pushed her sleeve back down. He let her, because seeing all the marks on her arm was making him furious.

He stuffed his hands in his front pockets so he wouldn't reach for her again, and waited.

"West, it was nothing."

It had been a really long time since anyone—*anyone*—had not immediately done what he wanted. Not since he was too young and weak to make someone listen. He was coming to realize that the feeling of frustration he was experiencing was just as sharp as it had been all those years ago.

"Was it your boyfriend?"

"What? *Nee*! I don't have a boyfriend."

He pocketed away that feeling of relief for a time when he could actually process why he cared so much. "Who then?" He stared at her closely. "Your father? Brother?" Unable to help himself, his tone turned harsher. "Is someone at home grabbing you? Hurting you?"

Her eyes widened. "*Nee*! It was just one of Alice's students' parents."

"Who is Alice?"

She sighed like he was one of her particularly slow customers. "Alice is my best friend, and she is a preschool teacher. One of her students' fathers was yelling at her when I stopped by her classroom. I got mad and interfered." Rubbing her arm, she looked a little rueful. "He didn't appreciate hearing what I had to say."

"Oh."

She smiled. "*Jah*. So"—starting to walk again, she said—"that is what happened. You see? I was telling you the truth. It was nothing for you to worry about."

"Is your friend all right?"

"Alice? I think so. She seemed more worried about the little girl than anything."

"You shouldn't have interfered."

She glanced back at him, her expression surprised. "Of course I should have. Alice is my best friend."

"But still, it was her problem. Not yours." That was how West handled his life. Shoot, that was how everyone he knew handled things. Interfering in things that weren't your business just got you killed.

"West, it was so terrible. Someone had to stick up for her."

West mentally catalogued the name *Alice* as

he was realizing that Irene was right. And just as soon as that thought passed, he admitted to himself that he had done much the same to Irene. He'd barged in and tried to help. Stuck up for her.

"Sorry if I overreacted." But instead of accepting his apology, she giggled. "What is so funny?"

Irene stopped again and smiled brightly at him. "You are, West."

"Because?"

"Because your apology sounded as rusty as an old nail left out in the rain."

"As bad as that, huh?"

Her eyes sparkled as she nodded. "I don't think you apologize much."

"I don't." At last allowing himself to smile, he admitted, "I think you are the first person I've apologized to in years."

She giggled again. "I'll take that. Now, I'm not sure why you came to Horse Cave, but since you brought us to this trail, would you actually like to walk on it for a spell?"

"Yeah. I'd like that."

She smiled at him again, then they resumed their walk. And because he couldn't help it, he followed. Little by little, he noticed the hollyhocks growing in between the ash trees. When she pointed to a pair of bright-red cardinals, and then a redheaded woodpecker, he caught himself scanning the dense foliage for other birds.

Slowly, the path narrowed and the vegetation got even more unruly and dense. Unable to help himself, he reached for her hand—just to make sure she was near him, in case something came out of the woods suddenly.

Her slight hand stiffened against his fingers before tightening. She didn't talk, though. Didn't say anything. Just seemed pleased to be holding his hand as they strolled on the trail in the middle of nowhere.

With some surprise, he realized that he felt the same way. No words were needed. Because at that moment he didn't want to do anything else.

CHAPTER 17

Friday night, February 23

C alvin opened the back door to his brother's house, took off his boots, then carefully closed the door quietly behind him. With luck, he would be able to wash up in the kitchen and sneak into his room without waking Waneta and Mark. He could leave his boots down by the door so neither would be surprised to discover he'd returned when they woke up in the morning.

Pleased with that plan, he ignored the hunger pains in his stomach. Any hunt for food would involve turning on a flashlight, lighting a lantern, or, at the very least, a couple of candles. Then, he would need to open multiple cabinets and drawers, which was bound to make a racket.

What he really needed was a shower, but that would make too much noise as well. He settled for dampening a dishtowel and rubbing it over his neck and chest, followed by cupping water in his hands and splashing it over his face.

"I didn't think you were getting back until later in the week."

Calvin jerked and got a neckful of the faucet's

spray for that action. Irritated with himself, he shut off the water and tossed the rag on the counter. Then, taking a breath, turned to his brother. Mark was standing at the entrance to the kitchen, holding a large, yellow, industrial-grade flashlight in his hand. The glow from it filled the room with shadows.

It also illuminated the smile playing across his brother's lips.

Calvin laughed softly. "You scared me half to death."

"You gave me a scare yourself. I wasna real excited to hear someone moving around my kitchen at two in the morning, you know."

"Sorry I woke you." Studying his brother, he thought Mark looked too thin and more than a little pale. Guilt flooded him. "I shouldn't have turned on the sink."

"You didn't wake me," Mark said as he set the flashlight on the counter, taking care to adjust the beam so that it faced the ceiling. The result cast a warm glow between them. "I've been up for a while."

It didn't matter how innocuous his brother's words were, they still brought forth a wave of worry. "You couldn't sleep? Why not? Are you in pain?" Calvin noticed that Mark was wearing an old pair of sweatpants, a T-shirt, and had one hand firmly gripped on the edge of the counter. "Hey, let's get you in a chair. Then I'll look at your prescriptions to see what you can have."

"I can read my own prescriptions, *bruder*."

"I know. But sometimes, if you ain't feeling a hundred percent, figuring them out can be difficult." Aware that Mark had raised his eyebrows, Calvin snapped. "And, yeah, I know I don't know anything about reading prescription labels, but I'm sure I'm right."

"Even if you're right, I don't reckon you need to start telling me what to do."

"I'm trying to help."

"You are. And while I appreciate it, *mei frau* is already fussing over me enough. Half the time, I feel like the dog is watching me like a hawk. You don't need to start managing me, too."

Hearing Mark's gruff-sounding whine was so unexpected, Calvin almost smiled. "Sorry, but you don't have a choice. Waneta asked me to be here, so you've got to take the good with the bad."

"You're bringing Waneta into this?"

"Of course I am. She's smart." Just to needle him a bit, Calvin added, "Some might even say she's smarter than you."

Mark sighed. "That she is." Then as he stopped resisting and grinned full-out, he grumbled some more, "I know the bad is listening to you fuss. What's the good?"

"I'm here, aren't I?" Calvin said with a smile.

And, though reluctantly, a smile also formed

on Mark's lips. "*Jah*. That is *gut*, for sure." Then he took a step, winced, and gestured to the chair. "Help me with that, 'kay?"

Calvin pulled it and curved a supportive hand around Mark's arm. Bearing some of his weight, he helped him sit down.

Mark blew out a burst of air—and seemed to be avoiding Calvin's eyes.

Seeking to change the focus of their attention, Calvin said, "You know, it always catches me off guard when I see you dressed like this."

Mark looked down at his clothes. "Sweat-pants?"

"Englisher clothes."

He shrugged. "Sometimes the sight of it catches me off guard, too. But these are comfortable around my middle and easy for Waneta to wash."

"If your hair was shorter, someone might mistake you for me."

Mark's lips twitched. "Perhaps. Until they see your eyes. My eyes are a simple brown."

"Now that you're here, I was just thinking I'd get something to eat. Do you want anything?"

"I could eat a turkey sandwich. You making them?"

"I am." Pleased to do something that was actually helpful, Calvin opened the refrigerator and started pulling out all the ingredients. His stomach growled again, offering its agreement.

"You hungry?"

"Yeah. I didn't want to take the time to eat before getting on my way."

"Really? You couldn't even run by a drive-thru on your way down here?"

Calvin shrugged, not wanting to share that his mind had been pretty occupied with West, becoming a lieutenant, and worrying about how he was ever going to extricate himself from the Kings. "I guess not." After placing two pieces of bread on each plate, he said, "You still like mayonnaise on yours?"

"*Jah*. And Swiss."

"And lettuce?"

"Uh-huh."

Calvin finished putting the two sandwiches together, neatly sliced Mark's in half, and set it in front of him. "Here you go. What do you want to drink? Milk?"

"Water's good."

After Calvin got him a glass, he got to work putting all the ingredients back where they belonged.

"You can do that later. Come eat."

"I'll eat in a sec. I don't want to get Neeta in a tizzy."

As he'd hoped, Mark chuckled.

"Appreciate that," Mark replied, then took a bite. "It's *gut*."

"It's just a sandwich." When Calvin couldn't put it off any longer, he took a chair and dove in, too. The sandwich was good. He figured it had something to do with Neeta's homemade bread, the Amish cheese, and the locally smoked turkey.

Or maybe it was simply because he was sharing a meal with his brother in the middle of the night. Just like they used to do so many years ago. But this time, he had been the one to take care of the food and his older brother was the one who was the recipient. There were some days when he was a teenager that he would have taken an extra beating just to be the one to do something for Mark.

"What do you do when you're out of town, doing your Kings business?" Mark asked, breaking the silence. "Or can you not talk about it?"

"I can talk about it." Some of it anyway. "I went to the warehouse where some of the members were. My boss was there, so I spent time with him."

"You had to go all the way there just to talk to him?"

"I didn't expect him to be there, but it was good he was. He gave me a couple of jobs."

"Jobs, huh? What kind of jobs?"

Images flashed in his head. The threats he'd made. The money he'd collected. The delivery West had asked him to make late last night. "That, I can't talk about."

Mark pushed his plate away, his sandwich

only half-eaten. Calvin realized that he'd already wolfed his down while he was talking. He didn't know how that happened.

And felt embarrassed, because he was now looking at the rest of Mark's sandwich with longing just as he was realizing that he had likely taken away his brother's appetite. "I know you don't understand my life, but it can't be helped."

"You're right, I don't understand it," he said with obvious impatience. "I also don't agree. I bet you could be doing something else. If you wanted."

"It ain't that easy." Which was an understatement.

"Maybe it ain't that easy because you make it hard. But doing the right thing is always better."

"Save your words of wisdom for your future *kinner*, Mark. I'm too old to do anything different and you are too old to be acting like you can tell me what to do."

"I only want to help you. This cancer, well, it's scared me. Made me see that we only get a set number of days to live on earth. You don't want to waste them."

His brother was right. It was actually one of the reasons why he'd jumped at the chance to be an informant for the DEA. But he couldn't reveal that truth to anyone. Calvin knew that not only his own life but Mark's and Waneta's lives depended on him keeping that secret. "Who says

193

I'm wasting anything? I've got a good life, Mark. It ain't easy, but yours ain't, either." He stood up abruptly. "Now, can we talk about something else?"

Mark flinched. "How about we try to get some sleep instead? It's got to be real late now."

"Yeah. I need some sleep." It was obvious to both of them that there were still things between them neither was ever going to understand. For a brief moment, he mourned the fact that his brother thought he hadn't changed at all.

But there was nothing to be done about that— and all this wishing for something different would only get him a night filled with regrets.

He had enough of those to last a lifetime.

Moving to Mark's side, he carefully curled his hand around his elbow. "Here, let me help you get to bed."

Mark pulled his arm out of Calvin's grasp. "I've got it," he said sharply. "I don't need your help getting up, or walking down the hall to my wife."

That mention felt purposeful. Calvin wondered if it was. That Mark felt the need to remind him how much better his life was? Of course, it didn't matter if he had or hadn't. He was well aware that he didn't have a home or a wife. "Good night, then."

Mark walked a couple of halting steps before

turning back to him. "Calvin, are you going to see Alice anymore?"

Calvin felt his body tense up. "I don't know. Why?"

"It's just . . . She's a nice woman. A preschool teacher."

"I know. She's told me all about her job."

"She's been well protected. She ain't worldly, neither. From what her brother Edward has told me, she's always been that way. She never ran around much."

"So she probably could never understand the things I've done?" he asked, choosing to fill in the gaps of what Mark wasn't saying.

"*Nee*, what you've done and *are still doing*. She ain't going to understand your choices."

Calvin realized that his older brother's tone wasn't full of condemnation. Instead, there was a fair amount of worry in it, too. "Are you hoping that I don't hurt her . . . or that she doesn't hurt me?"

Mark hung his head before replying. "I'm not sure. Maybe both."

Looking at his brother, Calvin saw several things in his expression. Despair. Hope. Worry for him. And, yes, irritation that Calvin was making him explain himself.

"*Danke*," Calvin said at last. What mattered was that Mark cared.

His brother simply turned and walked down

the hall to his bedroom, the flashlight in his hand casting a beam in front of his path. Calvin watched him, making sure that he got into his room all right.

Calvin pulled out a lighter to help get to his room. Lit a thick lemon-scented candle Waneta had placed on the top of his dresser and moved it to the bedside table.

Then he sat down on the bed.

There wasn't a thing in the room that was the same from when he was a young boy. New bed, new desk and chair. A new dresser and rag rug on the floor. With the lemon scent filling the space, it certainly smelled better.

Pulling off his clothes, he slipped between cool sheets, enjoying the soft cotton on his skin. Waneta kept a fine home. It was comfortable and clean. Filled with goodness and love. It was exactly the place for his brother.

But for once, instead of thinking that he would never deserve such goodness again, he wondered what it would feel like to be the recipient of similar gifts.

With that in mind, he blew out the candle, then closed his eyes, allowing himself to think about a home of his own. To imagine returning to his house, to a woman of his own. A partner and helpmate. A wife with light-brown hair and bright-blue eyes.

Imagining that, imagining Alice in his life, he

finally fell asleep, secure in the knowledge that no one but himself would ever realize that he dreamed about such things. After all, he knew for certain that such a dream could never come true.

CHAPTER 18

Saturday, February 24

Feeling pleased with herself, Alice took a moment to admire the pan of blueberry muffins that she'd just pulled out of the oven. Oh, they did indeed look fine! They were *packed* with berries, and the crumb topping had browned nicely.

Why, they might even be the best muffins she'd ever made.

After waking up earlier than usual, she'd decided to make something for Waneta and Mark and take it over. She'd spotted a plastic container of blueberries in the back of the refrigerator and decided to put them to good use.

She wasn't a particularly good cook, but she could make a handful of things and was proud of them. Blueberry muffins were in that select group.

Still feeling pleased—and perhaps a bit too prideful of her small accomplishment—Alice placed the warm muffins in one of Bethy's pretty baskets, covered them with a clean dishcloth, then headed across the street.

And stopped right in the middle of the road.

She saw that Calvin's truck had returned. Not sure if her pulse was racing because she was anxious to see him or because she was worried how he would act when he saw her, Alice changed her plans. Instead of going inside and chatting with Waneta for a few minutes, she was going to drop off the muffins and leave.

Yes, that was the right thing to do, anyway. Mark might be home from the hospital, but he was still under the weather.

Glad to have a new plan, she trotted up the steps and rapped her knuckles twice on the door.

When it opened, Alice smiled, ready to greet Waneta or maybe even Calvin.

However, it wasn't either of them. Instead, it was Mark Fisher himself.

And that? Well, that left her dumbfounded.

"Why are you out of bed?" she blurted before she thought the better of it.

Mark blinked, as if he needed a minute to process her words. Then he grinned. "Hiya, Alice. It's *gut* to see ya, too. Come on in."

"I'm sorry I was so rude," she said, feeling clumsy. "I have a bad habit of saying what is on my mind. I need to learn to hold my tongue."

"Do you think so? Huh."

Before she knew it, she had walked right in and he had closed the door behind her. "I brought you some blueberry muffins," she said awkwardly as she thrust the basket at him. "They're still warm." When he didn't reach for them, she began to feel awkward. More tongue-tied. "They're real good. I mean, I ate one of them already. I mean, I make real *gut* muffins." Oh, for heaven's sakes! Had she just said that?

He smiled. "That's good to know. *Danke.*" At last, he took the basket and set it on the kitchen counter.

It was all she could do not to roll her eyes. No doubt Mark was *real glad* to know that she made good muffins. He was also probably glad he had found out that she had terrible manners. Now he could warn Waneta away from her.

Alice wasn't sure how to salvage this awkward, one-sided conversation, but she reckoned she had better try.

"Um, I came over to see if I could help you or Waneta with anything. And, of course, bring you muffins." Yes, she'd just mentioned them yet again.

The corners of his lips twitched. "I'll tell her you came by."

"*Danke.*" After looking down the hall, half hoping to spy Calvin but seeing no one, she edged toward the door. Coming over had been a bad idea.

"You leaving so soon?"

She felt kind of sick. "I think it would be best." Mark nodded. "I think you are right," he said slowly, "especially if you came over here to see my brother."

"Calvin?" Oh, did she really make that sound like a question? Was she really going to act as if she didn't know that Mark Fisher had only one brother and it absolutely was Calvin?

And then, just as if her subconscious had conjured him, there he was.

"Hey, Alice," Calvin said as he walked into the room. "What are you doing here?"

That seemed to be the question of the morning. "I brought over muffins."

"They're blueberry. I heard they're real *gut*, too," Mark murmured.

"Yeah?" Calvin crossed the room, pulled one out of the basket, and took a bite of it. A few crumbs fell onto his white T-shirt before drifting to the floor. "You're right. This is tasty. Did you make them?"

"I did." Feeling the men's silence practically swallow her, she added, "Muffins are one of my specialties."

Calvin's smile expanded into a full-fledged grin. "We are truly blessed then. *Danke*."

She was fairly certain he was teasing her. She didn't blame him, either. How could she sound perfectly calm and poised with a group of four-year-olds but like a ditsy girl in front of these two men? Feeling even more awkward, she glanced around the room. She didn't know whether to smile, get down on her knees and clean up the crumbs, or scoot out the door before Mark started studying her again.

Calvin turned to his brother. "What's going on? Did you offer Alice a cup of coffee? And how come you aren't sitting down? Does Waneta even know you are up and wandering around the house?"

Mark's expression tightened. "I'm feeling well enough to answer the door and haven't had a chance to offer her a cup yet. I don't feel like sitting, and Waneta is asleep."

"Sounds like I got ho— I mean, back here just in time."

"What is that supposed to mean?" Mark snapped.

Looking between the two men and their bickering made Alice feel uneasy. Growing up with two brothers, and witnessing their jokes and jabs at each other all the time, she'd thought nothing could surprise her. Males were rough with each other. But this interaction between them was different.

Actually, it seemed as if there was something missing between Mark and Calvin. Oh, she didn't think love was missing. But maybe it was trust?

Or perhaps it was something that had always lain between them that she was ignorant about. No matter what, it was obvious that it was time to go. "You know, I think I'll go ahead and leave you two," she said nervously. "I'm sorry I barged over here the way I did."

Calvin whipped his head around to her. "No. Wait, Alice. You don't need to leave."

She eyed Mark nervously. "I don't want to be in the way."

"You aren't in the way at all." Calvin held out a hand. "Come on, let's go sit down in the living room. I want to hear what you've been doing. Don't worry about my brother's sour disposition. He doesn't mean anything."

She ignored his hand but nodded.

He smiled in obvious relief. "Good. Go have a seat. You want a cup of coffee? I really need one."

"*Nee.* I don't want a cup."

"I'll be right back." He held out a hand, almost as if he was trying to mentally push her into the other room.

Alice went into the living room and sat down. As Calvin returned to the kitchen and prepared a cup, she looked around the room. It was pleasing. She vaguely recalled Edward mentioning that when Mark returned to Horse Cave, he tore out most of the old floors and cabinets and replaced them all with fresh new items.

She guessed that when he married Waneta, she did some additional decorating. A bookshelf made of fine cherry filled half of one wall; on another was a blue and yellow quilted wall hanging. Also in the room were two comfortable easy chairs, a cherry rocker, and a game table, too. She liked how functional each piece was, like it had been chosen for its use and not just its looks.

"Sorry about that," Calvin said as he sat down in the chair across from her, a large mug in his hands. "Now, how are you?"

"I think that is what I should be asking you. After all, you're the one who has been gone. I hope your trip was *gut*?"

He rubbed one of his shoulders with a hand. "It was fine. Busy."

"What did you do?"

"Do?" He rubbed his shoulder again. "Nothing special. Just my job."

"Ah." Feeling foolish, asking questions that received no answers, she was starting to wish she'd accepted his offer of coffee. At least then she'd have something to do with her hands.

"What Calvin is trying not to say is that his work wasn't anything to be proud of," Mark interrupted as he approached. "When Calvin left our way of life, he turned the corner and never looked back."

Mark's voice was so caustic, Alice was taken aback. "I don't know what that means."

"It means he doesn't like who I've become," Calvin said.

"Who have you become?" she repeated, still

feeling like she was missing an important piece to their relationship puzzle.

Calvin leaned toward her. "All you need to know is that I would never hurt you," he said quietly. "I like our friendship. I value it."

She wanted to relax and take his words at face value, but doing so made her feel uneasy. It was obvious that he was lying to her, telling her things he wanted her to believe so that she would not ask him anything else.

Although . . . perhaps she was asking too much of him? After all, they didn't know each other. Not really. Who was she to expect so much? "I like our friendship, too." She heard her words, but they felt hollow—and maybe they were. They seemed to be five simple words that yearned to convey so much, but ultimately fell short.

Just as Calvin opened his mouth, obviously ready to tell her something else, Mark interrupted again. "I canna do this. I can't stand here and watch you manipulate her, Calvin." His voice turned hoarse. "Or worse, make her think that you are someone she should be spending any time with."

While she gaped, Calvin got to his feet. They were now standing face to face, both over six foot tall. Glaring at each other. The tension and hurt that flowed between them was tangible and more than a little frightening.

"Alice ain't your business," Calvin said.

"Alice is a nice girl. If you continue this game of yours, you're going to hurt her."

"I'm not playing a game."

"If you aren't, that's even worse. Are you really going to let her imagine that she could one day have a future with you?"

"We might have one," Calvin countered.

"You better not."

She definitely did not care to be talked about like she couldn't speak for herself. And what was all of this about her and relationships?

Standing up, Alice pushed her way in between the two men. "Mark, as much as I don't want to take a side, I have to agree with Calvin. I don't think it's your place to tell me who I should be friends with."

Looking stunned, Mark's expression faltered. "I'm sorry, Alice. I know it seems like I am over-stepping. But I don't want to see you hurt. And if you continue to persist in this relationship, you will be."

Puzzled, Alice gazed at Calvin.

He closed his eyes briefly before looking like he had come to a conclusion. "Leave us alone, Mark. Or, if you can't do that, let me know and I'll speak to Alice outside."

"What are you going to talk about? Are you going to tell her the truth about who you are?"

"I'm going to tell her what you believe to be true."

Mark shook his head. "The day you speak like a normal person is going to be a *gut* one." He threw up his hands. "You know what? Do whatever you want, I don't care. Plan a future that ain't never going to happen, if that's what you want."

After taking a step away, Mark turned to her. "Just don't say no one warned ya."

Neither she nor Calvin said a word as Mark trudged back to bed. Alice closed her eyes. What had happened? And just as importantly, why had it happened? It seemed as if the devil himself had gotten into her day's agenda and took pleasure in turning it on its ear.

Becoming even more uneasy, Alice glanced at Calvin, not daring to say a word. Though, what else could she say?

Calvin must have sensed that, because he guided her to the couch, sat down close to her, and sighed. "I bet you're wondering how your good deed turned out like this."

Alice wanted to laugh off the conversation, to tell him that she was sure that his brother was just saying things he didn't mean because he was feeling badly. But she hadn't missed the flinch in Calvin's expression when Mark accused him of keeping secrets.

He was keeping something from her. Something important that she obviously needed to know. "You might as well tell me what Mark was talking about. It's going to always be in between us until you do."

His mouth opened, then shut before he caught himself. "All right." He stared at the quilted wall hanging. Exhaled. Then looked at her directly in the eye. "I am in a gang, Alice."

She had heard of the word, of course. She might be Amish, but she didn't live in a cave. But that said, what he was saying didn't make a bit of sense. "I don't understand."

"I'm sure you don't," he said derisively. "My work . . . well, it's with some men who don't always function on the right side of the law."

"You break the law?"

"Sometimes. When I have to."

When he *had* to? What kind of man did such things? Gazing at him carefully, she realized that he was holding himself in a stiff manner. He was waiting for her to put him down. Or maybe even walk away?

That vulnerability she spied gave her the strength to carefully weigh her words, and maybe have more patience with him. "Calvin, I'm not trying to be difficult. But you need to be more clear. Just tell me."

"I could try to sugarcoat it and tell you I belong because the gang is all about brotherhood, but it ain't. It's a business." After looking at her again, he looked away. "We supply weapons to various other groups in the state. It's all illegal."

"So you are a dangerous man."

He nodded. "I am. I'm a dangerous man who does a great many things I shouldn't because I get paid well to do them."

She felt goose bumps form on her arms as everything he told her sank in. Mark had been right. She needed to stay far away from him. Calvin Fisher represented the opposite of every-thing she believed in. Everything her family did. Why, what would her brothers or parents say if they knew she'd been alone with him? They'd have been scared, and terribly disappointed in her, too.

She got to her feet. "I think I had better go home now."

Calvin didn't move. Kept his eyes averted, like he could hardly bear to look at her. "I understand."

She walked to the door, half listening for Calvin to call her name and beg her to stay. To say that he needed her friendship. To tell her that he wanted to change.

But he didn't do any of that.

Only silence met her back as she walked out of the house.

It suited her fine. She was in a daze.

Until she realized that Sheriff Brewer was parked outside her house.

CHAPTER 19

Saturday, February 24

C alvin was torn between throwing his coffee mug across the living room and breaking down into tears. Neither was an option. He hadn't been accidentally violent or done any crying in years. He'd learned over time to hold in his emotions, expect little from anyone, and never to plan for the future.

Heck, he'd learned all that from the time he was eight or nine years old. His father loved to dispense lessons through his fists while their mother had excelled in neglect. He'd learned from watching his older brother that no good came from letting his guard down. Things only got worse when you expected something better than was happening.

The only way to survive was to hold his emotions tight inside, pretend nothing mattered and bide his time. Those lessons had enabled him to go undercover in the Kings organization. He'd actually begun to feel pretty proud of himself for learning to hide his emotions so well.

Until now.

Seeing the horror on Alice's face was excruciating. Almost as hard as hearing the loathing in Mark's voice when he talked about his choices and decisions.

And just like that, every doubt he'd ever had about himself came back. Tenfold. What was he trying to accomplish, anyway? It wasn't like he could betray an illegal organization and then suddenly become a man who was worthy.

He cradled his face in his hands and tried to get his bearings. Since he was alone, he let himself relax enough to face his insecurities. Allowed himself to feel scared and disappointed. Allowed himself to admit that he *had* hoped Mark was finally coming to see him as someone worthwhile.

Admit that he *had* hoped he could be the kind of man that Alice would want to depend on.

The truths were difficult to face and harder to admit. They felt crushing. But perhaps they were cleansing, too. After all, it was so rare that he could be himself, even if for just a few minutes.

"Calvin, why are you sitting like this?" Waneta asked as she walked into the living room.

He popped up. "Hey, Neeta."

She stopped directly in front of him, her face a wreath of concern. "Calvin, Mark just stomped into our bedroom and glared at me when I tried to help him lie down. What happened?"

"Nothing happened that hasn't happened

before. Your husband is annoyed with me."

"That may be true, but I'd rather hear the truth," she said as she sat down.

For a moment, Calvin considered simply assuring her that everything was fine. After all, she had more than enough to deal with. But he just wasn't up to it. He felt alone and almost scared. Not for himself, but for the damage he was doing to his brother and to Alice. Even to Waneta. And Andrew, to whom he owed so much

If he didn't get himself together, he was going to hurt himself and put everyone he cared about in danger.

"I feel like I'm drowning, Waneta," he said frankly. "I can't tell you all the details, but I'm in a pretty rough spot. No, a *really* rough spot. If I do something wrong I could hurt a lot of people."

Her eyes widened. "Even Mark?"

"Yes. And you, too."

"And Alice?"

With reluctance, he nodded.

After gazing at him for a long moment, she spoke. "Calvin, when I first started working with Mark, I was a little afraid of him."

"Because of the rumors about his past?"

She nodded. "*Jah*. Not only was I wary about him being once taken in for questioning by the sheriff, I was uncomfortable about the way he made me feel."

"Why was that?"

"He made me feel different than any other man had before. I thought we were so wrong for each other . . . but I still thought about him all the time. In spite of my best intentions, I would find myself dreaming about being in a relationship. About having a future where I wasn't alone."

"So love happened in spite of yourself."

She smiled. "It did. I can't help but wonder if you are feeling some of the same things."

His knee-jerk reaction was that his feelings were completely different. He wasn't dwelling on love and attraction and hope. He was worried about causing someone to get seriously hurt, abused, or to die. But then he realized that there was a part of him that did feel the things she was speaking about.

"I've been alone for a long time, Neeta."

"I know." Looking sad, she said, "You know what? When one is alone, one doesn't have to worry about what other people do. There's a measure of control there that feels comfortable."

"I don't want to be responsible for other people's pain."

"But have you considered that even when you try so hard to carry all your burdens on your own, other people are still affected?"

"Unintentionally."

"*Jah*. To be sure." Her eyes widened. "But does that really matter? Pain, whether it was caused intentionally or not, still hurts."

"You are right. Right about that. Right about a lot of things, but it doesn't really change anything."

She nodded slowly as she walked over to the coffee pot on the kitchen counter and poured herself a cup, stopping to stare out the window for a moment.

Calvin watched, thinking as he did that Mark had chosen well. Waneta was the perfect woman for him. She was kind and had a calm, compassionate nature about her that drew him closer. No doubt it was because he'd had so little of that growing up. He'd physically ached for love and affection.

Still staring out the window, Waneta sipped her coffee. "Calvin, you are welcome to disagree, but as I think of all the events that brought your brother and me together, I can't help but realize that all of my hoping and planning and hesitation didn't do any good."

"But what choice is there?"

"First, we could put our troubles in the Lord's hands. He's strong enough to carry the burden."

"I believe in God, but I don't know if I'm ready to assume that He is going to watch over my mess and protect the ones I love." That was a lie, he *knew* he didn't believe that. After all, if the Lord was so good and caring, why hadn't He protected him and Mark when they were little boys?

"All right, then," she said, still staring out the

215

window. "How about this? I believe that life and love and hope and pain are going to exist no matter how hard we try to fight them. Just like we don't cause all the hurt in our life, we can't prevent it all, either. Not even when we walk on a tightrope across the crevice of our insecurities."

Calvin got to his feet. He was slightly taken aback that she had an answer for everything. But he was even more irritated by the way she was staring out the window instead of facing him again.

"I'm getting the feeling that you are avoiding looking me in the eye. What is so interesting outside?" he snapped.

"Oh, nothing much. I'm just watching Alice speak with the sheriff."

"What?"

At last she turned around and looked at him. "The sheriff's SUV is parked right in front of her house. Alice has been speaking with Sheriff Brewer the whole time we've been talking."

"And you didn't think to tell me?"

She raised her eyebrows. "Well, I'm telling you now. And I tried to tell you earlier."

"No, you didn't. You were standing there, offering platitudes."

"*Nee*, Calvin. I was trying to tell you that you can sit on my couch with your hands over your face for as long as you want. But that doesn't stop the rest of the world from moving along."

He opened his mouth. Shut it, and felt like a guppy. Then he went to pull out his boots from their mudroom, sat down, and stuffed his bare feet into them. "You know, I had no idea you were such a know-it-all."

She chuckled. "I fear that it came as a surprise to Mark as well. It's his cross to bear."

"I'm going out there to see what happened," he said unnecessarily. Already every worry that he'd been pondering was jumping around in his brain. He paused, half waiting for her to give him more advice or warn him off.

But instead, she simply nodded. "I know you need to do that. You care about her."

He did. But he was old enough to realize that just because someone cared, it didn't mean that their concern was a good thing.

Neeta spoke up again just before he could say something too revealing. "Let me know if I can help you, Calvin."

As he walked out, both the sheriff and Alice paused in their conversation to watch him cross the street.

And that was when Calvin Fisher knew that he shouldn't have acted so impulsively. He had no idea what he was walking into. He only hoped that he wasn't about to get arrested.

CHAPTER 20

Saturday, February 24

H ere comes Calvin," Alice blurted as soon as she saw him walking across the street. His presence was exactly what she needed to get through this horrible moment.

Sheriff Brewer turned to watch him approach. "I didn't realize you knew each other." Looking back at her, he murmured, "Y'all close?"

His question caught her off guard, both by his interest and the fact that she wasn't sure if they were actually close or not. "We're pretty close. He's becoming a good friend."

"Is that right?"

She was getting so spooked by the sheriff's tone, she blurted the first thing that came to mind. "Maybe he heard about my schoolhouse and is coming over to check on me."

"That would be real thoughtful of him. 'Course I can't think of how he would know about it already. Can you?"

Oh no! Had she just made Calvin seem guilty? "*Nee*. Not at all. I mean, I'm not sure. I mean, I guess we'll have to ask him."

The sheriff narrowed his eyes as he watched Calvin stop to give Valentine a scratch behind her ears. The silly cat was lounging on a rock next to the mailbox. "Yeah. Sure, we can do that. We can ask Calvin if he knows anything at all about the damage done to your school."

Sheriff Brewer's voice was quiet and low-key; his Kentucky drawl softening the consonants should have made her feel more at ease. But, unfortunately, it did just the opposite. Why had she even brought up Calvin now, connecting him with the damage to her school? "Calvin is a good man. I'm sure he'll tell you if he does."

Her pulse fluttered as Calvin neared. She noticed that his expression tightened as he got closer. It was obvious that he'd heard the last of her words. "What will I tell you?"

She hated how defensive he sounded. She knew he was scared, though. Of what, she wasn't certain. She didn't think he was afraid the sheriff was going to arrest him. But if not, she had no idea what could be on his mind.

He was definitely afraid of something. Really afraid. "Calvin, have you ever met Sheriff Brewer?"

He stuffed his hands in his pockets. "Yeah. We've met. Is everything all right?"

Sheriff Brewer glanced her way. "I hope so. I stopped by to speak to Alice here about some damage that happened to her school building."

Everything in Calvin's body language changed. Much of the guarded expression on his face disappeared as he stepped closer to her. "Why? What happened?"

"Looks like someone broke down the front door and pulled things down from the walls." The sheriff shifted. Rolled his shoulders. It was obvious, to Alice at least, that he was attempting to sound offhand. "Looks like it happened last night."

"Someone messed up a nursery school?" His expression was incredulous. "Who would want to do such a thing?"

"That's what I'm trying to find out," Sheriff Brewer said. "It's kind of an odd place for vandals to target."

While Calvin seemed to need another moment to digest that information, Alice spoke quickly. "There isn't anything of value inside. Well, not beyond everything that I made." As she began to mentally catalog all those things—the animal shapes out of cardboard and construction paper, the pretty calendar that her father had helped her make out of old plywood, the magnets, and the letters—it felt crushing. All of those things were personal and had taken a lot of care.

Was *any* of it left?

To her surprise, Calvin pressed a hand on the center of her back. "I'll go over there and work on that door."

"You will?"

A fiery, almost hurt expression burned in his eyes. "Of course I will. Did you really think I wouldn't help you?"

Immediately she felt warmer. Though, whether it was from embarrassment or happiness, she wasn't sure. "I didn't want to assume."

"I'm going to help you as much as I can."

"But your brother . . . I don't want to interfere."

"Mark's sleeping most of the time. He'll be all right."

"I was just asking Alice if she knew of anyone who might have done such a thing," Sheriff Brewer said. "Can you think of anyone?"

Calvin's expression tensed again before he relaxed. "No. I haven't lived here in years. I don't really know anyone around here anymore." Rubbing her back gently, he said, "I really don't know anyone who would want to damage a preschool."

Sheriff Brewer nodded, as if he'd thought the same thing. "If you discover anything odd when you're cleaning up, let us know, Alice. Otherwise, I'll swing by the school in a couple of days to check on you."

Feeling like the sheriff was taking note that Calvin's hand was still resting on her back—and maybe remembering the way she'd told the sheriff they were pretty close—Alice felt her neck warm. "That's mighty kind of you, Sheriff Brewer. Thank you for stopping by."

He smiled as he tipped his hat. "It's my job." Darting a look Calvin's way, he said, "Give me a call if you can think of anyone who could be responsible."

"Will do," Calvin said.

"All right, then. I'll be in touch," Sheriff Brewer said as he strode to his vehicle.

Still taking comfort in Calvin's presence, Alice watched the sheriff start his SUV, speak into his radio, and drive off.

Then the reality of what had happened hit her hard. Someone had broken into her little school. The place that she'd worked so hard to make into a happy, nurturing space for her tiny scholars. Now it was tainted. Feeling almost violated, she fisted her hands so she wouldn't burst into tears.

As the SUV disappeared from view, Calvin shifted his arm to curve it around her shoulders. Alice knew she should step away. His touch was far too familiar, both for their strained relationship and because of the fact that they were standing outside for the rest of the neighborhood to see.

But she wasn't strong enough to care about all of that. All she did care about was that she wasn't standing by herself, wondering how she was going to have to go ask her parents for help.

She bit her lip. But of course she was going to

have to speak to them. And her brother John, too. If she didn't, they would soon hear that the sheriff came to her house, and immediately assume that she was hurt or injured.

"What do you want to do first?"

Leaning closer, she rested her cheek on his chest. "You were speaking the truth? You really will help me?"

"Of course. I wouldn't have lied to you about that. When do you want to leave?"

Something blossomed inside her. It felt warm and comfortable, like she'd just donned a warm sweater. That was what Calvin's friendship was becoming, she realized. Comfortable and comforting. Something she was starting to think that she could reach for and feel better.

Realizing that he was still waiting for her response, she pulled away and gathered her thoughts. "I can be ready as soon as I gather my purse and my keys."

"Let's drive over in my truck. That way if we need to run to the hardware store for supplies we can."

"I need to visit with my parents and my brother John sometime today, too."

His expression turned carefully blank. "Why is that?"

"They'll have heard about the sheriff's visit. I need to give them an explanation before they make up their own."

"All right. We'll go to the school for a couple of hours. Then I can drop you off on the way home."

She knew what he was trying to do. He wanted to avoid her family. Not because he didn't like them, but because he didn't know if she would want him there. Alice decided to ease his mind by injecting a bit of humor. "Oh, no, you won't. You're coming with me, and there's no getting out of it, either."

"You sure about this?"

"I'm sure."

He gestured to himself. "They're probably not going to like that you've been hanging out with me."

"After I tell them how helpful you've been, they're going to want to thank you."

He rolled his eyes. "I ain't so sure about that."

Obviously, it was time to pull out all the stops. "It's going to be hard for me to tell them about the damage. I know I'll feel better if you are there. Please, Calvin?"

Twin spots of color appeared in his cheeks. Alice wondered if this was the first time in his life that he'd blushed. He stepped awkwardly to one side, then nodded. "I'll go get ready, too, and meet you in ten minutes."

"And I'll be ready, Calvin. I'll be standing here, waiting for you."

He didn't say a word, just turned and walked back across the street.

But as Alice went inside and got her things together, she realized that her mood was light and she was actually optimistic. She wasn't going to have to face the vandalism of the school all by herself. She wasn't going to have to worry about fixing the school's door on her own, she wasn't going to have to face the mess or her parents by herself.

Calvin Fisher was going to be with her. And no matter what happened, he wouldn't let anyone get the upper hand or run roughshod over her. He really had become her warm sweater.

CHAPTER 21

Saturday, February 24

Alice had hoped and prayed the whole time they were riding over that the damage to her classroom wasn't as bad as she feared. But the moment they walked toward the front steps, Alice knew she'd made a mistake in her prayers.

It wasn't as bad as she'd feared.

It was a whole lot worse.

Even Calvin seemed surprised. His footsteps had slowed as she was pointing out the yellow crime scene tape across the doorframe. Then they went up onto the porch and stopped—stood together, silently staring into the classroom.

It was obvious to Alice that Calvin was trying to gather his composure so he didn't frighten her any further.

But he needn't have worried. She didn't think that there was *anything* he could utter or accidentally say to make things worse. She was devastated.

When he finally did speak, his voice was strained. "I'm really sorry," he said at last. "To tell you the truth, I didn't think things were going to look this bad."

"I didn't think so, either." Wiping stray tears that had filled her eyes, she swallowed hard. "I don't know who would do this."

"I don't know either, but I'll figure out who did," he said, his voice hard. "I promise you that."

Alice had always believed in turning the other cheek and trying to look on the positive side of things. Actually, she relied on her beliefs when she taught her tiny scholars. How could she think otherwise?

But as she stood on the porch looking into her classroom through the taped-off door, seeing the picture books ripped, the pictures torn off the wall, the toys and easels broken, she secretly hoped that Calvin would find the person who had done all the damage. She wanted to yell at them. And, secretly, maybe she wanted Calvin to punish them, too.

As terrible images flooded her head, she whimpered. What was wrong with her? Reaching out, she rested her hand on the doorframe.

"Alice?"

"I'm all right, Calvin. Just a little dizzy."

"Of course you are." Before she could say a word, he swung her up into his arms. Her hands flew in the air before looping around his neck.

He pulled her a little closer, making her feel cared for. Almost better. Which was disconcerting, too.

"Calvin, you need to put me down."

"I will. But we're going to sit down," he said as he turned from the door and carried her back to the porch steps.

She held on tight, trying not to contemplate just how pleased she was to be in his arms. She felt safe and protected. She felt like she wasn't part of a half anymore. Almost like she was now part of a whole.

After they turned away from the door and got to the top step of the porch, both of them breathed deep. The cool air felt fresh and untainted. Cleansing.

"I'm going to put you down now," he murmured as his actions followed suit.

With care, he slowly released her legs, then lowered her. After another couple of seconds, he released his arms. Alice found herself having to remind herself to let go, too.

But he was still acting as attentive as a sweetheart might. Holding her elbow, he bent forward slightly in order to peer into her eyes. "Better? Or do you still feel dizzy?"

"I'm better." She breathed in and out again, slowly taking stock of how her body was reacting. Her shakiness was done. Her world had stopped moving. The numbness she had felt in her fingers and toes had subsided. "I feel much better. Sorry about that."

"You don't have a thing to be sorry for. Anyone would have been upset."

She realized then that while she physically did feel back to normal, the rest of her felt off. It was her viewpoint. No longer was she looking at her world through her optimistic perspective. She now felt bleak. It was as if the person who had torn apart the room had pulled away all the color also.

"I don't want to sit down. I need to go back in and start cleaning up now. It's Saturday and my students will be here on Monday." And that felt like another punch in the stomach. What was she going to tell her little scholars about the vandal?

"That might not be possible."

"It has to be. It's going to be hard enough to talk to my students about the damage that was done. I couldn't bear them having nowhere to go, too."

"I understand that, but what you want and what you can do are two different things." His voice softened to near a whisper. "Alice, I'm sorry but there ain't much left."

She knew he was trying to protect her, and maybe being completely honest, too. And maybe she did need some time to plan and make things a whole lot better before she had the children join her here again.

But with a new sense of urgency, she realized that that wasn't who she was. She was not the type of girl who backed down without a fight. "I'm going to do this."

He stared at her and nodded. "Then we need a list. You stay here while I find something for us to write with and write on."

She didn't argue. And had no desire at that moment to walk into that room. A few minutes' time would be soon enough, and she sat down on the porch step.

Calvin came out with two fine-tip markers and a piece of pink construction paper. Sitting down next to her, he pulled the cap off the blue pen. "How about this? We write down twenty things that need to get done, then we'll prioritize them by numbering them with the red pen."

"Calvin, there are many more than twenty things to do."

"I know, but we can't do everything. We can only do some things."

She liked how that sounded. His words made sense and made her realize that everything wasn't going to be perfect when her students came on Monday. Not even close.

But she could make it be good enough.

Steeling herself, she said. "All right, then. First, we need to fix the door."

Calvin smiled. "Good job. I'll write the next one. We need to sort all the furniture."

"And throw away what can't be salvaged."

"There you go," he murmured.

And so they continued. Back and forth they went, calling out tasks to do. With Calvin writing them down and encouraging her to limit the jobs, Alice felt like they'd made great strides.

Next, they prioritized the list. That was unexpectedly easy, with Calvin pointing out that the children's safety needed to be the priority. When they finished numbering, Alice realized that she was actually excited to go back inside and get to work.

"Better?" Calvin asked.

"*Jah*. Much. *Danke*, Calvin."

"You don't need to thank me. I am simply glad to be here with you."

"If you weren't, I think I would have fallen apart." She smiled sheepishly. "At least for a few minutes, anyway."

"Let's go to the hardware store and pick up everything we need, and stop somewhere to get you some food, too."

"I could stay here while you go. I mean, I could give you some money."

"No."

"No to the money?"

"No to leaving you here by yourself."

"Calvin, I know I lost myself for a minute or two, but I'm better now. I can handle working here on my own."

"Nope. It ain't going to happen. We don't know who did this or where they are now. As far as I'm concerned, you might be in danger."

She was just about to argue her case when two buggies pulled up, one of which was pulled by a black gelding with four white stockings. She would know that horse anywhere. It was her brother's horse and buggy. And . . . yes, those were her parents by his side. "Prepare yourself, Calvin. My brother and parents have arrived."

Watching them, Calvin said, "On the bright side, their being here saved us a trip to their houses."

"There is that."

As if on cue, John called out, "Alice, I heard the sheriff was at Edward's *haus*! And now there's yellow tape here. And a broken door. What's going on?"

"Someone broke into my nursery school, John!" Under her breath, she muttered, "Obviously."

"When were you going to tell us?" her father asked as he and her mother strode toward the porch.

"I was going to stop by later."

"Later?" her mother questioned. "Surely, you know better than that."

"I've been a little busy, Mamm."

All three of them came to a stop and gazed at Calvin. "Alice, who is this?" her mother asked.

"I'm really sorry," Alice murmured under her breath to him. "They can be a little over-whelming."

Calvin didn't answer her. Instead, he stepped forward, going down the steps to meet her parents. "Hello. I'm Calvin Fisher."

Her father looked him up and down. "I'm Moses Yoder. Who *are* you?"

"He just told you, Daed," Alice said, then joined Calvin.

"I'm Mark Fisher's brother," Calvin said easily. "He lives across the street from your other son, Edward. Since I've been visiting and Alice has been house-sitting, we've been getting to know each other. We've become friends."

John looked at Alice, then back at Calvin. "John Yoder. Good to meet you."

Calvin smiled. "Same, though I'm real sorry about the circumstances."

"What exactly has happened?" Mamm asked.

"Sheriff Brewer stopped by Edward's house and told me about the vandalism," Alice said as patiently and succinctly as she possibly could. "Calvin came over when he saw the sheriff's truck. When he learned what had happened, he offered to drive me over here."

"There was no way I was going to let her handle this on her own," Calvin supplied.

"It would have been better if you had come to us first."

"I don't think so," Alice said. "Calvin has been really helpful."

Before her parents could argue that point, John walked up the steps and peered inside the classroom. He whistled low. "Whoever did this spent a lot of time inside."

"I thought the same thing," Calvin said.

Afraid that her mother was going to start asking her a bunch of questions about the building, the sheriff, *and* Calvin, Alice said, "We were just about to go get some lunch and go to the hardware store."

John stared at her intently. "Do you plan to have your students back anytime soon?"

"Monday."

Her mother shook her head. "Alice, I'm sure that isn't possible. It's too much work for you."

Knowing that if she didn't take a stand right that minute, her mother would be holding out her hand to take and moving her back home within the hour. So Alice crossed her arms over her chest.

"Mamm, it's important to me. I need to do this."

To her surprise, it was her father who came to her rescue. "You know what? I agree. How about John stays here with you, I go with Calvin to the hardware store, and your mother goes home, makes us some lunch, and brings it back."

"That sounds *gut. Danke*," John said quickly.

Alice thought it sounded good, too, as long as they hadn't scared Calvin away. Turning to him, she studied him closely. "Will that be all right with you?"

"It's absolutely fine."

Now that they were all armed with plans, they split up. Right before Calvin turned away, he placed a hand on her shoulder. "Are you feeling better?" he murmured. "If not, I can raise a stink and get them all to leave."

She giggled. "That's mighty kind of you, but I'm good now. Actually, I think I'm going to be just fine."

After giving her a gentle squeeze, he nodded and walked to her father's side.

After her mother left, John said, "Do you want to talk to me about Calvin?"

"*Nee.*"

He laughed. "I figured you were going to say that. But sooner or later, you are going to have to talk to me about him."

"Since we have a school to clean, I would say that we have far more important things to do first."

Wrapping an arm around her shoulders, John pressed a kiss to her temple. "Can't argue with you there, Al. Let's go get started."

And so they walked in. At last, she felt ready for anything.

CHAPTER 22

Saturday, February 24

By the time Alice caught a glimpse of her father and Calvin returning from the hardware store, three parents of her students had arrived to help with the cleanup. News of the damage to her little school had spread like wildfire through Horse Cave.

Just like Alice, they'd first been stunned by the destruction that had taken place. However, in no time at all, they rolled up their sleeves and got to work.

Alice never asked who had told them about the damage or how they'd known that she was at the school on a Saturday morning. Years ago, Alice had given up trying to understand how rumors happened. All she did know was that she was grateful for the helping hands.

Thanks to Calvin's guidance, she'd been able to show the new volunteers her list and started assigning tasks while she and John cleaned and sorted toys and materials.

When Calvin came inside the school with her *daed*, he introduced himself to the volunteers, then walked to her side. "You doing all right?"

Alice instinctively knew that if she said she wasn't, Calvin would do whatever it took to make things better. It was humbling to realize that he always wanted to put her needs first.

She was relieved to be able to look at him and smile. "I'm doing a lot better." Leaning a little closer so no one else would hear, she asked, "How was the trip with my father?"

He grinned. "*Gut.*"

Obviously, there was a story there. "Did he ask you a hundred questions?"

"Not a hundred. Only a couple of dozen or so."

"I'm sorry." She could just imagine how the car ride had been. No doubt Calvin had been answering question after question while her father fired off one after another.

Calvin reached out his hand as if to touch her, then dropped it to his side abruptly. "There's no need to apologize. He cares about you."

"He can also be overbearing."

"I can take care of myself, Alice."

It was becoming apparent that he could. "Are you going to work on the door now?"

"Yep. And then I'm going to do the next chore on our list."

As much as she appreciated that, she knew his brother was home and might need him. "If you need to leave—"

"I'm not leaving. I aim to stay here as long as you'll let me."

"All right. *Danke*."

When Alice turned away, she noticed two of her students' mothers looking at them with interest. She stiffened, half-ready to be questioned. But instead of doing that, they only smiled and continued on their projects.

She relaxed and continued sorting through a pile of books that had been torn and ripped.

Eventually, her mother arrived and they all stopped to eat—she had made enough for half the town. A while after that, the children's parents left. Eventually her parents did, too, with her father taking the damaged wooden calendar with him.

By this time, it was after four o'clock and everything was in much better shape. Just as John was taking his leave and saying good-bye to Alice and Calvin, a black SUV pulled into the parking lot.

Alice tensed. That was the same vehicle that had passed her on the road three weeks ago. And the one that had driven slowly on her street and scared her half to death.

"What is that car doing *here?*" she murmured.

Beside her, Calvin tensed. "I'll deal with it," he said.

Both his voice and his body language had changed. He suddenly seemed bigger, harsher, more formidable, and less approachable. If Alice hadn't come to trust him, she knew she would have been afraid.

When a man got out, all muscle, brawn, salt-and-pepper hair, and sunglasses, John glanced at Calvin. "Is that man a friend of yours?"

"Yeah," Calvin said. Just before he was about to walk away from John and Alice, the man walked around the front of the truck, then opened the passenger door and let out Irene.

Alice gasped. "Why is Irene with him?"

"I'd like to know that, too," Calvin said. "Wait here, Alice."

"Oh, no. I'm coming with you," she said as she watched Irene and the man stare back. When the man leaned down to say something to Irene and *another* man got out of the vehicle, then moved to one side, Alice became even more worried. She started walking, too.

Calvin reached out one hand. "Hold on, Alice—"

She sidestepped his touch. "Calvin, I'm *not* gonna just stand here and watch," she said before he could start treating her like a child. "Irene is my best friend. If she's here, she's here to talk to me, not you."

Leaving John behind, she and Calvin had only gone a few feet when he stopped and spoke. "I know you want to be in charge, but now ain't the time. Trust me on this, okay?"

His voice was firm and quiet, but there was a new tension underlying it. This man was important to him. "Okay," she replied easily as they both walked on.

Calvin was staring straight at the man as he increased his pace, definitely concerned. On edge. Was it because Irene was with him? Did Calvin think that this man had something to do with her school?

Or could something have happened that was even worse?

CALVIN HADN'T THOUGHT it was possible to feel both relieved and scared at the same time. Seeing both West and Smith on the grounds of Alice's preschool proved him wrong. He didn't know whether to guard Alice with his body or act as if she didn't matter so West wouldn't notice her.

Of course, the realization that he could never pretend she didn't matter hit him hard. Alice *did* matter to him. A lot. Maybe even too much.

No matter what West had to say, Calvin knew he would look after her safety and comfort first.

"Everything all right?" he asked after Alice and Irene greeted each other with hugs.

West tilted his head to one side, almost as if he needed to think about his answer. "I'm kind of thinking that I should be asking that of you." Pointing toward the schoolhouse, he said, "It's obvious that everything isn't all right. What happened?"

"Someone broke into this little school and did quite a bit of damage."

Calvin could practically feel Alice wiggle restlessly next to him. She reminded him of a puppy that had recently been taught to sit still. She was following his directions, but it was obvious to all of them that she wasn't comfortable with the idea.

He figured he needed to let Alice speak before she ignored his request completely. Gesturing to Alice, he said, "This is actually her school. Alice, this is West. He's my boss. West, this is Alice. She's a friend of mine."

Alice smiled at him shyly. "Hello."

West nodded his head. "Good to meet you. Shame about the circumstances, though," he said in a soft and gentle tone that Calvin hadn't known he was capable of. "I'm real sorry."

"*Jah*. Me, too."

Irene spoke up. "Alice, what happened?"

"Someone broke into my schoolhouse and caused a lot of damage. Lots of damage," she said quickly, like she was afraid Calvin was going to stop her before she could get out all her words. "First the sheriff came to my house and told me. Then Calvin drove me here to look at it. After that my parents and brother John, and a couple of my scholars' parents, came over to help me clean it up."

242

"We can help, too," Irene said with a soft smile in West's direction. "That's why we came over."

Calvin stiffened. "How did you hear about the vandalism?"

"Does it matter?" West asked.

Wondering if West had had someone tracking him, he nodded. "Yeah, I think it does."

A muscle in West's jaw jumped. Calvin could practically feel him stiffen.

"We heard at the diner," Irene said, easing the tension between them. "I worked the morning shift. West came in to have breakfast."

"He came for breakfast?"

"That's what I just said, Calvin," Irene emphasized. "West *and* Smith. Anyway, everyone at the diner was talking about it. He offered to take me."

Alice curved a hand around Irene's arm. "Come with me and I'll show you the inside." And without looking in West's direction, they walked to the schoolhouse, leaving Calvin alone with West.

Maybe now he could hear the real story.

"Didn't know you started driving so far for breakfast," Calvin blurted before he remembered who he was talking to. No one used that tone with the head of the Kings.

West, to Calvin's amazement, looked chagrined. "Yeah, well, don't tell anyone."

"Has anything happened? Do you need me back in Louisville?"

West shook his head. "I told the truth. I came here to see Irene." Glaring at him, he said, "And don't go asking me why I'm visiting her. I don't know."

No way was Calvin going to risk challenging him again. "Yes, sir."

West rolled his eyes. "Anyway, Irene was worried about Alice, so we came over." Looking Calvin up and down, West's expression sharpened. "Want to tell me why *you're* looking at me like that?"

"Sorry, boss. I, uh, guess I'm just surprised. I didn't know you knew Irene well."

"You have a problem with that?"

"You're my boss and the president of the Kings. I don't have a problem with anything you do."

"Oh, yeah? You've got me curious now. What would you tell me if I wasn't your president?"

Calvin felt like he was barefoot crossing a rickety bridge covered with broken glass. One false move was going to cause him a lot of harm and pain. "If you weren't, then I'd probably ask you to take care with her. She's a sheltered girl who doesn't know a lot about the outside world."

West relaxed. "I realize that. I don't intend to hurt her."

But Calvin knew he would. That was how West was, how the gang was. Their very existence stemmed from the leadership wanting things that hurt other people *and* brought on lethal consequences. He also knew that because he was no doubt already hurting Alice with his secrets and lies.

West gestured to the splintered door that was lying nearby. "So who did this?"

"I don't know."

"Huh. Think it could have anything to do with you?" West asked.

"I don't think so," Calvin said, hoping he wasn't wrong. "If someone is pissed at me, there's a number of ways to get to me that are a whole lot easier and less messy."

"So it's someone local."

"I reckon so," replied Calvin. "I've been looking for any sign of who could have done this as we cleaned, but I haven't found a thing yet."

West's expression darkened. "What do you still need to do?"

"I patched the door with Alice's father. I was hoping this would hold until I had time to replace it. But if you want, we could take care of that now."

West nodded slowly. "Sounds good. There's a builder's supply off the highway about ten miles back."

Calvin thought this was almost too easy. Hoping that he was imagining things, he forced himself to do what he needed to do. "Let's go and get the measurements. You can see the rest of the damage up close, too."

"Who's the guy the girls are talking to now?" West blurted.

Calvin turned to follow his gaze. "*That* is Alice's brother John."

"Her *whole* family came right over to help . . ."

"Oh, yeah. As Alice said before, they did and a couple of her students' parents came, too."

Still carefully watching Irene, Alice, and John, West mumbled, "Things are real different here, aren't they?"

West looked and sounded completely confused. For the first time since he'd seen the truck pull up, Calvin was able to breathe easily. This was something he could relate to. It was also the first thing that he knew had come direct from West's heart.

"Yeah. Things are really different here." He would have been most comfortable simply leaving it at that, but West was still looking at him for an explanation. Calvin dug a little deeper, trying not to feel like he was betraying part of himself as he began describing the concept of Amish community and family.

"You see, with the Amish, it's typical to focus on a church community. It's made up of any-where between eight and twelve or fourteen families. Everyone gets real close. The bishops and the church elders determine what is allowed and what isn't. So all that is real important."

West's expression eased. "It's like the Kings."

It wasn't. The Kings was made up of a group of men who had joined the club for a variety of reasons, none of them good. Some had been betrayed or hurt by their families. Some men wanted to live a dangerous life. Or an illegal one. About the only thing they did have in common was that joining was for life and leaving wasn't really an option. That and the fact that there was a group of elders—in the Kings' case, only one, West—who made all the decisions.

But because he wasn't dumb enough to flat-out disagree with West, he tempered his words. "You're right. It's a lot like the Kings. Things here are just a lot more secluded." And legal. And meaningful. "Also, family is everything."

"Even when the family isn't good?"

"Yeah. Even then. But, um, most are pretty good. I mean, sure, everyone is human and makes mistakes. But by and large most of the Amish parents do right by their kids."

"Except for yours."

"Yeah. Except for mine."

"And Irene's."

That surprised him. "I don't know about Irene's family, West."

West looked over to where the women were talking, seeming just about to say something. Then he shrugged. "Never mind. It ain't like it matters."

Calvin almost sagged, he was so relieved.

After getting John's input and using a measuring tape that he'd brought, Cal and West got the dimensions and walked over to talk to the girls.

"Irene, we're going to get Alice a new door," West said, his voice soft. "You stay here."

"All right," Irene said.

But because she was Alice, she couldn't leave well enough alone. "A new door? But that isn't necessary. You and Daed fixed it just fine."

"Not for the long term. This is a good thing," Calvin said. "Accept the help, okay?"

She nodded. "All right. Thank you."

"You're welcome," West said with a smile.

Calvin would have gaped if he wasn't so used to covering up his feelings. When they got to the truck, Smith joined them again. "Where do you want me, boss?"

West glanced Calvin's way. "You armed?"

Calvin nodded. "Yeah." He almost hadn't put on his gun that morning, but he had learned the hard way that it did no good to ever assume anything was going to go as expected.

"Smith, Cal's got my back. You stay here with the women."

"Sure thing, boss. You want me to keep my distance or help them out?"

"I have a feeling they're going to need all the help they can get."

"Sure thing."

Calvin noticed Smith didn't seem all that upset to be hanging out with the women. A flicker of unease trailed down his spine before he pushed it away. Smith was dangerous, a trained killer, and only loyal to one person in the organization. That said, Calvin also knew that members weren't just loyal to other members, they were loyal to their women as well. Whether they realized it or not, Irene and Alice were now in that group.

The realization should have shocked him.

Instead, it felt almost right.

CHAPTER 23

Saturday, February 24

The moment they were alone inside the school, Alice grabbed Irene's hand. "Why were you with him?"

Irene looked uncomfortable. "I thought he was here to see me, but I'm not so sure now. He doesn't usually bring Mr. Smith."

Alice peered out the windows until she spotted the unfamiliar man. He looked to be even bigger than Calvin, was wearing sunglasses, dark boots, and a ski cap. He seemed to be wandering in a circle around her building. But instead of looking for damage, he was looking at the bushes and trees that surrounded it. "He seems odd."

Irene chuckled. "That's because he is odd. I've only actually talked to him once before. West says he's no one for me to be afraid of, though." Lowering her voice, she said, "Mr. Smith is his bodyguard. Isn't that something?"

There were so many things wrong with that statement, Alice hardly knew where to start. "Irene, how many times have you seen this West?"

"I don't know. About five."

Alice knew Irene was lying. Oh, maybe not about how many times she'd seen him. But she was definitely acting far more offhand about this relationship than it actually was. "I know we've both been busy, but why haven't you ever told me about him?"

"There wasn't anything to tell."

"Yes, there was. He's an Englisher. He seems scary. He has a bodyguard. He works with Calvin. I think there's a lot to tell. Irene, you need to stay away from him," she said as forcibly as she was able. Why, it was the same tone she used with her tiny students when they ran with scissors!

When Irene merely lifted one eyebrow, Alice reached for her hand. "Listen to me. He's not someone for you to be around. He could hurt you."

Irene pulled her hand away. "I've said the same thing about you. Calvin Fisher isn't exactly someone *you* should trust, Alice."

"He is completely different. He's one of us."

"*Nee*. He is not. He was dressed a lot like West and Mr. Smith. He knows them. He works for West doing who knows what."

Remembering how sweet he'd been to her today, remembering how worried he'd been about his brother, she shook her head. "He's different. He used to live across the street from where my brother lives now."

"That don't mean anything."

"Fine. He might not still be Amish, but he knows our ways. His brother is Amish. He's kind, too."

"Do you hear yourself?" Irene asked, exasperated. "You are making him into some kind of hero."

"I'm not." But she couldn't think of anything else to say about that because a part of her suspected Irene was telling the truth.

No matter how many ways she could try to make Calvin into someone like her, even she knew that pretending that he wasn't really like his boss was wrong. Calvin wasn't like her. Maybe he had never been.

After glancing outside and seeing that Mr. Smith was now sanding some wood, she continued sorting toys again. "What happened to us, Irene?" she asked quietly. "I thought after our *rumspringa* we would never stray from what was good and right again."

Irene shrugged as she picked up some scissors and started cutting out letter patterns. "I don't know what happened. Maybe we aren't actually as good as we think we are. Maybe there's still a part of us that likes testing the boundaries instead of doing only what is safe and proper."

"Do you think that's why we haven't married yet?" she blurted.

Irene chuckled. "*Nee*. We haven't married yet

because the boys we grew up with turned into men we don't want to marry."

"You may have a point," she said with a reluctant grin. "Our choices haven't been all that *gut* in Horse Cave."

"All the good men have been snatched up."

She sighed, realizing that even the men who had married hadn't been for her. With that knowledge came the strong feeling that only one man was for her, and he was extremely unsuitable. "Do you ever think about marrying a man like West?"

"*Nee.*"

Irene had answered that really fast. "Are you sure?"

"I need to be. I don't want to marry him." Looking embarrassed, she said, "I don't even think he's the type of man who wants to marry."

"You should stop seeing him."

"I can't, Alice. I like being with him too much." She bit her lip, then said, "Remember when we went off with those English kids and ended up in some apartment complex in Bowling Green?"

Remembering how helpless she had felt, Alice flinched. "I was so scared. I didn't know who we could trust." She lowered her voice. "For a while, I didn't think we were going to be able to leave."

"If we hadn't met that one guy, things might have gone a lot worse." Irene wrinkled her nose. "I can't believe it, but I forgot his name. What was it? Adam?"

"Able. It was Able, and he had grown up Amish. Remember? We kept whispering to each other that God must have sent him to watch over us."

Irene looked at her intently. "I think he is why I have been able to trust West. Able looked just like the rest of those creepy kids. He was friends with them . . . but he was different, too. He helped us get out of there without anyone noticing. He put us in his car, and drove us home."

"All he said was for us to not go back. He wouldn't even let us pay him for gas, and the car trip took two hours."

"I'm not saying that West is going to be my savior or help me get through anything really hard. But I am going to give him the benefit of the doubt, Alice. I'm determined to not judge him until I know different."

"I understand now."

Irene's expression eased. "So you agree with me?"

"I should. He and Calvin are spending their day replacing the door to my schoolhouse. That says it all."

Looking calmer, Irene said, "Who do you think could have done this damage?"

"I've talked to everyone, and I keep saying the same thing. I really have no idea who it could have been." Looking around the room, she added, "Calvin said he was worried about me. He is afraid that someone is really mad and might come to my house next. Well, Edward's house."

"I hope not."

"Me, too," Alice said fervently.

"Do you want to stay in my apartment with me? You can if you'd like. I'd love the company."

"*Danke*, but I am not going to let a bunch of what-ifs drive me away. Plus, I feel pretty safe at Edward's house. Calvin is right across the street."

Though it was obvious that Irene wanted to do some probing of her own about Calvin, she simply nodded.

Which gave Alice the feeling that at least one part of her life was still the same. No matter what happened, or what direction either of them eventually went, they would always have each other.

CHAPTER 24

Saturday, February 24

They'd stayed at the school another two hours. West helped install the new door, sweep the floors, and haul a bunch of debris to the dump. It had been a long time since he'd done physical labor like that.

Thinking about it, West mentally corrected himself. It hadn't been labor, exactly. His mother would have called them chores.

Allowing himself to picture her, he almost smiled. His mother cursed like a sailor, favored bleached blond hair, too-tight clothes, and was the hardest worker he'd ever known. She'd also been a particular fan of giving her four children chores to keep them out of trouble. It was too bad that hadn't worked out all that well.

Realizing that thoughts of home would only bring on sleepless nights, he turned to look at Irene, sitting beside him in the car.

She was as different from his mother and his two sisters as could be . . . except that she seemed to possess that same hidden iron will that they'd had in spades. Maybe that was what drew him to her. Or it could have been her beauty. She was such a pretty thing.

As if she was feeling his gaze on her, she smiled at him tentatively. "Everything okay?"

"Yeah." He didn't bother to explain himself. There was no need for her to know the things that filled his head.

After searching his expression, she nodded, then faced front. Seemingly content with the silence.

He'd never been a big talker, but West knew that this was bothering her. And because he knew that he was about to hurt her, he elected to stay silent.

It wasn't much, but it was something, he figured.

IRENE USUALLY ENJOYED being alone with West. He was attentive and asked questions about her and her life, like he really cared. Sometimes he was quiet, but he didn't brood like he was doing now, during the entire time in the car. He remained quiet even as they walked to her apartment. Feeling dismayed—especially after the way she'd defended him to Alice—she turned to him after he helped her unlock her door. "Well, good night—"

"Can I come in for a minute before I go?"

"Are you sure you want to?"

He looked down at his boots before meeting

her gaze. "I know I was pretty quiet during the drive over here. Sorry."

"Well, all right, then." After West followed her inside, she turned on the lone gaslight in the main room, then leaned out the door to West's body-guard, who was standing on the stoop. "Smith, would you like to come inside, too? It's awfully cold out."

He looked at her in surprise before shaking his head. "Thanks, doll, but I'm fine right here."

"Would you like some coffee? I could make some."

Before Mr. Smith could answer, West guided her back inside. "I'll bring him some coffee when I'm on my way out."

"Okay." Realizing then that she needed to go make that coffee, she smiled nervously. "Want to come into the kitchen with me?" Even as she said it, she felt herself blush. Her kitchen was simply the back corner of her apartment. The whole place was barely four hundred square feet. Even her bed was right there for anyone to see. Thank goodness she believed in making it neatly every morning.

He didn't answer, just continued to look around as he followed her across the space. He leaned on the other side of the kitchen counter while she prepared the percolator.

Looking at it closely, he said, "I've never seen one of those outside of the old movies."

"It's all I've ever used at home. The diner has a regular drip coffee maker."

"You ever wish you had that here?"

"Not really."

"No?"

"This makes good coffee, and that's what really counts. And as far as doing without goes, this is nothing—compared to, say, not having a cell phone or a computer."

"I guess you're right."

Now that they only had to wait for the coffee to brew, she walked around the counter so it wasn't in between them. The moment the barrier was gone, she felt better. Closer.

Irene had no idea why this man had made such an impression on her, but he had. She hadn't been lying when she'd told Alice that she couldn't imagine they'd be friends for anything other than a short amount of time.

But she hadn't felt compelled to tell Alice that she hoped West felt the same way . . . or that she was pretty sure she was going to be disappointed when their friendship had run its course.

"Did you want to talk about anything in particular, West?"

"Yeah." Looking at her intently, he said, "Seeing you and your friend Alice today . . . well, I'm afraid Calvin and me might have given you the wrong impression."

"Oh?"

"Yeah. Irene, I don't want you to expect that there can ever be anything between us."

His statement hurt. " 'Anything' covers a lot of ground," she said lightly, hoping that she was fooling him at least a little bit.

He narrowed his eyes. "Are you teasing me?"

"Maybe a little." When he continued to glare, she smiled. "Maybe a lot."

"Oh, Irene."

And . . . there went another little zing of pain. She loved moments like this. Moments when they seemed so close. When she did or said something that caught him off guard. She had a feeling that such things rarely happened to him.

He looked even more disgruntled. "I'm trying to be serious here." He closed his eyes, then said, "I mean, I'm trying to do the right thing."

She attempted to smile, but all that happened was that her eyes started tearing up. Here was this man, this brawny, strong, powerful, violent-looking man . . . and he seemed all twisted inside, in knots. It was so unexpected, she couldn't help but smile. "I know you are," she said at last. "And I appreciate it, too."

"Then why are you looking like that?"

"Maybe because you're trying so hard to spare my feelings. I think the only other person who has ever tried to treat me with such care is Alice."

A muscle in his cheek jumped. "You deserve

better than that. You should have had lots of people all your life looking out for you."

Just the other day, she'd begun thinking the same thing. That maybe she was worth more than she'd been led to believe. "West, I don't know why the Lord decided you and I should become friends. Maybe I'll never know. But I've decided to simply appreciate it for what it is."

He was staring at her closely. "And what is it?"

"Well, that our Lord God must have wanted us to know each other right now, at this time."

He stared at her closely, as if he was trying to read her mind. "Do you really believe that?"

"How can I not? There is no reason on earth that the two of us should have ever met each other, let alone have something to actually say to each other."

He rubbed the back of his neck. "You're right. It doesn't make sense."

"It doesn't make sense at all." Thinking of Able, Irene knew she had rarely believed anything so wholeheartedly. "But I don't need for it to make sense. I just need to accept it."

"Are you able to do that?" West asked.

"That's what faith is. Ain't so?" Because he still looked confused, she said, "Faith is believing in something without needing proof. It's simply accepting that it is so." She nodded. "I have to believe that. It's okay if you don't."

He stared at her, looked like he was about to

nod, then seemed to catch himself. "Irene, you are the most surprising girl. Every time I think I'm prepared for something you're about to say, you go in the opposite direction. You're really something else."

"I'm a lot of things, I guess. Do you remember when I first told you that I had a bad time of it growing up?"

"I do."

"Well, as bad a time of it as I had, Alice lived the complete opposite. She had a charmed life. Wonderful parents. Wonderful brothers. A cozy, nice home. Pretty looks, too."

"Why are you bringing her up?"

"When we were seventeen, we both ran off for the night. We didn't mean to get into trouble, but one thing rolled into the next. The next thing we knew, our bad decisions had snowballed. Do you know that feeling?"

"I've experienced it a time or two."

She figured that was an understatement. "Well, in our case, we ended up at a party in an apartment where we didn't know anyone. People were doing and saying things that made us uncomfortable. We were scared."

West was staring at her closely now. As if there wasn't another person in the world he needed to listen to right at that moment. "What happened?"

"A boy showed up. His name was Able, and he looked as 'English' as any of the other kids there, but he'd been raised Amish. He led us out of there and got us home safe."

"I'm not following you."

"West, he appeared in my life when I needed him. I never saw him again after that, but here I am, after all this time, talking about him to both Alice earlier today and now you. I'm thinking that you are going to have that same kind of impact on me. One day, years from now, we'll understand why we met."

West swallowed. Seemed to think about that for a moment, then, to Irene's surprise, nodded. "As much as a part of me wishes things could be different, I'm okay with that."

She couldn't help it, she chuckled again. "Me, too."

"You still going to give me a cup of coffee?"

"Do you still want to be my friend?"

"Don't even start asking me stupid questions like that. Now, how about that cup?"

"And then?"

"And then we're gonna sit down on this uncomfortable-looking couch of yours and talk about nothing." He eyed her again. "You good with that?"

Slowly, she nodded. "*Jah*, West. I am."

CHAPTER 25

Thursday, March 1

Almost a week had passed since the school had been vandalized. All their hard work on Saturday, cleaning and straightening up, paid off. Alice greeted her tiny scholars bright and early on Monday morning. For the first few minutes, she'd been wary, afraid that they would have heard about the damage or would be upset that everything wasn't the same as it was before.

But instead of focusing on the differences, they'd greeted the new door, calendar, and decorations with wide-eyed excitement. Alice was so relieved that she ended up making a game out of it. They played *I Spy* for a full half hour, clapping every time one of the students located something new and different.

So, despite her many worries, school had been wonderful.

Calvin had been, too. He stayed in town all week, watching both his brother and her with care.

In fact, everything would have been wonderful-*gut*, if she hadn't felt like she was being watched.

Nothing had happened that she could put her finger on. If there had, she would have either told Calvin or paid Sheriff Brewer a visit. Instead, it was more like she sensed shadows outside the school where there didn't used to be, or twigs cracking outside her bedroom window that couldn't be explained.

She knew her mind had to be playing tricks on her.

But because of that feeling—and because she knew she needed to start acting more self-reliant—she kept her worries to herself.

She also only went to school and back to Edward's house. And when she was at the house, she kept all the windows and doors tightly locked.

Anything to feel safe and secure.

Because of this self-imposed isolation, Alice hadn't seen Calvin, Irene, or her family. She didn't go to the diner or stop by her parents' house on the way home from school like she usually did from time to time. She didn't even glance out the front windows in an attempt to spy Calvin. Being visible from the street felt like a bad idea, too.

That was why she was caught off guard when Irene walked into her classroom just moments after Alice had hugged her last student good-bye.

"What are you doing here?" she blurted when they were completely alone.

Irene shrugged. "I figured I better come over

here since you've been staying away from the diner."

"I haven't been staying away. I've just been busy."

"I bet." Bending down, Irene picked up a couple of fallen plastic letters from the floor and set them on one of the tables. "But I still thought you might have stopped by. You aren't mad at me or anything, are you?"

"Of course not."

Looking like she was bracing herself, Irene continued. "Oh, *gut*. For a while, I was starting to worry that you were upset that I was friends with West Powers."

"I'm not." Though she had thought their friendship was odd, Alice knew better than to say anything else. After all, she hadn't liked Irene talking bad about Calvin.

But since she'd brought it up, she eyed Irene carefully. "Do you really like him *that* much?"

"I think I do."

"He sure acted like he liked you."

Irene's expression lit. "Do you think so? I think he's handsome."

"He is at that. He seemed nice, too."

"He has been. But, what I really like is that he doesn't act like I'm damaged."

Taken by surprise, Alice set the tablet of paper she'd been holding on a table. "Goodness, Irene, I never knew you felt that way."

"I don't feel that way all the time. When I'm alone in my apartment, I feel at peace." Her friend's mouth tightened. "I know you think you know how bad things were at my house, but I promise, you don't. Not really. When I think about those days, living the way I'd been forced to . . . well, I've learned to be thankful for a peaceful life."

"I don't think West's life is all that peaceful," Alice pointed out gently.

"You're right. It ain't. But I'm willing to be okay with that because he makes me realize that although I'm not perfect, there's still a lot of me that is good."

"If he makes you feel that way, then that's wonderful, because there's a lot of good in you, my friend. I'm happy for you."

Irene's light-blue eyes searched her face, obviously looking for subterfuge. "You mean it, don't you?"

She nodded assuredly. "I mean it."

"*Gut*, because I came over here to see if you wanted to go to that new coffee shop that opened. I hear that they have some great scones and cookies and cupcakes. You want to go get some hot chocolate, tea, or coffee—and eat things we shouldn't? My treat. I got some good tips the other day."

Alice smiled. "Sure, but first I have to clean up."

"I can help you do that." Reaching down, Irene

picked up a stray yellow crayon. "What should I do first?"

"If you could do what you're doing, that would be wonderful-*gut*. I get so tired of collecting things off the floor."

Holding a magnetic letter *P,* Irene smiled. "Everything is so cute and small. I don't mind doing this. It's kind of fun to see how you spend your afternoons."

"Have at it, then. I always put out everything for the next class. It won't take me but fifteen or twenty minutes."

"Go on, then. I've got this."

Alice chuckled as she walked back to her desk, feeling like a weighty load had just been lifted from her shoulders. She really should have swallowed her pride and gone over to visit Irene. After all, it was none of her business who Irene liked.

She had enough to worry about with her own love life, anyway. Calvin Fisher was the type of man her parents had always feared she would date. No, that wasn't quite right. They'd always assumed that she would stay away from men like him and do exactly as they wished. For the longest time, she had done just that.

But all that had gotten her was a lot of lonely days and nights.

"Hey, Alice? I found something I think you should see."

Putting her pencil down, she walked across to see what had Irene so concerned. It looked like she was holding several crumbled pieces of paper. "What is all that?"

Irene held one of the sheets out to her. It was obvious that she'd recently worked to smooth it flat. "This."

Puzzled, she took the paper from Irene's hand. Within seconds, she realized it wasn't a scrap piece of paper, it was a letter. One addressed to her that she had never seen. As she read the words written there, she was glad she was only seeing it now, with Irene by her side and not before class started.

It was a horrible note, written in large, scrawling, angry print. Calling her all sorts of terrible names and threatening her.

It was from John Yutzy.

Tears formed in her eyes. Not because of the words, but because it was obvious that Mr. Yutzy's daughter, Mary Ruth, knew it was mean and didn't want to show it to her teacher.

That poor little thing. First, her father had ignored Alice's directive and had continued to send her to school. Now it was obvious that he was giving her this burden as well. What must her home life be like? She already knew her father's letters to her teacher should be something to be avoided.

"Are they all from John Yutzy, Irene?"

"*Jah.*"

"She must have been crumbling them up and hiding them in her cubby so I wouldn't see them."

Irene look confused. "But she couldn't have read the notes, could she?"

"*Nee.* But I think it's obvious now that she knows her father doesn't do nice things. Or, who knows? Maybe he was in a rant when he was writing them and she sensed they would be upsetting."

"What should we do?"

"*We?* Nothing. *Me,* I don't know."

"He grabbed my arm. And, well, we both know that he's going to hate us for the rest of his life."

"He might not hate us . . ."

"Alice, you can pretend that everyone lives like you do, in a happy preschool cloud, but most of us are well aware that some people are evil and mean."

"I don't live in a happy cloud." And, well, she *was* pretty shaken up. "You know what? I don't want to stay in this room here anymore. Let's go."

"Are you sure? When are you going to prepare everything?"

"I'll come in early tomorrow." Realizing that her hands were shaking, she said, "I need a brownie."

"All right, then. I'll buy you two."

She folded the terrible notes and slipped them in her purse. Then put on her bonnet, cloak, and mittens as quickly as she could.

Minutes later, they were walking down the hill and toward Floyd's Pond.

CHAPTER 26

Thursday, March 1

Even though John Yutzy's awful letters were tucked in her purse, Alice felt lighter than she had in days as she walked toward town at Irene's side. In an obvious effort to lighten the mood, Irene told her a funny story about Mr. Lehmann, who owned Blooms and Berries, and also happened to be Mark and Waneta Fisher's boss. Practically the moment Mr. Lehmann had ordered Bill's famous pepper steak special, another man got the last helping. Mr. Lehmann started bartering for the meal, offering all sorts of things, including potting soil, a dwarf rosebush, and a watering can he'd been trying to get rid of forever.

The customer didn't want any of that, but was willing to trade for a tree.

Alice had giggled. "Never say Henry Lehmann wouldn't give up a tree for a plate of Bill's steak and peppers."

Irene nodded. "It was a crabapple one, too."

"But those are expensive."

"Oh, yes. They are! But Henry was deter-

273

mined to get what he wanted, and he wanted that special."

"I wish I had been there," Alice said as they crossed a field and approached Floyd's Pond. "I would have ordered it just to get a tree."

"I know, right? None of us could believe it. Bill said that event was going to be talked about for years from now."

"Oh, I bet Mark and Waneta are going to give Henry a talking to. Mark thinks of Henry as his father."

"If he does, I doubt Mr. Lehmann is gonna listen. He really enjoyed his supper."

Chuckling, Alice said, "I'm so glad you came to the school. This is just what I needed to take my mind off things."

Irene's smile faltered. "What 'things' are you speaking of?"

"Oh, you know. The break-in . . ."

"Has something else happened that you aren't telling me?"

"*Nee.* Of course not."

"But you would tell me if there was?"

"*Jah.* Of course." Stopping at the bank of Floyd's Pond, Alice pasted on a smile and hoped it looked more at ease than she felt. "After all, we've been through too much together."

Irene's smile faded. "Are you talking about our *rumspringa*?"

"*Nee.*" Alice gestured toward the ice. "I'm talking about how I taught you to ice skate."

"Argh! Only you could bring up something more embarrassing than our teenaged years."

"Teaching you to skate wasn't embarrassing."

"Not for you. Because you knew how to skate. You could skate like the wind. I could not."

Alice giggled. "It just took you a while. That's all."

"It took longer than that, Al."

Alice couldn't completely disagree. In truth, it had taken Irene forever to get the hang of gliding across the ice on skates. No matter how hard she'd tried, Irene wasn't able to do it and wanted to give up.

But Alice wasn't inclined to do that. She turned it into a personal battle, wanting to help Irene succeed no matter what. She ended up helping her for hours, holding on to her hands—and getting pulled down every couple of minutes because Irene jerked her to the ground.

Other kids watched. Some had offered to help, a lot more simply snickered. Irene was beyond embarrassed. She saw her inability to skate as a glaring symbol of how she wasn't like everyone else. They had siblings and parents who helped them learn to do things.

She had next to nobody.

Staring at the ice now, Irene smiled. "You never gave up on me, Alice. No matter how hard it was, or how many bruises you got, you stayed by my side."

"I did. But you are forgetting something, Irene."

"What is that?"

"You did learn to skate. And then once you learned, you skated better than me."

Looking a bit dreamy, Irene sighed. "And your parents bought me those beautiful ice skates for Christmas when I was twelve. I haven't thought about that winter in years."

"We should go skating again soon."

"When we find some skates on sale, let's get them, okay?"

Alice nodded. With a wink, she said, "We can show all those teenagers how it's done. They'll be so impressed."

"Not hardly, but we'll have a good time. Ain't so?"

Just imagining it, Alice tapped the ice with a toe. "I wish we had skates with us now."

Irene shook her head. "No way. Do you spy that crack over near the middle? I don't think it's thick enough for skating."

Alice frowned. "You're probably right. Still, it would be fun . . ."

"Even if the ice was thicker, I'd still rather go eat brownies while sitting down someplace warm."

Feeling so much better, Alice wrapped her arms

around her. "That is why you will always be my best friend, Irene. *Jah*. Let's go eat brownies." When they pulled away, she noticed that Irene had tears in her eyes.

"Why are you crying?"

"I'm just so relieved that we're back to normal. God is so good, Alice! I'm so thankful He guided us right here so we would remember how precious our friendship is. Friends like you are what is important in life."

"Now you're going to make me cry." Tugging on Irene's hand, she said, "Come on. Let's go buy brownies and coffee, then go to your apartment. It's close by."

"That sounds perfect. We can sit on the couch, eat brownies, and drink lattes—and I can show you my latest knitting project. But if we do all that, it's going to be dark. How will you get home?"

Alice smiled. "I can call Calvin and ask him to pick me up."

"He'd do that?"

"*Jah*. He said that he didn't want me walking home by myself until he takes care of that vandal." Realizing that he was probably driving over to the school right then, she winced. "Uh-oh. We better hurry. If I don't call him real soon, he's going to think something happened to me."

Irene nodded. "We can walk as fast as you

want. It's awfully cold. Come on. I'll race you," she said with a grin.

Alice laughed. If they hurried, she could maybe catch Calvin before he got to the school. He usually gave her an hour after school let out to clean up and prepare for the next day's lessons.

"You girls need to stop right there," a voice said from behind them.

Releasing Alice, Irene spun around and then gaped.

There, standing in front of them, was John Yutzy. He was staring at the two of them, pure venom in his expression.

He was also holding a rifle and pointing it straight at them.

CHAPTER 27

Thursday, March 1

Calvin had always assumed he wasn't going to have a long life. He'd endured too many nights as a little boy with next to no food, and had a father who was so angry at the world that he thought nothing of taking that bitterness out on his sons.

Later, Calvin was sure his dumb mistakes would lead to his downfall. He'd drunk too much and tried too many drugs when he'd been alone, hurt, and afraid.

Most recently, Calvin resigned himself to the fact that he was going to die working for West's organization. He was in over his head, and certain that sooner or later he was going to make one mistake too many. He'd simply started hoping that his death wouldn't be too hard on Mark.

But now, as he stood in the woods by the skating pond, watching John Yutzy point a gun at Alice and Irene—Calvin felt as if he'd never looked at death as closely as he did that very minute.

West had shown up at Mark's house just as

Calvin was getting into his truck to pick up Alice. He was alone for once, having ignored Smith's concerns about traveling without a bodyguard. If that hadn't been confusing enough, West then invited himself to go along with Calvin, since he'd heard at the diner that Irene was with Alice.

Calvin felt vaguely as if they were going on a double date . . . until West started listing jobs he wanted Calvin to work on. Knowing West didn't repeat himself, Calvin concentrated on his boss's instructions.

But all thoughts of work and dates disappeared when they found the school empty, with two pairs of footsteps leading toward Floyd's Pond.

Calvin cussed a blue streak as they strode off to find the girls, deciding to walk and follow in their footsteps. He'd told Alice not to go anywhere by herself.

West grinned. "But she's with Irene. You know that's what she's going to say."

"That doesn't make me feel better," he'd said right before they heard a man yelling, followed by the faint murmur of women's voices.

They picked up their pace, then started flat-out running when they heard a gunshot.

Now they stood on the outskirts of the pond, half-hidden by a cove of scraggly trees. Both were assessing the situation while staring in shock at Alice and Irene. The women were standing on the ice. They were visibly afraid and holding on to each other. An Amish man who looked vaguely familiar held a gun on them. After a moment, Calvin realized it was John Yutzy. He and John had once been asked to work on a charity project when they were twelve or so.

John was yelling at the girls, the majority of his words drifting toward them like oncoming traffic.

"You never changed! Even after almost killing me, you still acted like you were better."

"I never thought that," Alice said.

"Of course you did. I saw how you treated Mary Ruth. Giving her gifts like I couldn't take care of my own."

"You know it wasn't like that," Irene fired back.

John responded by waving the rifle in the air. "Don't talk anymore. Don't say another word."

Irene complied, but her chin lifted as she stared back at him in open defiance.

Calvin winced. "Sure wish they were still looking scared. Yutzy seemed a little calmer then."

West's expression was murderous. Pulling out his gun, he said, "We've got to get over there now."

"Hold on," Calvin said. "Not yet."

Pure fire lit West's expression as the ice cracked loudly enough to make one of the girls gasp. "What are you talking about? We can't just stand here doing nothing. Those girls are going to fall through the ice."

"I don't think so. The girls grew up here," he said in a rush before West could interrupt him again. "They know that pond as well as anyone. They know where not to stand or walk."

"He's got a rifle pointed at them. They're not going to be thinking about anything."

Calvin knew everything West said made sense. And if they were in the middle of downtown Louisville or on the streets of Cincinnati, he would have absolutely followed every directive that West gave.

But he knew this area, knew the girls, and he had a pretty good idea of how awkward John Yutzy was feeling at the moment. Men in Kentucky grew up hunting and fishing. They knew how to handle a rifle and were confident when it came to hunting deer and turkey.

But raising it to his shoulder to shoot two women in cold blood?

"We don't have time to plan," West practically growled.

Calvin feared if they didn't take a moment to gather their thoughts, John would get spooked and do something even crazier. "I hear you, but hold on."

"I'm not just going to stand here while they are in danger."

Lowering his voice, Calvin said, "Look at

282

what's happening. The girls are talking to him. Everyone's calm. Give me a second to think this through."

West placed his finger on the trigger of his gun. "You've got one minute, then I'm going in."

Calvin braced himself, then realized he didn't care about anything anymore. "I am going to text Sheriff Brewer." Without waiting for permission, he quickly ran his thumb across the screen and typed out a quick missive. The moment he pressed Send, he felt better.

West narrowed his eyes. "You have the sheriff's number in your phone?"

Calvin had a feeling he'd just given himself a death sentence. "Yeah," he said. "I grew up with a girl who is married to Deputy Beck now."

West narrowed his eyes again. "Is that so?"

"That's so." It was clear that West wasn't buying the story. Calvin didn't care. All he cared about was getting Alice off that ice and shoving John down to the ground. "I'm thinking that we should divide up. I'll distract him, catch him off guard. You go in behind him and take him out."

Suspicion still clouded West's eyes, but he nodded. "That's better than my plan, which was shooting the guy and then drowning him in the middle of the pond for good measure."

Calvin wasn't going to lie. West's plan didn't sound all that bad to him. And it was then that Calvin realized just how much West cared for

Irene. Cared about her more than killing Calvin on the spot for betraying him. That was saying something. Of course, once Irene was safe, all bets were off. But he was going to have to worry about that later.

"I liked her," he said.

"Irene? Yeah, I know."

"No. I liked her a lot. Maybe even could have loved her, if things had been different."

Calvin would have gaped at him if he wasn't so worried about the girls. In all the time he'd known West Powers, he'd never seen him sound so vulnerable. "No need to talk in the past tense, boss. Maybe something can still work out with y'all."

"I'm president of the Kings. I can't leave my life for some innocent Amish girl. I sure can't bring her into my world. I'd ruin her." He swallowed hard before continuing. "I knew it was wrong, but I did it anyway."

"Don't give up hope. I know she likes you, too. Alice told me that."

"Your Alice told you that," West repeated. After a beat, he looked at Calvin directly in the eye. "Who are you?"

He *knew*. West knew he'd been lying.

Please God, he prayed. *Don't let West kill me before I help Alice and Irene.* Playing for time, he said, "You know who I am. I'm your newest lieutenant."

West cursed under his breath. "I bet you had quite a party the day I gave you the news."

" 'Course I did. A lot of guys in the organization work their whole lives to be in your inner circle."

"Cut the crap, Calvin. I'm talking about you and whoever you are working for."

Realizing he had nothing to lose, he shrugged. "I made my peace with what was going to happen if you found out a long time ago." Feeling West's fury, Calvin knew that all of them had just run out of time.

Just then, John's voice cut through the air. "Are you takin' me serious now?"

Calvin started walking. "Do what you want to me when this is over. Right now we have to work together to rescue the girls."

"Agreed," West bit out.

Increasing his pace, Calvin weaved his way around an old band of rusty barbed wire and walked over a rocky shallow creek. West stayed firmly by his side, his movements smooth and fluid.

As they got closer, they heard John Yutzy ranting. Talking about how unfair his life was, how so many women had played a part in hurting him.

It was time to split up. Calvin gestured to the more direct path toward the ice. "You go to the right. If you stay on this path, it will keep you hidden until you can approach Yutzy from behind. I'll wait a minute, then start walking toward him on the ice."

"He's going to shoot you."

"He might. If he does, it will save you the trouble," Calvin said with a grin. "Look, you're a good shot. If Yutzy kills me, you shoot him . . . but make sure the women are safe."

West eyed him closely. "No. I'm going on the ice."

"No. That wasn't what we decided."

West grunted. "Do you think I actually care about that?"

"But—"

"Who are you working for?"

"The DEA," he said reluctantly.

West laughed under his breath. "At least it wasn't the cops." Then he turned and started walking.

"West—"

"You got two women to keep safe. Maybe even me, too. Go do your best, Undercover Cal," he said over his shoulder.

Calvin waited the beat of a heartbeat, then tore forward. He didn't allow himself to think about anything but getting to Yutzy.

With each step, all he heard were the girls' voices. The rustle of the bushes and brush around him. The frost in the air. Just as he was about to call out to John Yutzy, like a scene out of a movie, West strode out onto the icy pond like he owned it, his gun pointed at Yutzy.

Calvin broke into a sprint as pandemonium broke out.

The ice cracked. Irene cried out. Yutzy raised his rifle and with a shaking hand, started screaming obscenities.

He took a shot, but thankfully it missed everything but the ice. Alice and Irene screamed and fell to their knees. West took his shot, but his foot slipped. His arm went wide as he, too, fell. A second later he scrambled for his footing.

Yutzy fired again, but it went wide. When he attempted to reload, it jammed.

Alice tugged at Irene, but Irene was fighting her. To his amazement, Calvin realized that she was struggling to get to West.

It seemed Irene cared for West as much as he did for her.

Before he could say a word, West called out to her. "Irene, go on now."

She shook her head. "Not without you."

He tried to get up and go toward her, but the ice cracked again. "I can't worry about me if I'm worried about you. *Go!*" West yelled, his voice firm.

"West—"

"Now!" he ordered before his tone turned almost tender. "It's going to be okay."

Yutzy was furiously jacking his rifle, trying to clear the jam. Calvin had to stop Yutzy before he could get his rifle working again. His lungs were on fire as he ran. Why hadn't West waited? If only he'd stuck to the plan!

Fifty yards to go. Forty. Adrenaline propelled him along, over tree roots and over an outcropping of rocks.

Irene and West were still visibly straining to get to each other. "Please, be careful," she called.

Just like that, an expression of vulnerability raced across West's face. It passed so quickly that, if Calvin hadn't witnessed it, he would have sworn that it couldn't have happened. Then the hardest man Calvin had ever met looked like he had tears in his eyes.

Suddenly, West tugged off his coat and threw it on the ice. Tried to get it under his feet, so the fabric would provide his boots something to grip. He was able to, and got up, started toward Yutzy, surefooted and determined, even though each pounding step created more cracks in the ice. He lifted his gun and took aim.

As did Yutzy. He'd finally cleared the jam.

Calvin ran harder. Just ten more yards . . .

Yutzy fired just as West pulled the trigger of his weapon. With a wounded cry, John fell backward onto the ground. The women screamed.

Relief surged through Calvin as he stopped to throw Yutzy's rifle far from his body, then continued running toward Alice. He just needed to hold her. To make sure she was all right.

West seemed to have the same notion about Irene. He had tucked his gun back into the waistband of his jeans and set his sights on Irene. Then everything seemed to slide into slow motion. He didn't seem to even notice the blood soaking through the front of his shirt.

"West!" Irene cried out. "West, you're hit."

As though shocked at the idea, he glanced down.

But he didn't answer, because right then the ice gave way and he plunged into the water. Within seconds, the whole area of ice around him shattered into a thousand pieces, just like broken glass.

Calvin didn't break step as he ran toward him. Didn't stop at Irene's terrified shrieks. Didn't stop when the freezing water shocked the breath straight out of him. Didn't stop when Alice's voice pleaded with him not to go in.

He couldn't think about Alice right now. If he did, he'd turn back to her, grab hold of her, and never let go. He swam toward the spot where West had gone under, Calvin's skin feeling oddly numb and on fire at the same time.

"Calvin!" Alice screamed.

But he couldn't stop. Not even after he dove under the ice—five, six, seven times into the bone-chilling darkness. Not even knowing that the man would likely kill him if he survived the light of day.

Calvin knew he could take the easy way out and just let West go, let him and the secrets they shared die in this pond.

But Calvin wasn't that man. Maybe he had been at one time, but he wasn't anymore.

"Calvin, please!" Alice was calling out. "Please come back! I need you."

His heart clenched as he reached the surface of the water. It was over. West couldn't have survived. He was gone and Calvin was going to be unable to save himself if he didn't get out of the water.

Feeling as desolate as he ever had, Calvin raised himself out of the water and headed over to Alice, each muscle in his body screaming with the effort. When he got to her, Alice reached for his hands and pulled him closer. "Oh, Calvin!" she cried through her tears. "I thought I'd lost you."

He was vaguely aware of sirens approaching. Of car doors slamming. Of Alice covering him with her coat, then wrapping her arms around him.

But all he seemed to realize was that Alice was crying.

He knew why that was . . . because he was crying, too.

CHAPTER 28

Thursday, March 1

"Here, honey," the female EMT told Alice as she pressed a thin brown wool blanket around her shoulders. "You must be freezing."

With a murmur of thanks, Alice gripped the blanket and cuddled into its warmth. It did feel good, but to be honest, she hadn't noticed the cold. Ever since she'd run onto the ice with Irene, realized that Mr. Yutzy intended to shoot them, and then experienced the nerve-wracking, horrible, terrible moments when Mr. Yutzy was waving his rifle and West fell into the frozen pond, she felt as if she was in a daze.

She probably was. All she could do was stare out to the pond. To the water, the break in the ice-covered pond where West had fallen, which now looked smooth and tranquil. So deceptive. So horrifying to realize that West was somewhere in its depths.

Oh, that poor man!

He'd risked everything in order to save them. And he had. He had given the ultimate sacrifice for her and Irene. It was humbling and heart-breaking, too. She knew she would be saying prayers for him and the family he left behind for the rest of her life.

But as for Irene?

Alice looked over in her direction. Irene was sitting next to Deputy Beck and crying inconsolably. She was heartbroken that Calvin hadn't been able to save West. That, combined with the guilt Irene said she felt, was a terrible burden to bear.

Alice knew Irene was going to be having a difficult time for many weeks and months to come.

"Here you go. It's hot tea with some honey in it," another emergency worker said, pressing it into Alice's hands. "Are you sure you don't want to wait in the ambulance?"

"I'm sure. I'm not sick or hurt."

The worker hesitated, but nodded. "All right, then. I was told the sheriff wanted to speak to you after he speaks to the man over there. Then you'll be free to leave with your family."

That penetrated. "I'm sorry, I don't have a way to get home."

"You don't have to worry about that," the lady said, a smile brightening her face. Pointing just beyond them, she said, "They're over there. Along with about half of the population of Horse Cave."

Alice craned her neck and was shocked to see

that the field just beyond them was filled with cars and buggies, and groups of people standing around and watching everything with interest. She couldn't exactly see her parents or her brothers, but she was sure they would be there. Knowing that, she relaxed. Her family would help her understand why everything happened and how to move forward.

Glancing at Irene, she wished her friend was feeling the same way. She'd had a bad home life and now lived in a small apartment by herself. Of course she would help Irene as much as she could, but would that be enough?

With effort, she forced herself to look at the second ambulance. Its lights weren't flashing, and there were a number of people surrounding it. That was where John Yutzy's body was.

She didn't feel as if she knew all the details, of course. All she could remember was that West had shot John Yutzy before falling through the ice. When the sheriff first arrived, he'd grabbed Calvin roughly, even though he was soaking wet and near freezing. Alice and Irene both screamed to let Calvin go, frantically sharing bits and pieces of what had just happened.

When Sheriff Brewer and Deputy Beck finally noticed the rifle lying next to John Yutzy's body, they'd sent Calvin with one of the EMTs to the ambulance.

At least for a while.

Dwelling on that, she glanced over toward Calvin. The workers had given him a pair of scrubs to change into and placed several warm blankets around him. He looked pale, but otherwise not too worse for wear after his plunge in the pond.

Sheriff Brewer was still talking to him and writing notes. But another man had joined them. This man wore a black slicker with the letters DEA imprinted on the back of it. When the man patted Calvin on the shoulder, then handed him a cell phone, Alice wondered what was going on.

Hopefully, he wasn't in trouble for shooting his gun?

Surely, the sheriff discovered that Calvin had fired his gun in self-defense?

Still watching Calvin speak on the phone, Alice wished he could come over to her and tell her what was happening. Instead, she sipped her tea and continued to wait.

As if he sensed her staring at him, Calvin glanced over at her. Immediately, his expression softened. Right then and there, Alice saw pure honesty in his face. Calvin really cared about her. And he was worried about her, too.

She wouldn't have thought it was possible, but she managed to smile at him, too.

Oh, but God was so good. Here, even in the worst of situations, He was giving her a glimmer of hope.

Just as she watched Calvin continue to talk to the man in the slicker, Sheriff Brewer approached her. He had on a black baseball cap and a fuzzy parka-type coat over his usual uniform. Thick rubber boots were on his feet.

He looked serious but calm.

Alice hoped that she would be able to talk to him about whatever he needed so she could get on her way.

"How are you doing, Miss Yoder?" he asked as he drew to a stop in front of her. "I know some people have been giving you hot drinks and blankets. Do you need anything else?"

"*Nee.* I'm doing all right."

"Right. I'm sure you are more than ready to get out of this field, so I won't keep you long."

"I understand. You need to do your job."

He pulled out the notepad and pen that she'd noticed he was holding when he was talking with Calvin. "Tell me how you got out here."

"Irene came to my schoolhouse. After we talked for a while, we decided to go to some new café that just opened. We took a shortcut through the field and stopped at the pond because we used to skate there when we were little girls. Then John Yutzy showed up and made us go out onto the ice."

"Any idea why he was so upset with you?"

She swallowed. "At first I thought he was mad at me because I was teaching his daughter, Mary

Ruth. But while we were standing out on the ice, he told us what he was so mad about."

"And that was?"

Hating that she was going to have to share so much about her past, she mentally closed her eyes and forced herself to continue. "When Irene and me were seventeen, we did some stupid things. We took risks. One night we ended up at a party where a lot of kids were drinking. Some were doing drugs."

"Ah."

Feeling even more embarrassed, Alice glanced at his expression. To her surprise, she didn't see any recrimination there. Instead, his face looked tense, as if he was worried about other things than her history.

Which was how she should have been thinking.

Feeling a little ashamed, Alice realized that she should stop thinking only about herself. It didn't really matter if the sheriff was shocked about her past, or how he would think about her in the future.

All that mattered was that two men were dead.

All of the truth needed to come out.

"I wasn't doing drugs," she said slowly. "Irene wasn't, either. But we had been drinking. We weren't really drunk, but we had too much. It was a really bad mistake."

The sheriff wrote down some notes. "And then?"

"Well, we wanted to leave. We were scared. Then a man named Able took us home. Able grew up Amish and said that he knew that we were in over our heads." She cleared her throat, sensing that the sheriff was getting impatient for her to get to the point.

"Well, um, when he was taking us home, it was real late. It was foggy out, it was real hard for any of us to see." Through the lump in her throat, she forced herself to continue. "I guess you can guess what happened next. Able hit a man coming on his bicycle."

"Did he die?" The sheriff's voice was urgent, almost like he was dreading to hear the rest of the story.

"*Nee*," she said carefully, not even caring that she was replying to him in Pennsylvania Dutch. "But he was hurt pretty badly."

"What did you do?"

"Do? Well, Able got right out of the car, of course." Thinking back to that evening, she amended her words, feeling like the sheriff needed to hear every detail. "Actually, we all did. Able offered to help the hurt man, even take him to the hospital. But instead of accepting that offer, the man just yelled at us. First he called us a bunch of bad names in Pennsylvania Dutch. But then Irene had had enough of him saying all that, so she talked back to him."

"So he discovered you were Amish."

"*Jah*. By that time, he had gotten to his feet. He was scraped up and bruised, but we could all see that he didn't have any bones broken."

"And then?"

"Then? Well, we knew who it was. It was John Yutzy."

"Your friend."

"Oh, we weren't friends. Irene and I knew him, but we'd never been close. I . . . well, I just had never liked him."

"Why? Did you have a reason?"

"*Jah*. He, well, he'd always looked down on Irene because she was poor. He would whisper nasty things to her, talk about her behind her back. I didn't like that."

"I bet." Sheriff Brewer wrote down more notes. "And then?"

Returning back to that night, Alice said, "And then Able offered to drive him home. But John wouldn't have any of that. He started saying mean things again. He said he knew who we were. He knew that we'd been drinking." Not wanting to share out loud the cruel, disparaging things he'd said, Alice shivered. "He said a lot of awful things, Sheriff Brewer. He talked to us like we went out and drank too much all the time. Like we fooled around with a lot of boys, too."

"Did you take him home?"

"No. Actually, Able dropped us off on the street near my house. Irene and I ran into the field, changed back into Amish clothes in the barn, then we each went home. I went to my room and fell asleep. That was the end of it."

"But not for John Yutzy?"

"No, I guess not. I avoided him as much as I could after that. At first, I thought he was going to show up at my house with his parents and tell on me, but he never did. I just assumed he didn't want his parents to know he was out riding his bicycle in the middle of the night."

"My deputy is speaking to Irene now. Do you think she'll say anything different?"

"I can't imagine that she would." Thinking about Irene, she hesitated. "She might have more to say, though. She and I had different home situations—and like I said, he used to make fun of her a lot."

She was suddenly exhausted. "Sheriff Brewer, Mr. Yutzy recently yelled at me at school. Just this afternoon, I discovered that he had been writing me notes, too, which his daughter had been hiding. I have some in my purse that I can give to you."

"Thank you. I'll take them before you leave." Looking at his pad, he sighed. "Are you sure you can't tell me anything else?"

Alice shook her head. "I think only God knows why he went after me and Irene. Or maybe you will discover more when you go to his house or something. All I know is that we were crossing this field, he started yelling, we ignored him, and then things escalated from there."

Just when it looked as if he was going to ask her more questions, Calvin approached. "I'm thinking Alice can answer any more questions you have tomorrow, Sheriff. She's exhausted."

The sheriff's whole demeanor changed. "Yeah, I'm guessing you're right, Calvin. You need to get home and put on some warm clothes, too."

Calvin shrugged, like he couldn't care less about what clothes he had on.

Sheriff Brewer swallowed. "Y'all about done here? Do you need anything else from me?"

"You could ask, but I don't think so."

"All right, then." Sheriff Brewer turned back to Alice. "I appreciate you speaking to me. I know it wasn't easy. Would you like me to walk you to your family?"

"I'll take her," Calvin interjected smoothly.

"Good enough." With a brief tip of his hat, the sheriff turned and walked over to the DEA agent.

"You ready?" Calvin asked as he reached for her arm.

"In a minute. Calvin, what did the sheriff mean when he asked you about that man?"

His expression turned guarded. "What do you mean?"

"Please don't play games. You know what I'm talking about. He was acting as if you were part of the investigation." When his body tensed, she began to get confused. "What's going on?"

He rolled his shoulders and looked away. "Alice, maybe we could talk about this tomorrow."

"Talk about what?"

"Talk about my connection with that officer over there."

Maybe it was because so much had happened, or maybe it was because she'd just been reminded that nothing mattered more than the men's deaths. "It's okay if it's upsetting, Calvin. We're close enough now to always tell each other the truth, right?"

To her surprise, he looked even more uncomfortable. "All right, then. Alice, you need to know something about my relationship with West Powers."

"What about it?"

"It was complicated. What I told you earlier was true. I really was in his gang. He was the president of the Kings, and on his orders I did a lot of things I wasn't proud of. But there's another side to it."

"Which is?"

"A while back I became a confidential informant for the DEA. For the Drug Enforcement Administration."

"You still sound like you are speaking in riddles. What does that mean?"

"It means that I only pretended to be a member

of the Kings. What I really did was share secrets and details about the Kings' operation to the DEA. I have been giving them information so they could eventually bring them down and arrest the men in charge."

"Which was West, *jah*?"

"Yeah."

"Calvin, you weren't his friend at all."

"Well, I was and I wasn't. I liked West. I really did. But he was a criminal, and I had no choice in the matter." He grimaced. "You see, before I got myself cleaned up, I made a lot of mistakes. I took drugs. I sold some, too. And I owed a ton of money. When I connected again with Mark last year, I started realizing that I wanted to be different, but it wasn't that easy. I owed the Kings that money and if I didn't pay it back, I knew they'd kill me . . . or go after Mark."

She shuddered, thinking about his situation. "So you did what you had to do."

"Yeah." He sighed. "It was hard, but the DEA offered me a deal. They would pay my debts if I agreed to go undercover for at least a year. That deal was so good, so much better than I thought, I took it."

"This whole time I thought you were involved in a dangerous gang."

"I was. Make no mistake, Alice, I was involved. I had to do a lot of things that I'm not proud of. But I wasn't all bad."

"But you lied to me."

He shook his head. "I didn't lie. I just couldn't tell you the truth."

"But we became close," she whispered, thinking of all the hours she'd spent trying to come to terms with the fact that she'd been falling in love with a criminal. Of all the hours she'd spent worrying about him.

"We have, and I've been so grateful for that. Our relationship has been really special to me. You are really special to me."

His words were sweet. And she knew that she should be relieved that he wasn't a gang member.

And she was.

But she also felt as if she'd been falling in love with just the shell of a man. He'd never allowed her to see his whole self. And, if this whole terrible situation with John Yutzy hadn't happened, he would still be keeping his true identity a secret from her.

Maybe he would have kept it a secret for a lot longer. Maybe even years.

"I . . . I think I need to go on home now."

"Of course you do. Let's find your family, then."

"There's no need. I can go by myself."

"Your dress is wet and you've just been through a terrible time. I'm going to help you."

His voice was firm and unyielding. Still feeling in a daze, she let him take her hand and guide her to her parents.

After he brought her to their side, she thanked him and got in their buggy.

On the way home, she rested her head on her mother's shoulder and pretended to sleep so she wouldn't have to answer their many questions.

Or wonder why she suddenly felt like she'd lost so much more than West that day. She felt as if she'd lost part of herself, too.

CHAPTER 29

Friday, March 2

The phone's ringtone rang loudly in his bedroom, jarring Calvin from a deep sleep. Feeling around on his bedside table, he looked to see who was calling.

When the number registered, he answered right away. "Hey, Andrew."

"Calvin," his voice boomed on the other end. "Good to hear your voice. How are you?"

Calvin's whole being felt raw, but that wasn't something he was eager to share. "A little groggy, I'm afraid. I was asleep. Sorry."

"No problem." For the first time ever, Calvin heard concern in his boss's voice. "Want me to call you back?"

Calvin sat up and shook his head to clear it. "No, sir. I'm fine. I appreciate you calling me so quickly."

"There's nothing to thank me for, Cal. We're all still talking about what a fine job you did yesterday. You took down the head of the Kings and saved two innocent women from some crazy Amish man. As far as we are concerned,

305

you have more than repaid your debt to us."

Everything Andrew was saying should have made Calvin happy. He was free now. Free to live the life he wanted, free of pretending to be someone he wasn't. Free to start pursuing his own dreams.

But all he felt was empty.

Maybe he shouldn't have been all that surprised. For the last year, he'd had a new sense of purpose. He'd had goals. Yeah, it had definitely been hard, pretending to like things he didn't, and pretending to be someone he wasn't. But because his alias wasn't all that far from the man he'd used to be, he'd been able to fit into that role without too much worry.

Of course, it wasn't like he'd had much of a choice anyway. He'd owed a ton of money to the Kings and if he hadn't done a good job for the DEA, he could have either died at their hands or eventually gone to prison for the crimes he'd committed for the Kings.

"That's good to know," he said at last.

After a lengthy pause, Andrew spoke again. "You don't sound all that happy about it. Are you worried about the rest of the Kings coming after you?"

"I'd be a fool not to worry."

"All they know is that West died. He was here by himself, too, so no one in the organization knows what happened to him exactly."

Thinking about Mark and Waneta, he said, "I hope that's enough."

"We're still monitoring the Kings, so if we hear something, I'll let you know—or we'll put a guard on your brother and his wife. But for now, I have to tell you that I'm not worried. Men in those gangs are used to death and used to changes. No doubt several of the members are probably more interested in taking West's place than figuring out what happened to him."

"I hope you're right."

Andrew paused. "Is something wrong that we don't know about? Are you sick? Do you need to be in the hospital? Brewer told me you were in that frozen pond for several minutes."

"No, it isn't that." What could he say? It wasn't like he deserved any special words, thanks, or concessions. "I guess I'm just trying to get my head wrapped around everything."

Andrew chuckled quietly on the other end of the phone. "I can understand that," he replied, his voice easy again. "You know, I probably don't need to tell you that we don't get to make too many calls like this to our informants."

"Oh? What usually happens?" The moment he asked, he wished that he could take back his words. Did he even want to know what could have happened to him?

"Usually, our informants can't figure out how

to switch their loyalties. Then they can't figure out how to make better decisions."

"I'm sure it ends badly for them."

"Yeah, it does. I like you, Calvin. I'm not going to lie. At first I thought you going undercover was a terrible idea. However, you surpassed my expectations. You have grit and character."

"Thank you."

Andrew paused. "Look, I know we're going to be meeting again several more times to get the evidence and information we need to take down the rest of the gang, but let me tell you this now. Keep my number. If you ever need me, or if you ever want to do more work for us in the future, give me a call or email me."

"I don't think I'm ever going to be ready to go undercover again."

"All right. But maybe you can do something more than that."

Calvin was pretty sure Andrew was talking about being an actual employee of the DEA. "That's an option?"

"I think so. No promises, but if you ever aren't opposed to putting on a uniform, I think you might find that you've got a place with us."

A few moments later, Calvin hung up feeling like he'd just entered someone else's life. Had that really just happened? Had Andrew just encouraged him to work for the DEA?

After tossing his phone on the sheet beside him, Calvin lay back down.

With some surprise, he realized he had a headache. He closed his eyes, hoping for sleep, but instead of rest, all that came to mind was the memory of what had happened long after Alice, her family, and the majority of the bystanders had left.

A van had arrived with divers on loan from the Louisville P.D. They'd come to retrieve West's body.

Even after multiple people—Sheriff Brewer included—had encouraged him to leave, Calvin sat down on a rock and watched. He couldn't bear the thought of West's body being pulled out with only strangers surrounding him. He deserved far better than that.

After Deputy Beck pressed a thermal cup of hot coffee in his hands, Calvin sipped the liquid and watched the divers stride out across the ice, then dive into the hole in the middle of the pond. One by one they entered the water and disappeared into the pond's dark depths.

Feeling as if he was there with West, Calvin felt the cold surround him again. Felt the chunks of ice brush his skin. Breathed in water that tasted of algae and decay. Shivering, he'd inhaled deeply, then took another sip of coffee as he watched bubbles appear on the surface.

Not ten minutes later, the divers rose. One of

them held West by his chest, almost as if he was a wayward rag doll. Calvin made himself gaze at him.

Though his face looked slightly swollen, the frigid temperatures had kept West from looking too terrible. His eyes were closed, his lips slightly parted. He almost looked like he was asleep.

Almost.

Eventually, they dragged him onto a dinghy they'd pulled onto the ice.

Sitting in bed, Calvin gasped, then started coughing. With a start, he realized he'd just now forgotten to breathe.

He scrambled out of bed, thankful that he'd slept in a pair of Mark's sweats. At least he wasn't freezing in the chilly air of the house.

Just as he slipped on a pair of thick wool socks, Waneta knocked lightly on his door. "Calvin, may I come in? I have some *kaffi* for ya."

He opened the door for her. "Did my phone's ringing wake you?"

"Of course not. It's after eight." Looking a bit pensive, she handed him the cup. "Here ya go."

"Thanks." Gratefully, he sipped, studying her face. She looked a little pale and was watching him with big eyes. "You all right?"

Crossing the room, she sat in the oak wooden rocking chair in the far corner. "I was going to ask you the same thing."

He sat down on the end of the bed to face her. "I've got a headache, but other than that, I'll be all right."

"Mark and me are tired, but I think we'll be all right, too. Eventually."

There was so much honesty in her face, so much compassion, it nearly took his breath away. "Yesterday was a tough day."

"We were worried sick. Mark, especially, since he had to stay home while I went to Floyd's Pond with Lora. It's such a blessing that you weren't injured or didn't end up in the hospital."

"It is." Deciding to be honest, he said, "I'm pretty rattled and upset about what happened. West, the man who died, wasn't a good man, but he had good qualities. He didn't deserve to die like that."

"Of course not. But he gave his life for all of you, so he didn't die in vain."

"No, he didn't."

Looking reflective, she said, "We didn't want to press you too much last night, but we'd sure like to know more about what you were really doing."

"I'll be glad to share what I can with you."

"Mark is really proud of you, Calvin. You did a very brave thing out there on the ice."

Calvin's first instinct was to shake his head. But then Waneta's words sank in and the tears came. He couldn't remember another moment when his brother had been proud of him. "Thank you for saying that."

"It isn't just words, Calvin. It's the truth." Hesitantly, she said, "When you are ready, I know your brother wants to tell you that himself."

He stood up. "Give me a few minutes and then I'll be right out."

Looking pleased, Waneta walked up to him and wrapped her arms around his middle. "You mustn't forget something, Calvin."

"And what is that?"

"You are never alone, my brother. Not anymore. We're your family."

His family.

He realized then that she was absolutely right. He might have lost West, he might even have lost Alice, but he'd gained something, too. His brother. His own flesh and blood. Waneta, too. Never would he distance himself from them again.

Their love, it was worth any risk. It was worth everything.

CHAPTER 30

Saturday, March 3

She was home again. Back in her own bed. Two days had passed. Two nights as well. Forty-eight hours of tears and nightmares, gazing off into nothing, and wondering how Calvin and Irene were doing.

And always, always trying not to think about West falling through the ice and John Yutzy bleeding on the bank of the pond. It didn't matter how hard she tried not to remember, though. Every time Alice closed her eyes, the images flashed by, vivid and bright and awful.

That would lead her to curling into a ball and crying.

Two whole days had passed, but Alice thought she would have been able to handle things better by now. She wanted to feel better for her parents' sakes, if no others'.

As if they heard her thinking about them, her mother knocked on her door and stuck her head in without waiting for Alice to answer.

When she saw Alice curled into a ball, her

expression fell. "Ack. You having another tough day, child?"

"*Jah*." Struggling to sit up, she attempted to look at least a little brighter than she felt. "I'm sorry, Mamm. Every time I think about leaving my room, it seems like too much trouble. All I want to do is lie here."

"No reason to apologize, but we're all worried about you."

"I know. It's just been really hard, you know?"

Her mother's expression turned distant as she sat down beside Alice and rested a hand on her shoulder. "Oh, I know, child. Never in my life would I have ever imagined that such a scene would have happened here."

When her parents had met her at the pond, they both enfolded her in their arms and brought her back home. She'd been too cold and shaken up to protest. Frankly, she'd been so happy to see them, she had wanted to be coddled a bit.

But after she got home, took a hot bath and ate some soup, she realized she just wanted to be alone.

Her parents tried to understand, but she knew they didn't. It wasn't in their nature to keep silent. They wanted to know every bit of what had happened.

She began to realize that they thought of it all as rather exciting. And while they didn't offer any criticisms or judgments, she resented their need to know everything.

It felt too fresh and raw.

She still felt that way.

"I actually came here to tell you that you have company."

"Who is it?"

"Calvin Fisher." Her mother's expression turned pinched. "I almost sent him right on his way, but then I thought that you might want to speak to him." Before she could answer, her mother added, "If you'd rather not, I can tell him that. I don't mind."

Alice didn't need to be a mind reader to know that her mother wanted her to stay far, far away from Calvin Fisher. She would probably be right, too. After all, her brief, intense friendship hadn't exactly brought her a lot of happiness.

But one thing overruled everything.

"Mamm, Calvin saved my life. Of course I want to see him."

Her expression fell. "Of course. We *are* grateful, but perhaps you should wait until you are feeling better?"

"Grateful? Mamm, Calvin saved my life." She got off the bed. "Please tell him that I'll be right there."

Her mother got up slowly. Walking to the door, she clasped her hands tightly in front of her. "Alice, I'm sorry, but I'm just going to say this. Just because some people do good deeds, it doesn't mean they are good for us."

Alice couldn't disagree with that statement. But she didn't think it made any difference. What mattered was how she felt. She could practically feel the Lord whispering into her ear, reminding her that it was not her place to judge. What mattered was what was in her heart.

"Mamm, all I can say is that I know you are right."

She relaxed slightly. "Then?"

"But then, my heart is telling me that it doesn't matter if you are right or wrong."

She nodded. "I'll go tell Calvin you'll be right out."

"*Danke*." When her door was closed tightly again, Alice unpinned her dress and slipped on a fresh blue one. Then she smoothed her hair as best she could and put on her second-best *kapp*. The one she'd had on was sorely wrinkled. For a moment, she gave in to vanity and wished that she had a mirror in her room. There was one in the bathroom, but she didn't want to run down the hall to check herself. That would be too much.

She ended up reminding herself that her looks were not what was important. Just as Calvin's appearance wasn't what drew her to him, either.

She hoped by the time she met him in the living room that she would actually believe that. After all, Calvin Fisher, with his dark hair and amazing eyes, was still the most handsome man she'd ever met.

All thoughts of her looks faded when she walked into the room. Her parents were sitting side by side on the couch staring at Calvin, who was sitting in the most uncomfortable chair in the room—a dark wood monstrosity of a chair, all hard wood and planks.

To her knowledge, no one sat in it unless there were no other options.

Here he was, obviously treading someplace where he wasn't exactly wanted, seated in an uncomfortable chair, stared at by her father—and how did he look?

Her father looked as if he was completely at ease and wouldn't want to be anywhere else.

"Alice," Cal said as soon as he saw her. Immediately, he got to his feet and strode over to her. Then, as if he didn't realize her parents were standing there—or maybe he simply didn't care—he reached for her hands. "How are you?"

She was so taken off guard, she let him. Then she was glad she did. His hands now felt familiar intertwined with her own. She loved how rough his calluses were, how he held her hands securely but without any force. There was no doubt in her mind that if she tugged on her hands, he would release them immediately.

Raising her head to meet his eyes, she realized that she hadn't replied. "I'm okay. And you?"

"Me? Oh, I'm fine."

She hated how he was surprised that she would ask. Suddenly hated that he wasn't going to tell her the truth.

But maybe it was up to her to be the brave one for once. "It seems that we're both choosing to lie, then."

"Alice!" her mother chided.

Which brought them back to the present.

Looking down at their joined hands, she squeezed lightly. "Would you like to go to the back hearth room to talk? We could have some privacy there."

"That probably ain't the best idea, Alice," her father said.

Finally, pulling her hands out of Calvin's, she turned to face her parents. Her father was still sitting, but her mother was hovering at his side, looking vaguely like a sparrow eager to be of assistance but unsure of what to do next. "If I was John or Edward, you wouldn't be acting this way. You would be giving me the privacy I deserve."

"You are not them," Mamm said. "You should be chaperoned."

It was such a ridiculous statement that Alice grinned. "Yesterday, I almost died in the middle of Floyd's Pond. Don't you think my reputation is the last thing we need to be worrying about?"

"Hush, now, Alice," Calvin murmured. "Let's just go to the other room."

"You know what? Let's go to your house. I suddenly have a need for space."

Calvin darted a look at her parents, then shook his head. "That isn't the way I want to do things. I don't want to disrespect them that way."

At last her father lumbered to his feet. After rubbing his palms down his pant legs, he held out a hand to Calvin. "You are a good man, Calvin. Thank you for thinking of us right now. And thank you also for putting your life on the line for our Alice." With a sigh, he turned to her. "Alice, you're exactly right. You are a grown woman and we should be treating you as such."

Not daring to look at her mother, Alice hugged her father. "*Danke*, Daed."

After kissing her brow, he stepped back. "I put a log and kindling in the hearth room earlier but never started the fire. Maybe one of you could do that."

"I'll take care of her," Calvin said quietly.

Alice felt a lump form in her throat, knowing that Calvin was speaking about so much more than just that afternoon. When he gestured to her to lead the way, she did just that.

Then, in the back room, she lit a kerosene lamp while Calvin knelt down in front of the fireplace, struck a match, and gently coaxed a roaring fire.

"You have a way with people," she commented.

He chuckled. "I think I'm just used to fitting in with others." After a second, he said, "I mean, I'm used to fitting in with people who want me to fit in with them."

She realized that wasn't always the case. Remembering when he'd told her how hard his childhood had been, she felt embarrassed that she'd gotten upset with her mother for being so overprotective of her. "I guess you think I take a lot for granted."

Sitting down on the couch, he lifted an arm and rested it on the back of it. "All I'm thinking about now is how, at last, I can get you to sit down next to me. What's it going to take, Alice?"

She might have felt a little insecure. Maybe felt a little bit bashful. But she would never make him ask twice. She took a seat, enjoying how it felt to be next to him in the cool room. Appreciating how it felt to have his arm around her.

"How are you, really?"

"I'm having trouble sleeping. Every time I close my eyes, I think of what happened."

"I've been doing the same thing."

"Truly?"

"Of course." He stared at her. "I don't know how to get over something like that. Do you?"

Feeling even more unsure, she shook her head. A dozen questions came to mind, but she couldn't bring herself to ask any of them. They all felt too personal. Or maybe too invasive?

Whatever the reason, she elected to remain silent.

He shifted. "Alice, I don't know what to do about us."

"Is there still an us?"

"I hope so. I want there to be." His gaze rested on hers again. "I've fallen in love with you."

Alice couldn't remember if anything in her life had ever sounded so sweet. But though his statement was wonderful, it didn't make her feel as secure as she would have hoped.

Why was that?

After a couple of seconds, Calvin shifted. "You act surprised. Did you really not realize how I felt about you?"

"I knew you cared." She swallowed. "I care about you, too."

He smiled slightly. "Well, caring is something. Ain't so?"

Alice folded her arms around her middle. Everything inside of her wanted to proclaim her love for him, and promise to be by his side no matter what their future had in store. But what if she wasn't strong enough to do that?

"Calvin, as much as I care for you, I'm also feeling confused."

His body next to hers relaxed a bit. "I'm not surprised about that. You thought I was someone really different."

"I don't know if the person I thought you were

and who you seem to be now are that different. I liked you then, even when I thought you were bad for me."

"And now? Do you still think I'm bad for you?"

"I don't know. I don't know how to trust you again."

"Would it matter if I swore to you that I wouldn't lie to you anymore?"

Could it really be that simple? Could one promise that dozens of lies didn't count anymore? She wasn't sure.

Staring at him closely, she saw a yearning in his eyes. A vulnerability that spoke to her own heart. He'd already been through so much. His terrible childhood, losing his parents, living on the streets, working undercover. She wanted to make him happy.

"I know this might make me sound harsh, but I don't know if I can believe that promise right now."

"I told you the reasons for what I did, Alice. I told you I didn't have a choice. Why can't you trust me now?"

He sounded frustrated. Almost impatient with her. So different than the man who'd picked her up in his truck when she was walking home alone that first evening. So different than the man who'd told her to hide in her house when West first showed up. Who had spent a whole day helping her put her school to rights.

Was the man who had done all those things the same person who was sitting next to her? Or had he been playing a role then, too?

"I'm trying to trust you."

"Then trust me."

She wanted to . . . but if she'd learned anything over the last few weeks, it was that wanting something and being able to have it were two very different things. One couldn't force the other.

Taking a deep breath, she said, "Calvin, I'm sorry, but I don't know if I can simply accept things and move on. Maybe I need time?"

"Time for what?" he asked, his voice impatient again. "To get used to the idea that I'm not in a gang? To get used to the fact that I love you?"

She flinched. "Of course not. Of course I'm glad you aren't in a gang. Of course I love that you love me."

"Then what's the problem?"

"Maybe I need to make sure that the man I fell in love with is the man who is sitting by my side."

"It is. I'm still the same."

In a moment of clarity, she realized what was holding her back. All of the events that had just occurred had changed her.

Just like how that awful night when she was seventeen had changed her, the events that occurred on Floyd's Pond changed her, too.

She couldn't help but wonder if that was a sign. After her *rumspringa*, she'd tried to be so good. Maybe the recent events were a sign that she needed to continue to be careful.

Holding out her hand to him, she said, "Calvin, I really do care about you. Actually . . . I think I love you, too. I'm just asking for some time. Can you give me that?"

He clasped her hand between both of his and squeezed gently. "Yeah. I can give you that. But don't give up on us. Will you promise me that?"

Feeling better than she had in days, she nodded. "I can promise you that, Calvin. I won't give up on us."

She just hoped that was the right decision.

"BY THE EXPRESSION on your face, I'm guessing it didn't go well," Mark told Calvin when he walked into his brother's kitchen.

"You would be guessing right. She said she wasn't sure if she could still trust me." Rubbing a hand through his hair, he added, "Even though she said she thought she loved me, I think she's not even sure if we have a future."

"She told you that she loved you?"

Calvin nodded. "And I told her that I loved her. But maybe she's right. Maybe that isn't enough."

"She's wrong."

Calvin stared at him in shock. "I expected you to tell me the opposite."

"Calvin, you're my brother. I'm always going to be on your side. But in this case, after everything all of us have been through? I know she is very wrong. Life is full of unexpected twists and turns and bumps and disappointments." He stood up. "Actually, there's so much bad that isn't our fault. So much that we have to put up with, sometimes I think it's hard to believe that anything good *can* happen. But when it does, it's worth grabbing ahold of."

"I'm worried Alice might not ever be able to forgive me for lying to her."

"But surely she likes who you are now?"

"She does . . . but she still seems so confused. I just don't know."

"Calvin, you can't erase the past. We both know that."

His brother's words were true. And even though they might seem harsh, they were exactly what he needed to hear. No matter how much he might want to change things with Alice, it wasn't possible.

"You're right. I need to be the person it's taken me twenty-four years to become. Plus, I haven't told you this, but Andrew has hinted that I could have a long-time job with the DEA. I could become a man who makes a difference. I could be a man of honor."

"I think you already are. But if that happens, I know we would all be proud of you."

"So what do you think I should do?"

"I think you should talk to Andrew and see what you need to do to be the man you want to be."

"And Alice?"

"When things calm down, I bet Alice will come around."

"And if she doesn't?"

Mark winked. "I'll have to start figuring out a way to *show* her that you're a man worth fighting for."

Calvin was humbled by the things Mark was saying. A little bit skeptical, too. But then he thought of West and how he was willing to give up his life for Irene and Alice. And that was when he knew that he couldn't give up a future filled with everything he'd ever wanted so easily.

Anything worth holding on to was worth risking it all for.

CHAPTER 31

Thursday, March 15

It had been two weeks since Irene had watched West die, and each day had felt like a carbon copy of the previous one. It didn't matter what the weathermen said was happening, whether the skies were blue, filled with fog, or twinkling with snow and ice, it all felt dreary and gray to Irene. No matter how hard she tried, she couldn't escape the feeling of emptiness that filled her heart and soul.

Though, to be honest, she didn't try all that hard.

Instead, she concentrated on her job at Bill's Diner and her faith. Both seemed to help her get through each day a little easier.

She didn't know if she had ever prayed so much before. The prayers seemed to help, at least momentarily. But then in the middle of the night, when she would relive the same episode again and again and again?

She would wonder if the Lord had run out of answers for her.

She'd begun to find comfort in herself. It

seemed as if no one really understood her pain. Most of her friends had no idea just how close she'd been to West. And while this was a time when she might have leaned on Alice, Alice seemed to be fighting her own demons.

That was why she didn't know what to say to Calvin Fisher when he was waiting for her at the end of her shift. She'd heard that things between him and Alice were strained. She supposed that was to be expected, given that all of them had gone through a terrible ordeal. However, it still seemed like a shame. If the last month had taught them anything, it was that life was short and happiness was fleeting.

After she collected her tips and gathered her cloak and mittens, she approached Calvin, taking notice of the dark circles under his eyes. "Hey."

"Hey, yourself."

His voice sounded like sandpaper. "You hanging in there?"

He shrugged. "I don't know. You?"

"About the same." Suddenly feeling exhausted, she said, "Calvin, I'm sorry, but I don't know how to help you with Alice. I have a feeling she just might need some space to process everything."

Calvin's lips pressed together, but then his tension eased. "I didn't come here to talk to you about Alice. I wanted to talk to you. Do you have time?"

She really didn't want to talk about West, but she couldn't escape the pain in his eyes. "I have time."

He glanced around the empty diner. "How about we talk in my truck? I'll drop you off at home when we're done."

She wasn't all that eager to be trapped in Calvin Fisher's truck with him for an extended conversation at nine at night. But she did trust him. At least there was that.

"All right."

When they got to his truck, he opened the passenger-side door for her and held out his hand to help her get up. She didn't accept his help. Doing so would have reminded her too much of West.

Immediately, he dropped his hand and walked to the driver's side. They remained quiet as he pulled out of the parking lot. He turned down the highway and kept driving, passing all the rest of the side streets and exits for their area. She tried to care about where they were going, but she really didn't. Instead, she made due with staring listlessly at the passing scenery.

After another ten minutes, Calvin pulled into a motel's parking lot.

Suddenly uneasy, she turned to him. "What is going on?"

"Oh, settle down," he said with a tinge of impatience in his voice. "I meant what I said, I just want to talk to you. I was just going to drive around until we came to a park or something, but then I started thinking of this place. I thought seeing it might help you."

"Seeing this?" She looked out the window, finding nothing about the old motel with its faded paint, burned-out neon sign, stained walkways, and cracked parking lot that would help her at all. "What does the Hart Motel have to do with me?"

"Maybe nothing."

"It absolutely means nothing to me." Fearing that he'd mistaken her childhood poverty with loose morals, she lowered her voice. "Calvin, I don't know what you think I've done, but I've never been here before."

"I have." His expression turned bleak.

And just like that, all the bluster went out of her. "You have?"

"I was staying here the first time I came back to see my brother, Mark." He cast a quick glance her way before looking out the windshield again. "You see, I had made a lot of mistakes and was paying the price. I was in deep with the Kings, but not in a good way."

"What other way is there?"

"In a real bad way," he said lightly. "You see, I'd been using."

"Oh, Calvin."

Still staring straight ahead, he continued. "I'd been gambling, too. I owed them money. A lot. I

330

came back to Horse Cave to try to persuade Mark to sell the house so I could use the money to pay my debts."

"But he didn't do that?"

Calvin shook his head. "He not only didn't do that, he put me in my place. He made me see myself through his eyes for the first time. I was pretty disappointed with what I saw."

Irene unbuckled her seat belt. "Calvin, I'm real sorry to hear about your past troubles, but what does it have to do with me?"

"I ended up making a deal to work undercover for the DEA. They gave me money to pay my debts as long as I would report to them as much as I could about the Kings. And about West Powers."

"What are you saying?"

"That I was only pretending to be a part of the gang. I was there to take down West. If I succeeded, they would have arrested him. He probably would have spent the rest of his life in prison."

Pain knifed through her, hating that the man she'd befriended had been used like that by Calvin. Hating that West had probably deserved such a future, too.

It took her a moment to swallow around the lump in her throat, but at last she found her voice. "He's dead now. I guess that suits your plan."

"In a way it does." Wrapping his hands tightly on the steering wheel, he said, "Irene, you are probably the only person who might understand what I'm about to say. You see, I actually liked West. Even though he did a whole lot of bad, I knew him well enough to see the good parts."

"Truly?"

"Oh, yeah. Knowing that I was one day going to be responsible for putting him in a federal prison for the rest of his life wasn't easy for me to come to terms with." He flexed his fingers before tightening them on the wheel again. "Even though I was supposedly working for the good guys, it still made me feel dirty."

"But you were going to do it anyway."

"I was. Not only did I owe the DEA for covering my debts, it was the right thing to do. West wasn't all bad, but what he was doing, running guns and drugs, using force and intimidation to get his way? It wasn't right."

She couldn't deny his words, but to agree with him felt so hard. "He . . . He was kind to me," she said hesitantly. "I felt like he liked me."

"I know West cared for you." He paused, then said, "I also know that he didn't know what to do about that. He didn't want to disillusion you, but he couldn't change who he was. He couldn't have gotten out of that life if he'd wanted to."

Thinking about who West had been, and the future that had been in store for him made her heart hurt. "Being in prison would have changed him."

Calvin nodded. "I think so, too, Irene. It would have taken out the rest of the good and replaced it with all the bad. He had a lot of enemies, too. Someone probably would have killed him. Now? He died a hero."

Staring out at the broken-down motel, thinking of how desperate Calvin must have been when he'd been there, thinking how West had sat down next to her on that couch in her apartment and talked to her for hours—and how he'd saved them all from John Yutzy before dying—Irene felt her chest become tight. "I don't understand how things like this happen. What is God trying to tell us?"

"I'm not real sure, but I think it means that God hadn't given up on him. He took West's life early; that is true. But the West I knew wouldn't have regretted it. I think he would like being thought of as a hero." After he waited a moment, he added, "And maybe God was looking out for you, too, Irene."

"How so?"

"If West was still a part of this world, well, you might have decided to do something that you would later regret," he said slowly. "Now you can miss him. Be thankful for his friendship. Be grateful for him saving you. But not be ruined."

Tears were now falling down her cheeks. And

as she felt them, she realized that Calvin's story had pierced the fog that had cloaked her for the last two weeks. "Maybe God does have other plans for me."

"I kind of think He does. Irene, you and me aren't all that different. We were born to people who didn't know how to care for us, but we still grew and survived. We made mistakes that we regret. But instead of spiraling down, we pulled ourselves up. And now we have a future that is better than either of us ever dreamed."

"And we have Alice."

He smiled, the warmth filling his eyes. "That's right. She's a good friend to you. To me? She's my reward for doing something right in spite of myself."

"I'm glad you came home. And I'm glad you came to get me today. *Danke.*"

"Anytime. People like us? Well, we need to stick together."

CHAPTER 32

Friday, March 16

G ood-bye, little scholars. I'll see you next week," Alice said as she waved to the last of her students as they walked home. She was proud of herself for getting through another day.

Proud of herself for not crying. Proud of herself for not allowing herself to dwell on everything that had happened . . . or everything that had not.

Amazing how the world continued spinning even when hers felt like it was slowly falling apart. Calvin had been true to his word. He was giving her time.

But unfortunately for her heart, that also meant that she hadn't seen him. At first, she just assumed that he was giving her space and was, no doubt, busy.

But then she'd seen Neeta at Blooms and Berries and heard that he'd left town.

Had he already grown impatient with her? Realized she was just a small-town girl and that they had nothing in common?

Needing a break from the inside of her school-house, she sat down on the front steps. Resting her elbows on her knees, she closed her eyes, breathed deep, and prayed.

She prayed for West and for the soul of John Yutzy. She prayed for little Mary Ruth and for everyone who loved her, too. She prayed for Mark Fisher and his continual recovery, for her tiny scholars, and for her parents, her brothers, and their wives. Finally, she prayed for Irene and Calvin, asking the Lord to give them comfort and strength.

Then, at last, she gave in and asked Him to grant her those same things, too.

She'd always felt like she shouldn't ask for prayers for herself, but lately she was wondering if God was wondering why she didn't think her needs were just as important.

Maybe it was another thing to feel guilty about, but she poured her heart out to the Lord. At last asking for His help and guidance.

Because the truth was that she missed Calvin. She had fallen in love with him.

When she opened her eyes, she did feel a bit of peace.

She sighed, stretching her legs out. She needed to get up and go back to her classroom, to put to rights and then head home.

Just as she was attempting to do just that, a buggy pulled up and her brothers got out. Both of them, since Edward was now back from vacation. As she watched them approach, both so tall and handsome, happiness to see them warred with worry.

Something had to be wrong. She couldn't remember the last time they had both taken off work early enough to see her at school.

New tension spiraled through her as she studied their expressions.

As usual, Edward spoke first. "Hiya, Alice. What are you doing out here?"

That was what he had to say?

"I was just taking a little break after my students left," she said as she got to her feet. "Why are you both here? What is wrong?"

"Maybe we simply wanted to see our little sister," John said.

She noticed that the carefree words didn't match the look of concern in his eyes. "At three in the afternoon? I think not." Grasping at straws, she said, "Did something happen with Mamm and Daed?"

"*Nee.* They are fine," John replied as he sat down on the steps that she'd just left. "As usual, they are concerned about you."

"Me? I am fine, too."

Edward leaned against the banister. "*Nee*, I don't think so."

She didn't bother to deny it. "Why do you say that?" Before he could answer, she thought about all those days she'd been unable to get out of bed. Her parents had acted like they'd understood, but maybe they really hadn't. "Did Mamm say anything?"

He raised his eyebrows. "Mamm? *Nee*. Of course not. She is going to pretend you are fine as long as you are living at home, teaching school, and never doing anything out of the ordinary."

Alice was surprised to hear such criticism. "That sounds kind of harsh."

"It's true, though," John said quietly. "I'm even kind of embarrassed that until recently, I liked to think the same thing."

"And now?"

"Now I've come to the conclusion that you've got a bit more spunk and fire than I ever gave you credit for."

"Spunk and fire, hmm?"

"Okay. Maybe that ain't the best way to describe ya. But you know what I mean."

"Is that why y'all came here? To tell me that?"

"Not exactly," Edward said.

"Well, then . . . spit it out."

"We came to see how you're feeling about Calvin."

"Oh. Well, I don't know if it matters how I'm feeling. He left."

Looking pleased with himself, Edward said, "I know where he is. Bethy and me talked to Mark and discovered that he is in downtown Cincinnati this weekend, meeting with his boss in the DEA."

"I see." Her heart sank. So she did wait too long to reach out to him.

"*What* do you see?"

"That he didn't wait for me. I guess it's over."

"Is that what you want?"

"*Nee*," she said.

"What was that?"

She was getting irritated with them now. "No, of course not, Edward. I want to see him again. I want to tell him that I really do believe in him, and believe in us." Getting to her feet, she paced a bit. "I want to tell him that I don't just *think* I love him, but I *do* love him."

"Is that all?" John asked.

"*Nee*. I need to tell him that even though I'm just a preschool teacher, I'm tough, too. I might need some coaxing and a little bit of patience from time to time, but that isn't terrible."

Edward grinned. "Sounds like you've got a lot to tell him, sister."

"I do. And I would tell him that, too, if I had his phone number." Snapping her fingers, she said, "You know what? I'm going to go over to Mark and Waneta's house and ask for Calvin's cell phone number, and give him a call."

John whistled softly. "That sounds like a plan. Good for you."

"Why are you both grinning at me?"

"Because we had a plan in mind, too," Edward

said. After smiling at John, he pulled out an envelope.

"What's this?" she asked, reaching for it.

"It's everything for your trip to Cincinnati. Your bus is going to leave in three hours."

She drew her hand back like the envelope was on fire. "What?"

"Bethy and I talked with Mark and Waneta, then we asked Lora Beck to help us," Edward said, looking pleased with himself.

"Lora called a travel agent and helped arrange your bus trip and hotel room in a little inn in Cincinnati." He grinned as he continued. "Next, Lora and Edward called Calvin and talked to him. He's going to meet your bus tonight and take you to the hotel."

"Don't you think this is all mighty heavy-handed?"

John nodded. "It would have been, if you hadn't just given that little speech of yours."

Feeling kind of proud of herself, she grinned at her brothers. "I was about to take matters into my own hands, wasn't I?"

"You were. So, what do you say?"

Glancing back into her messy classroom, thinking of the lesson plans that weren't written . . . about how all she was going to have time for was to throw some clothes in a bag and hurry to the bus station, she smiled. "I say we better get on our way."

And with that, she went into her classroom, grabbed her cloak and bonnet, pulled her purse out of her desk drawer, and left her schoolhouse. At the moment, nothing mattered but Calvin Fisher and the future that was almost in her grasp.

CHAPTER 33

Friday, March 16

"Do you need anything, sir?" the porter in the bus station's lobby asked.

For a second, Calvin was tempted to look around to see if the guy was talking to someone else. He still wasn't used to being treated as someone easily approachable. "I'm good, thanks," he finally replied.

The porter nodded before approaching the next person.

Checking the clock on the wall, Calvin guessed he had about another ten minutes to wait until Alice's bus arrived. That was time enough to take a seat and allow himself to reflect on what had happened.

Two days ago, he'd received a message from both Andrew and Mark. First, Andrew said that his boss wanted to meet with him in Cincinnati, which was both scary and exciting to hear.

But it was Mark's message that had made his insides knot up. Edward Yoder wanted to talk to him about his little sister.

What was amazing was that both of the conversations had surpassed his expectations. He'd assumed Andrew and his boss, Mr. Perry, were going to say he was a free man . . . not offer him a job. He'd been humbled and honored.

Hours later, he'd taken Edward's call fully prepared to promise to leave Alice alone, at least for a while. But instead Edward had asked if Calvin loved her.

Admitting that he did had been practically the easiest thing he'd ever had to do in his life.

Now here he was, waiting for Alice to visit— with an ID card in his wallet saying that he was an employee of the Department of Homeland Security. Both his job and this upcoming visit went beyond his wildest dreams.

He only hoped God would help him say the right words to Alice in the next couple of hours. Feeling that he could never pray too much, he quickly closed his eyes and did just that.

The bus pulled into the station just as he finished.

Standing up, he anxiously watched the passengers disembark. When Alice wasn't one of the first ten people to appear, his palms started to sweat. Maybe she'd decided not to come after all. Or worse, maybe she'd gotten into some kind of trouble.

What if someone had harmed her at the bus station?

He pulled out his phone, checking for a missed message.

"Calvin?"

His head popped up. And there she was. Pretty, angelic Alice Yoder. Dressed in a pale-blue dress and *kapp*, with a black cloak. She stood out among the rest of the passengers like a beautiful lily.

To cover up the wealth of emotions he was feeling, he grinned at her. "You made it."

But in her typical Alice way, she simply tilted her head to one side and fired back. "Did you think I wouldn't?"

"I was afraid you would change your mind."

She looked wary. "I almost did. I've never gone so far by myself before."

Some of the tension that had been building in his shoulders eased. She hadn't said that she had second thoughts about him. Only about the trip. "Someone told me once that people underestimate preschool teachers."

She smiled. "Seems I need to listen to my own words."

"Maybe so. Let's find your bag and get you out of here."

She walked by his side and pointed to the serviceable black roller bag. "It's that one. I borrowed Edward's suitcase."

After checking for her name, he pulled out the handle and guided her through the terminal. More than one person watched Alice intently. Calvin knew no one was being deliberately rude. It was more that they had never seen an Amish woman before.

However, he still kept close to her side and didn't hesitate to give anyone who stared at Alice too long a cold look. If she noticed, she didn't let on.

Instead, she walked quietly next to him, allowing him to rest a hand on her back while they walked through the parking lot. When he helped her inside his truck, she smiled at him and pulled on the seat belt while he took care of her suitcase and got in on his side.

And then they were on their way. "I thought we could check you in at your hotel and make sure your room is okay. Then get you something to eat."

"I'm not too hungry because I ate on the bus."

"Oh." Now what were they going to do?

Obviously misinterpreting his expression, she groaned. "Ack! That was rude, wasn't it? Are you hungry, Calvin?"

Right at that moment, he couldn't eat a thing. "Actually, I'm not."

"Ah."

He couldn't think of another thing to say as he navigated the dark city streets. Lora and her brothers had found Alice a small inn on the outskirts of the city. It was pretty and was near the river. It also had an electronic gate, so it was safe. He was so glad she was staying here instead of in one of the large hotels in the heart of the city.

When they walked to her motel door, he said, "It's late and you had a long bus ride. Would you rather we talk in the morning? If so, I would understand."

"I don't want to do that."

"No?" His stomach dropped. Had she already decided that they didn't have a future?

"I could never sleep without talking with you first, Calvin. Maybe we could get some water or something and sit in one of the motel's main rooms?"

He exhaled. "Sure. Yeah. I mean, okay, we can do that."

Twenty minutes later, he was sitting in a back parlor with two cups of decaf coffee and a plate of warm chocolate chip cookies. When Alice appeared after checking out her room, she smiled at the sight of him.

"What?"

"Most of the time in Horse Cave, you always looked kind of scary to me. I was just thinking that if you had been sitting on a floral sofa, sipping *kaffi* and eating cookies, I might have thought differently about you."

He chuckled. "It wouldn't have gone too well with the role I was playing."

She sobered. "Tell me about your job, Calvin."

347

Slowly, he told her about the offer Andrew and Mr. Perry had given him. It was mostly a desk job in Cincinnati. But it included training and schooling, even a tutor to help with the gaps in his education. He hadn't been a good student in Amish school, and then had left home when he was so young.

"That's wonderful, Calvin. You must be pleased."

"I am. I . . . well, I never expected to have people like Andrew or Mr. Perry believe in me."

"Sometimes I wonder if you've ever expected anyone to believe in you."

She was right. That statement, and how close it was to his heart, caught him off guard. "I never felt good enough. Not by my parents, who didn't really want me, or by Mark who had to raise me because our parents wouldn't." After glancing at her to make sure he hadn't scared her off, he continued. "Later, after making so many bad decisions, I didn't think I deserved anything." Taking a deep breath, he forced himself to say it. "Most especially you."

"You deserve everything. We all do."

"I've started to realize that I'm a person of worth. But what I don't know, Alice, is if you and I will have a chance."

"Because I told you that I didn't know if I could trust you."

"Yes. And because I lied to you."

"Calvin, ever since that day at the lake, I've been having trouble sleeping. I've sat in bed at night, staring into the dark and thinking about everything that happened."

"I bet you have."

"It made me realize a lot of things about myself. Some of them are good, others . . . not so much."

"I see." He forced himself to remain still and proper, even though his insides were shattered.

Gathering herself, she continued. "For example, I realized that I've been something of a late bloomer. I was good at following directions, doing what I was supposed to do. Even if it meant I was lonely or felt out of step. I realized that I had been only living half a life."

She smiled. "Just hours before I first met you that night, I was praying in my empty classroom. I asked the Lord to help me. I . . . I was so sad thinking about having only taken care of my brothers' houses and sometimes looking after—loving—other people's children." A blush crossed her features as she continued. "I told Jesus that I didn't think it was right that I was twenty-two and had never even been kissed."

"So . . ." He was afraid to hope, but the waiting was driving him crazy.

"So, I am going to keep praying to the Lord. Ask Him to believe in me, even if I choose a life with you one day."

"You would do that?"

She nodded. "I'm here, aren't I?" Smiling, she shrugged. "Calvin Fisher, I kind of think I already have."

He was overwhelmed and overcome. Beautiful, strong, adorable Alice Yoder was going to be his. He was going to be enough for her.

He couldn't think of a thing to say that could come anywhere close to the gift she had just given him.

Except for one thing.

He got to his feet, stood in front of her. Reached for her hands and pulled her up against him.

Pressing her palms on his chest, she sputtered. "Calvin?"—and looked up at him, her blue eyes filled with longing, her lips slightly parted.

Then that telltale spark that was all Alice entered her expression.

And she knew what he was about to do.

Feeling that this was the first, most perfect moment in his entire life, Calvin cradled a hand around her jaw, guided her even closer, and leaned down. And kissed her.

She froze before relaxing against him. One of her hands reaching upward, curving around his neck. Silently asking for something more.

Which he was more than happy to give.

He kissed her again. Held her close to him. Attempted to convey the depth of his feelings as best he could.

And when they at last parted, he finally spoke.

"I love you, Alice Yoder. And now, no matter what happens in your future, you have officially been kissed."

Her eyes sparkled before she started giggling.

The sound filled the room, filling his heart, filling his world. Making him realize that every risk he'd ever taken in his life had been worth this moment. He gave thanks, and then did the only thing he possibly could.

Calvin gathered Alice into his arms and kissed her again.

Books are
produced in the
United States
using U.S.-based
materials

Books are printed
using a revolutionary
new process called
THINKtech™ that
lowers energy usage
by 70% and increases
overall quality

Books are
durable and
flexible
because of
smythe-sewing

Paper is
sourced using
environmentally
responsible
foresting methods
and the
paper is acid-free

Center Point Large Print
600 Brooks Road / PO Box 1
Thorndike, ME 04986-0001 USA

(207) 568-3717

US & Canada:
1 800 929-9108
www.centerpointlargeprint.com